"Don't you see?" Beeton said, half pleading and half angry. "Galaxies pass on. There is no longer any dust or gas to fuel the stars; even the planets are consumed in energy. Instead of being brilliantly alive—they are dead. Only their ghosts live on," he said earnestly. "The malignant spirits of once-living nebulae."

Ghosts of galaxies?

"You're crazy!" Johns exclaimed.

Beeton's control snapped. He jumped up and the flame leaped with him. "No, no!" he cried. "You have to understand, all of you. We are entering the time of ghosts. Within an hour or two. We have to stop the ship before it's too late!"

"The supernatural is no threat to the natural," Shetland snapped.

"Stop the ship!" Beeton screamed. "The ghost is out there—"

In a moment he would realize that the ghost was not *out there,* but *in here*—

"Anthony's description of the journey through the ghost universe is exceptionally vivid and rises to compelling heights."
— *Booklist*

Tor books by Piers Anthony

Anthonology
But What of Earth?
Ghost
Hasan
Prostho Plus
Race Against Time
Shade of the Tree
Steppe
Triple Detente

WITH ROBERT E. MARGROFF:

Dragon's Gold
Serpent's Silver
Chimaera's Copper
Orc's Opal
Mouvar's Magic
The E.S.P. Worm
The Ring

WITH FRANCES HALL:

Pretender

PIERS ANTHONY

GHOST

A TOM DOHERTY ASSOCIATES BOOK
NEW YORK

GHOST

Copyright © 1986 by Piers Anthony

Cover art by Don Maitz

A Tor Book
Published by Tom Doherty Associates, Inc.
175 Fifth Avenue
New York, N.Y. 10010

Tor ® is a registered trademark of Tom Doherty Associates, Inc.

ISBN: 0-812-52088-2
Library of Congress Catalog Card Number: 85-50315

First Tor edition: September 1986
First mass market printing: December 1987

Printed in the United States of America

0 9 8 7 6 5 4 3

Table of Contents

Chapter 1:_____Blimped

"How long has it been, sir?" the girl inquired.

"One year," Shetland said. He did not need to qualify that; this was the Space Service Outprocessing Clinic Satellite Station, SSOCSS, where spacemen first put their feet on the ground. As the saying went: "Ssocss before sshoes." The term "satellite" referred to more than orbiting bodies; this station had never been offplanet.

She considered momentarily. "Please strip, sir."

He glanced askance at her. "In your presence?"

She smiled professionally, without either malice or humor. She was a perfect young woman in her mid twenties, marvelously symmetrical in more than mere figure. Her full breasts were not merely appealing in a sexual sense; they were somehow precisely *right* and in proportion to her overall body structure. Her brown hair complemented the neutral color of her uniform and was coiffed just so. Some finer hand than man's had crafted her to be subtly esthetic. That was of course why she had this position.

Yet there was a single remarkable incongruity that loomed much more significantly than it should have, because it stood in such contrast to her physical poise: one eye was a lighter gray than the other. Perhaps only a spaceman would have noticed.

"It is the rule, sir. If you can't do it here, you will be unable to do it Outside. The Clinic will have to hold you for Leave Conditioning."

Because his year in space had deconditioned him for close association with the masses of Earth. He was out of touch with contemporary mores. If the current fad consisted of stripping in mixed company, failure to do so could lead to social embarrassment at best, and to personal hazard at worst. This appealing girl had evidently been placed to verify his adaptability.

Shetland hesitated. "I did not want to take Earth leave."

"Obviously, sir, since you went the maximum. Now you have to survive thirty days on Earth—or be cashiered from space. One of the little anomalies of Service."

"Hell for a month—or hell for life," he agreed.

She glanced down momentarily. "Would it help if I stripped with you?"

"Woman, do you realize that I have been denied—" He broke off. He had not been denied sex; the Operations Manual had made all women of space accessible to him, and all were smart and fit and skilled in the necessities. Yet he had *felt* denied; the purely physical possession of women who he knew had no real interest in him left him fundamentally unsatisfied. How much better merely to talk with someone in honest companionship, to feel the quickening of genuine mutual interest. In that sense a stranger became more alluring than a known woman, for apart from the novelty of first-liaison there was at least the delusion that a better relationship could develop.

This woman was also in the Service. She knew the manual. Therefore she would oblige him sexually without qualm if he asked. That made it pointless. He was sick of semi-professional sex.

"I admire your aplomb," he said instead.

And realized that he had uttered, in lieu of a lie, a half-truth. He envied the whole world its aplomb. The human sphere continued in what to him seemed grandiose insanity, yet it endured, satisfied with itself in myriad idiotic ways that *he* could never indulge in. The world had its niche; Shetland had not found his own. Space was only a substitute for the true companionship he craved.

"It is simply a matter of pride," she said seriously. He saw that this was no casual thing with her. She was performing her chore in a manner that reflected a deep, virtually innate, wholly attractive pride. He was reminded of the adage of all those dependent on machinery for their well-being, which meant every living creature in space. "A machine does not *care*."

Many people in space could hardly be differentiated from machines in that respect; they had allowed routine convenience to make them resemble automatons. It seemed to be a survival trait in the Service; a number of his onetime classmates of this persuasion now ranked him.

But this girl was dedicated. Whatever she might do, however trivial, had to be done with the proper flair. Yet that one discordance, the offshade eye, interfered. It provided for her an individuality of expression that set her involuntarily apart. She probably hated it, but he found himself attracted to that lone discrepancy far more than to her more conventional charms. Charms were commonplace; *all* young women were well proportioned these days. Few had the art or fortune to possess or even to desire nonconformity.

Did this person really care, or was it all a mask? Historically masks had been used to conceal expression, to hide the truly human feelings beneath. Today they emulated it, hiding the lack of meaningful personal interest. Unable to let it go, he played the game he disliked. "You don't know me. You could face an unsafe situation."

"Not at all, sir. I am certain you are a gentle man." She pronounced the last two words carefully, making clear they were two. That much he understood: a gentleman was by one aspect of reckoning a male gentile, or non-Jew. Therefore it carried a certain religious implication. Direct religious reference was rigorously excluded from casual dialogue. Yet this particular distinction was commonly ignored, and of course the majority opinion traced the true origin of the word to "gentle," or a well-bred person.

Did this refinement of usage on her part mean that she harbored a religious preference? Was it her way of expressing subtle objection to the law that had abolished all semblance of religious, social or sexual distinction?

Shetland frowned. How would this beautifully balanced creature react to a direct slur? Ordinarily he had no interest in baiting people, but this one intrigued him. Perhaps that interest stemmed chiefly from his desire to postpone his reckoning with the current society of Earth another moment. He preferred to think that it was because of that trifling shade of the eye. *Truth*, he remembered, *is a shade of gray*. Nevertheless it had taken hold. "I did not realize that the Space Service now employs professional mistresses."

"There are no such things, sir," she said without rancor, and he realized that she had fended off similar implications before. He had not been sufficiently original in his choice of insult. That was part of his problem. He was not an original man, despite his desire to be. "The exchange of sexual relations for money or material consideration was ruled unconstitutional last year. All things must be voluntary."

As well he knew—though in space these things were not voluntary but mandatory. The manual covered it all. "The Constitution is getting to be a comprehensive document," he remarked. They were of course referring to the World document, not the lesser one he had grown up with.

"The most comprehensive document in the history of our species, sir."

Shetland started to laugh, but choked it off. She was not joking.

After a moment, he asked: "What is your name?"

"Sosthenna, sir." She was not required to give her full identity; that would have interfered with her offduty privacy. But he pondered what she had provided, leafing through his mental dictionary of names. The name had originally been Hebrew—fittingly?—meaning a vigorous woman. Was she vigorous? Did she really derive from Hebrew loins? He suffered a momentary picture of a concentration camp, an ugly plume of thick smoke rising from a sooted chimney within it. Her parents could have lived in an age to experience that horror, or rather her grandparents; had they escaped the historical Nazi purge? He shut off the vision; his imagination had no right.

"You intrigue me," Shetland said.

"I am intended to, sir. Please strip now, or a line will form."

Hardly. Each officer of space received individual outprocessing attention, unrushed. Time was not of the essence; there was a certain irony there. But having failed to penetrate her emotional armor, he had no recourse. He stripped, hand-ing her the items of his uniform as they came loose. He did not balk at the underclothing. Soon he was no longer a Commander in the Space Service, but merely another naked man.

Sosthenna studied him carefully. "You do not appear to have suffered muscular deterioration during your long tour in space."

"Much of it was at one point five gee acceleration," he said. "We spun ship at other times, and followed the manual on exercise. There is never any need to deteriorate."

She smiled with just the right force. "That explains it. Not all spacers honor the manual that literally, and so some suffer tissue losses that make it harder for them on Earth for several reasons."

"If you do not get on with your business, I will demonstrate my health more tangibly."

"In that case I'd better hurry." But she had not been bluffed; his masculinity was obviously of neutral concern to her. Probably many men had indulged themselves with her, and many more had wished to; none had touched her where it counted.

She walked slowly to the wall where costumes were massed, and drew out one. "I think this is appropriate."

"Anything," Shetland said, becoming perversely impatient with the process. "What is it?"

"A blimped outfit." She pronounced it as two syllables, equally accented: blim-ped. "I think you can handle it, and it is excellent camouflage."

He considered it dubiously. "Knickers and sneakers?"

"And plastic jacket and mini-cap. No one will suspect you of being a space officer in this."

"Is this not somewhat extreme? This is not a hostile country; it is my homeland."

"It is extreme. This is not hostile country. It is your homeland," she agreed without inflection.

Shetland sighed and donned the outfit, transferring his identity tokens to it. "Exactly what does a blimped do?"

"Oh—you haven't encountered them? Public transport closed down entirely six months ago when its electric allocation ran out. Now it's every person for self." He noticed how she avoided the standard "he" so that no vestige of sexism showed. The language was accelerating its process of change! "The streets are so congested with cycles that it is hazardous for anyone not used to it. The blimped is the newest device, but it should get you there if the wind is right. That's blimp-ped: pedal blimp."

"Pedal blimp," he repeated. "I begin to comprehend."

"It can be strenuous, especially in contrary winds, but I believe you are up to it. We have several rental units on the roof. What direction will you be going?"

"From here? Southwest—if the volatile modern society has not changed the directions of the compass."

She smiled to the appropriate degree and touched a button on a column. Instant weather came on. "Storm approaching area of receiver, ESA 1700. LTA warning. Present 15K, veering SE and erratic at fringe. Repeat: LTA warning."

"That is not entirely clear to me," Shetland said. "We do not have much weather in space, and it was not an immediate concern to me on my last visit to Earth."

"Right now the wind is fifteen knots in exactly the direction you need, at ideal speed. But in one hour the storm will ground all small lighter-than-air craft. That means you had better hurry." Then she frowned. "Oops, I nearly forgot your briefing. The blimp will have to wait."

"My parents reside within fifteen miles of this station," Shetland said. "It is pointless to delay an hour when that will cost me perhaps as much as a day before the wind turns again." Actually he was not emotionally close to his aging parents, who had opposed his entry to space and also blamed him for a certain—but a kind of redness formed before him like a wash-technique painting, a malignant spirit, and he suppressed that concept immediately. He would merely introduce himself to them, suffer their cold welcome, then find other lodging. The remainder of his forced leave would not be as bad. At least Earth had good libraries. But it would not be politic to say all this openly, and it was not this woman's business. He must seem willing to go. "I am familiar with this area; I grew up here in the virtual shadow of the Station. I need no briefing."

"Oh, but you do, Commander," she insisted.

They were standing close together. He enfolded her and kissed her. It was not an expert job, just a rather hurried, sloppy effort.

Caught by surprise, she neither resisted nor responded. But he found her, even in the dishabille of temporary stasis, a very nice object to touch. He was tempted to remain longer, exploring the sensation, ascertaining whether her offcolor eye was merely the superficial indication of a lode that penetrated deep into her being, expanding into true individuality deep within, where the world could not know. But he realized that it probably was no such thing, and that she was likely as conventional as her exterior format suggested. This returned him firmly to his original objective.

He separated from her and proceeded to the stairs, and she did not oppose him. Better to leave some play for the imagination, to believe that there could be a real person in there behind the near-perfection, and that such a person could be genuinely interested in a difficult man like him. Illusion was at times a far sweeter thing than reality. The fact of illusion needed to be cherished as well as its content.

The stairs were a shut-off escalator. Energy had become far too precious to waste, and it would have wasted more energy to replace the machinery with a regular staircase or ramp, so the thing remained in place. Was this a fair analogy of contemporary society? he wondered. A thing that had run its dramatic upward course, going nowhere, and whose steps were now in stasis? It was another topic to meditate at leisure. He conserved such topics; they were valuable. To him, boredom was a greater evil than hunger or sexual frustration, for boredom signaled the waste of a mind.

There was no alarm. Sosthenna would not turn him in. She had told him to report for briefing, but enforcement was not her department. A man had a right to ignore what was intended only for his own good. Provided he wasted nothing and infringed the rights of no others.

He found the roof, pleasantly winded by his charge up four flights of escalator. Exercise was wherever one found it; this was also the essence of nonwaste. Conservation came naturally to those familiar with space, where life depended on making existing resources do.

The top of the building was covered with solar collectors, each unit enclosed by clear plastic so as to make an oven effect. The sunlight entered freely, but reflected out with much more difficulty when polarized, so heated the trapped air. The water circulating through the tubes carried away that captive heat for use by the occupants of the building. Other collectors were crystals that converted the light directly into electric power, efficiently. Only a narrow walkway remained for access to the blimp dock, and a sign said WATCH YOUR SHADOW.

Shetland obediently hunched down so as to minimize his

power-robbing shadow and hurried to the dock. The blimps
were there: three of them anchored to a rail on short leashes,
tugging like eager steeds in the breeze. Each had a dependent
apparatus, a framework of seat and pedals, with vanes on the
sides, a plane to the front and a large propeller fan behind.
No waste material; most of it was light plastic.

He was familiar with the basic principles of guidance in
atmosphere, and could see that the wind would be the overwhelming factor. The blimps were long and narrow, with
flattened sides, like freshwater fish, so as to provide maximum lift with minimum drag. He concluded that it should be
possible to tack into the wind in conjunction with the propeller. But far easier to ride with the wind, especially for a
novice.

He climbed into a pretty red blimped, fitted his arms into
the vane attachments, his feet into the pedal shoes, and
fastened the safety harness. The front plane was controlled by
shifts of body mass. The apparatus seemed simple enough in
theory to operate; the physics of it were elementary. And it
was essentially a ship. Shetland liked that. A ship, *any* ship,
was home, and it was nice to feel like a captain.

The wind was steady and strong, as the weather report had
promised, but the blimp did not respond properly to his
efforts as he made to cast off. He observed that his weight
was a little too much for it, so that the pedal housing was
snagging on the roof. He worked the valve to feed just
enough additional hydrogen into the bag to provide the necessary buoyancy. Hydrogen: there had been a year when this
gas was banned in favor of inert helium. But hydrogen had
greater buoyancy, and was easier to prepare—after all, most
of the universe consisted of it!—and the fire hazard had been
abated by making the system self-contained, with no leakage
of gas to the atmosphere. Of course the abolition of tobacco

smoking helped; today the average citizen was not an incendiary mechanism. Therefore blowups should be few.

When precise balance had been obtained and he hovered inches off the roof, he valved it down, cast loose the mooring and set off downwind.

It was, in its fashion, fun. He was floating, but not in free-fall. The effect was quite different from space travel, and somewhat eerie. For one thing, he was appallingly close to the planet. Fifty feet. Ahead of him a tall building loomed; the wind should carry him by it, not through it, but he didn't care to gamble. In space nothing changed direction of its own accord, so his reflexes urged action. He used his armvanes to guide to the side.

Nothing happened. He was drifting in air, and had no purchase. Hastily he pedaled. The fan pushed against the atmosphere, increasing his forward velocity. Now the vanes had some slight traction, and he wobbled over to the side, barely clearing the building.

"Birth!" a woman screamed irritably as the blimp almost sideswiped her window vegetable garden. "Get in your lane, purebred!"

Embarrassed, Shetland guided his craft into the airway he now discerned, marked off by a pattern of buoys anchored to buildings and utility poles. Faster blimps traveled higher, and traffic bore to the right. The street was east-west, not quite aligned with the wind, so he had to pedal and steer vigorously.

"Birth," he murmured, remembering the woman's curse-word. So reproduction itself had become anathema in some circles. "Purebred." That was a more established insult, more specific. He did not care to explain that he had been born before the law had changed. But this sort of language was all too typical of what he disliked on Earth; in space there was no parallel.

Below him were the massed cycles that Sosthenna, her of the shade of gray, had warned him about. There were thousands of them. Most were two-wheeled, but quite a number were one- or three- or four-wheeled: unicycles, tricycles, quadricycles. The last were actually pedalcars, some loaded with families, some even with solar collectors covering them. There were no fuel-powered vehicles at all.

No mystery about that. The energy-exorbitant last century had virtually depleted all ready sources of power. The developing crisis had been apparent for half a century or more, but nothing had been done until too late. The government of the world had finally reserved all remaining fossil fuel sources for offplanet use, at one stroke abolishing the age of the automobile, jet plane and powered watercraft. It had been desperation, not foresight.

Suddenly the pollution of the environment had decreased sharply, physical exertion had increased, and lives had lengthened. Serendipity: perhaps the loss of the use of fossil fuels had been a net benefit. Of course the average citizen had not thought so, and the public transport system had been strained—until its current had also been cut off, during his most recent tour.

Mad world! he thought. It seemed determined to do the right things for the wrong reasons, even though the right reasons were apparent. Space was more predictable and more reasonable. Or were those concepts redundant? Could there be unpredictable reason, or unreasonable predictability? Well, perhaps. Relativistic theory seemed very like the former, and as for the latter, he had experienced an event once that in retrospect—no, no, blot that out; it was too red, too—

"Watch where yer goin', prok!" a voice yelled in his ear.

Shetland looked about. He had drifted into the opposing air lane during his introspection, and was interfering with traffic.

In this fifteen-knot wind it seemed impossible to pedal a blimp northwest, but some were tacking west successfully. "Sorry." And what did "prok" mean?

"Sorry!" the other yelled indignantly. He was a young man, perhaps twenty, light brown of hue in the current fashion. He spun his blimp about expertly and flew alongside Shetland's craft, interfering with his wind. "*Sorry*! What are you—a waster?"

Waster—that was identifiable as contemporary slang. Waste had become the ultimate crime, especially in the eyes of those who had most freely practiced it until very recently. New converts were generally most vigorous—and obnoxious—in any pursuit.

"I have not used this type of craft long," Shetland explained, not wanting to get involved in an altercation.

"Then what in seg are you doing in mainline traffic, paleface?"

This time Shetland caught the insult squarely. Seg—that would be short for segregation, now a bad word. Paleface—the Amerind term for the white intruder, historically. Since Shetland was a very dark black man, this was a studied irony. Anything that called attention to the extremes of a person's racial characteristics was an affront, for it presumed he was of illegitimate birth. This despite the fact that the Miscegenation Act had been in force for only twelve years. Youngsters assumed that the present state had always obtained, even when they knew better; that was in its way also typical of this new culture.

Shetland ignored the obnoxious youth and steered away. But the other, his baiting spirit awakened, kept pace with him—an easy job, since he had preempted the windside. "Where you bin, glutton?" he demanded loudly. "Home on the range?"

More insults. Translation was becoming easier as the nature of the youth manifested. Food was scarce, so gluttony was an unforgivable offense. Obesity had disappeared. Those who could afford to eat well did not dare do so, lest they be lynched. The "range" was the old cattle-raising farm, before the consumption of meat was banned. To have a home on the range implied either criminal ranching for the black market meat market ("fenced" meat), or that a person was one of the cattle.

Understand a culture's insults, he thought, and understand the culture. How closely the two were allied!

Yet it was pointless to attempt to trade jibes with such ilk. The kid surely had a job, as there was now a hundred percent employment, and soon he would have to go to it. Shetland continued his flight. He had now gotten out of the city proper and was over the suburbs—where fifty percent of the terrain was garden. Corn stood between the houses, and cabbage ruled the back yards, and the front lawns were waving wheat. Regular grass had become uneconomical, since there was no fuel for power mowers. Today men used scythes—at harvest time.

"You jobless neuter!" the youth shouted. "What kind of a fish *are* you?"

Jobless—neuter—fish. The lad was really scratching for something that would hurt. It was time to shut him up. "A space fish," Shetland replied shortly—and realized immediately that he had made a bad mistake.

"Space!" the youth exclaimed as if this were another dirty word. Then, gleefully to the whole lane: "This character's radioactive! He's a spaceman!"

Immediately other blimps converged. Some of them were larger two-seater tandems. "Spaceman!" The word spread like news of a radiation hazard. Shetland tried to accelerate away, but his leg muscles weren't conditioned for this specialized form of exercise, and the others readily caught up. White, yellow and brown faces grinned maliciously.

"Hey, spacer! How much coal have you stole?" one yelled. Extracts of coal provided the bulk of the chemical propellants of spaceships. There was a lot of coal available, but processing it without destroying farmland was expensive.

"How much shale did you fail?" another demanded. The second major source of fossil fuel was shale oil, much of which did not make the stringent space standards. "Failed" shale served for much of Earth's essential industry. Most natives felt that the good shale oil should be reserved for Earthly use, so this was another source of ire.

"How much roent did you vent?" Radiation had of course become an obscene concept since the Atomic Act. To make the obscenity of it quite plain, the speaker issued a loud sound of crepitation, as of breaking wind.

"How much gas did you pass?" They were getting bolder; someone chuckled. The crepitation became a small chorus.

"How much work did you shirk?"

Shetland cut in the compressor circuit. The pedal resistance abruptly stiffened as the hydrogen gas was recompressed to liquid state. There was no immediate effect on the blimp; though its lift was finely balanced against its cargo, compressing hydrogen by hand was not a rapid process. He was getting hot, both from the exertion and the heat emitted by the compression cylinder. Not to consider the harassment. But by the time the punks realized what he was doing, he would be losing elevation at a rate they could not immediately match, and should be able to escape them by floating low.

It would be much faster merely to bleed some gas from the bag! But there was of course no way to do that short of punching a hole in the blimp, and it would be both wasteful and dangerous. It would be difficult or impossible to regain elevation later, even if the hole could be resealed, as the blimp carried only a minimal reserve. Waste was a crime, a sin, and a social indiscretion; that was a cultural view that Shetland shared completely. Even to break wind naturally had become an offense not so much against taste but against waste, as the taunting of the youths was making evident. Flammable gas was a planetary resource.

"Space, space, hide yer face!"

"Some other place!"

"Go find yourself another goal!"

"Go ram your pole!"

"Up a black hole!"

The supposed cleverness of that last impromptu jibe overcame them, and the whole gang burst out laughing. Shetland had to admit that it was an inspired juxtaposition of spacism and racism and perhaps sexism—and it didn't help that he was now echoing their doggerel in his own mind. With an effort he kept his face straight, for they had scored on his most vulnerable spot. *Black hole . . .*

They were using their planes to scoop down, buzzing him like so many monstrous flies. Flies were more common since the Insecticide Act that banned the use of all airborne poisons. But so, fortunately, were spiders and other fly predators.

"Space, spaced!" they yelled, now linking the space effort with the illegal use of consciousness-changing drugs. "Was'e, waste!" they chanted in unison.

Now they started bumping into his blimp, rocking it violently in time with the loudening chant. "SPACE—SPACED! WAS'E—WASTE!"

But the commotion had attracted official attention. A blue police glider looped down inquiringly. The crowd of blimps scattered, finding other traffic lanes with a facility Shetland could only envy.

Shetland slowly relaxed. What had started as mere harassment had been working into a dangerous situation. Had one of those attempted jostlings caused him to go out of control, with his present uncertainty of navigation, he could have taken a bad fall.

Perhaps he should have waited for the briefing Sosthenna had urged upon him. Like a typically short-sighted human being, he had ignored the warning until almost too late.

Chapter 2:＿＿＿＿＿＿Naiad

The glider moved on. It could not come in too low or close, lest it lose its airstream and have to land. But it had done its job of breaking up the harassment. Had the youths not scattered, it could have dropped tear gas, forming a cloud that would have changed the nature of the activity quickly enough. Rioting was a waste of energy, subject to immediate penalty.

Unfortunately Shetland had forgotten to cut out the compressor when the craft started nudging down. Now he had lost too much buoyancy, and could not regain altitude. He was dropping steadily toward the ground.

He stopped the compressor now, and the blimp shot ahead as his full pedal power returned to the fan. He valved more gas into the chamber, but it filled slowly: another built-in waste-reduction measure. Finally he leveled off with the help of his plane, barely twenty feet from the ground.

Only it wasn't ground. It was water. Preoccupied with the

harassment and elevation, he had not paid attention to direction, and the wind had taken him over a small reservoir. He was lucky he hadn't gotten dunked!

Still, it was bad enough. Sailboats were crossing the water, their masts rising above his own present elevation. Each sail bore a large L: these were learners, practicing maneuvers before risking the open waterways traffic. They would not be adept at avoidance. He was headed for one now. He didn't want his bubble punctured by the crossbar!

He worked his vanes and guided around, hardly hearing the sailsman's angry "Waster!" shout.

The blimp was finally rising. The stiffening wind was carrying it directly toward another hazard. On a rocky promontory extending from a small beach was a Darrieus hoop, a large modern windmill. Its shaft was vertical, with three ribbonlike loops of thin metal anchored at top and bottom. These were twisted to scoop the wind, making the whole structure rotate on its upright axis. In fact, it most resembled a thirty-foot-tall inverted eggbeater—going at full speed.

His little balloon was headed right for those flashing blades. Not only would they cut it to pieces—they would perform the same service for his body.

He could not rise above it in time. He veered to the side, but a sudden stronger gust of wind bore him straight into it anyway. The storm was developing!

Then he remembered to use his plane. The insulting youths had used their planes to swoop down quickly. Such motion required effort, as it was necessary to peddle strenuously, and the effect was temporary, but at least it was fast. He angled his plane down sharply—and offbalanced himself. These forces had to be applied cautiously!

He was not sure precisely what maneuver he performed, but he found himself skimming the water barely to one side of the eggbeater. He had cleared it, somehow! But now he was too low, out of control, and too close to the beach. People were on the shore, throwing themselves out of the way as he zoomed toward them.

His pedal framework snagged on the sand as he swept to shore. The blimp nosed forward and down, like a man tripping, and Shetland landed face down in the sand. His harness kept him seated, but his plane snapped off and his knees were dragging painfully.

Hands grabbed him, halting the rampaging blimp. Dazedly he saw girls: half a dozen nude nymphs, sunbathers. Every one was slender and pretty in an elfin way, as if newly formed from coalescing froth.

Oceanids, he thought. No, those were sea nymphs. These were freshwater. He flipped the pages of his mental dictionary, that had not been disturbed by the shakeup or the angle of his head, searching for the appropriate term, but couldn't find it.

Of course not, he reminded himself impatiently; he had to know what word he was looking for first. Dictionaries went from term to definition, not vice versa.

"Are you all right, blimper?" a worried girl inquired. She had sunbleached light brown hair, and the skin around her eyes was pale where habitual sunglasses had interrupted the tan. That was the only place on her body where her natural pure-white skin color showed through; she had probably been razzed about it, though she was at least three years older than the Miscegenation Act. Well, two years, perhaps. One, certainly. At what age did girls develop, these days? Possibly she felt an affinity to him, the "purebred" of another color.

"Shaken up," he muttered as she reached around him, unfastening the straps. It was necessarily an awkward position, but her tanned small breasts pressed against his side with more than casual force. Nymph she was, indeed; what *was* the specific term?

With inspiration, he looked up "Oceanid." Sure enough, its definition mentioned its complement, the freshwater nymph: *naiad*. "Naiad!" he exclaimed.

"What?" She paused, arms around him. She had a pleasant sunbaked smell, and her skin was soft.

"Naiad. Nymph of the lake and fountain. A fair young maid, mythologically. That is my impression of you."

She smiled. "Really? That's neat! And you're a handsome black devil. Would you like to sex me?"

Caution! The rapidly changing sexual mores of Earth could be disastrous for him. The costume-girl Sosthenna had already shown him that, telling him that he had to be able to strip in mixed company. He had known that such conventions were developing in members of the same race, since they could not marry within it, but this girl was of a different race. But young; what was the minimum age limit now? To "sex" her, as she put it—would that be tantamount to betrothal? Opposite races were under strong pressure to marry. She evidently thought he was a regular native, a dashing blimp-pedaler. Better to beg off, politely.

"I would like to sex you all," he said gallantly to the group of girls. "But in my present state I lack the capacity."

One of the brown nymphs laughed, her breasts jiggling. "Well spoke, bach!" To be a bachelor was now a mark of respectability, for it was assumed that he wasn't reproducing.

"But we could make it a groupie affair," another girl said brightly, running her left hand down the outside of her thigh as she rotated her hips, and sliding it up on the inside. The gesture had a potent effect on him. Oh, didn't they learn the sexual signals early today!

The others exclaimed with merry agreement, jumping and clapping their hands. Young but eager!

Joking or serious? Shetland wasn't sure. He was normally a lusty man, and this group of seemingly willing nymphs barely into their teens was very like some of his space-haul erotic fancies. He was sure now: age had become no barrier. Any individual who desired sex and possessed the physical indications of maturity was entitled to it, provided the proposed partner was amenable and there was no force or pain. All the girls would have been treated at menarche to prevent conception. These were fresh and clean and wholesome creatures, and there was no question of multiple marriage—though who could tell what the standard might be by the time of his *next* leave?! But after the harassment by the young men, he took nothing for granted. He could not enter into this under false premises.

"Ladies, I must make a confession," he said gravely, and they tittered with pleasure at the adult address. Observing the quivering motions of their pert mammaries as their pleased embarrassment manifested, he wondered whether he had just discovered the true origin of the term "titter." Tit—titter—titillate . . . of course his mental dictionary said that last word derived from the Latin *titillo*, tickle. But who could say where the tickling might be done? "I am of space."

All six young faces froze, eyes staring at him with that dainty fixity typical of shocked nymphs. In the past decade they might have reacted similarly had he confessed to being a pederast or a truant officer. Today pederasty was socially acceptable, even popular; school, less so. But not space travel.

Finally the naiad, the friendly white girl, spoke with difficulty. "I suppose *someone* has to go to space. When you get drafted, you just have to go, or—"

"I was drafted," he said. "But after my compulsory tour, I re-spaced. I am a career officer."

They were visibly torn between awe and horror. Space still had its fascination, perhaps because of its traditionalistic military aspects, but the phenomenal waste of energy associated with it dominated the popular conception.

"We should have let him drag," a black-haired nymph said bitterly.

"Let's be fair," a dark brown maned one said. "He landed here by accident. That wasn't his fault. He told us the truth when he didn't have to, so we wouldn't prok with a waster. We can't really blame him."

Prok—that word again. But this time it was in context. Prok—proc—procreation. A new four-letter term, signifying illicit reproduction, similar to the one he had been raised with. A word of many purposes, ambition mixed with negation. Sex was no longer suspect, but procreation was, especially between members of the same race. Since many people still opposed the Miscegenation Act, the only guaranteed good sex was sterile sex. Or so the polite-society myth went.

"We sure can't really praise him either!" another exclaimed. "A prokin' *spacer*!"

The white girl blushed, victim of her companion's lewd language. There was a brief silence.

Then the brown nymph, adept at compromise, said brightly: "Let's give him a five-second head start."

Smiles flashed. Recent improvements in nutrition and prophylaxis had given them all perfect teeth. "That's fair!" they agreed.

Shetland glanced around. Two of them held his blimp, their combined weight too much for it despite the tug of wind, though there were scuffly marks in the sand where gusts had made their feet drag. The storm was developing, blowing the girls' hair across their faces attractively.

Three others were stooping, gathering handfuls of sand and what stones they could find. Only the naiad remained aloof, gazing at him with such disappointment that he was sorry for her. Even one-minute heartbreaks were keen at that age. To find a kindred soul, to have the chance to engage in genuine adult sex with him, the dream of proclaiming afterward "I had it with a full-grown man, forty at least, and totally opposite race!"—and then to lose him to something as stupid as this! Shetland understood, for he shared the feeling, whether straight or mirror-image. Now she would have to participate in the witch-hunt, lest she suffer ostracism by her companions, and it might be *months* before she had another such chance. But condemnation by her peers was, of course, beyond her capacity to tolerate.

Would they try really to hurt him? If it was to be merely a matter of tackling him, getting him down, stripping him, rubbing sand in his hair, and perhaps playing a game of "Samson" by holding him down while they took turns playing with his genitals and concluding with a "rape" by the chosen nymph before they let him go . . . well, he had heard of such things, and would be willing to submit. But he had no assurance that they would not instead punish him truly, beating him as hard as they dared without killing him. That, too, he knew of.

He was a man in fit physical condition; they were freshly nubile girls. He could fight, using his training to knock them out in rapid order. He doubted that all six together could stand effectively against him if he chose that course. But he didn't want to attack these lovely little nymphs—especially if their intent was merely to play with him, in whatever manner.

That left only one safe and feasible course: the one suggested. The chase.

He leaped for the blimp. The two were too quick for him. Laughing, they let the craft go. Unburdened, it shot into the air, its broken plane dangling. He made a grab for it, but a yellow nymph blocked him, getting her illicit thrill as his body thrust against hers. Then the blimp was out of reach.

"You have wasted the balloon!" the naiad cried, horrified. "That's just as bad as what *he*—"

But Shetland's motion had started the clock. "One, two," the girls chanted in place, clapping their hands in the measured cadence. "Three, four, FIVE!"

He ran. The sand gave way under his feet, costing him traction. Barefooted, the girls were better off. A stone caught him in the back. It didn't hurt; it was too small, and lacked force. They weren't really trying to harm him, then, just to chastise him. It was a demonstration they had to make, to prove how they hated space. The waste of space!

Had he made a mistake, then, in running? Had he even advanced on them menacingly, they probably would have scattered in panic. All except the naiad, perhaps. But he, too, had a demonstration to make: that in no case would he hurt them. If he became certain that they were only playing, he might allow them to catch him, and he would submit with only token resistance to their "punishment." He had seen the forbidden longing in the naiad's face. Not merely sexual: one day she might even go to space herself, having seen the human side of it. There was so much he could tell her, in the guise of a casual erotic encounter. So much he might gain from her innocent but genuine attention. Her feelings were mixed but genuine.

He charged down the beach toward the Darrieus rotor. A mistake; there was no path beyond it, just the open water— and these nude girls could surely swim better than he could in his clothes. He would be caught in a drown-or-be-drowned situation, for their frenzy was building like the storm, becoming genuine. Water could be an excellent site for sexual games, but it was also entirely too dangerous. Already other naked sunbathers were joining in, male and female, and the naiad was falling back. That was the signal of the deteriorating nature of the chase. The pursuers had the land cut off; there was nowhere to go but toward the windmill.

Maybe that was their intent, if a forming mob could be said to have intent: to drive him into the rapidly moving blades of the mill. Then the people would be anonymous and blameless; it would be called accident or suicide. Murder was still a crime, for it was the wasting of human life, but suicide was legitimate so long as it did not destroy anything else of value. The murder of a spacer would rouse the enforcement agencies, and retribution would be severe; the suicide of the same person would not occasion much alarm on Earth.

The fair nymphs had been ready to engage in group sex with him. Willingly, joyfully, perhaps imaginatively, with the very human excitement of first significant experience, and perhaps some mind-to-mind camaraderie slipped in, as it were illicitly—the very kind of experience he craved. These girls were too young to possess the emotional control of the mature woman; their joys and hurts were openly expressed. Why hadn't he kept his mouth shut? He could have had it all, and gone his way anonymously. All seven participants would have benefited.

But of course he had the answer. It would have been dishonest to accept their ministrations under a false pretense. Though he liked genuine sexual interplay, integrity was fundamental. This was not a position many people understood or appreciated, but he knew he would never alter it. If he ever found a woman with a similar attitude . . .

Actually, he had found one, once. She had been, if anything, yet more set in this matter than he. She had even—*No, no! Block it out! Forget, bury, hide!*

He was panting now, but he had outdistanced the pursuit. His footwear gave him an advantage here on the rocky projection; their bare feet slowed them. He was a powerful man, with unusual endurance; that came of exposure to sustained high-gee acceleration. He also had inflexible determination, and could push himself, physically and mentally, much beyond the normal limits of others.

He was, however, coming up against natural limits now. The blades barred his further progress, and the lake on either side of the promontory limited maneuvering. No police glider was in sight this time. He would have to choose between his propensities for disabling hand-to-hand combat and his inclination to offer no resistance at all. The former was more likely, now that the group of girls had been supplanted by a different kind of throng, but also more complicated. He would be held accountable for any person he hurt, and the image of the Space Service would suffer yet another blow. But if he did not resist, he could get himself maimed or killed.

Now he saw that the mill rotor was set up on a substantial pedestal—in more than one respect, considering this culture's newfound worship of "free" power—in order to bring the blades into the wind properly. He would have to leap up to touch the dangerous part. That was fortunate, because the wind was now increasing to near-gale strength, with stronger gusts, making the blades sing with their special melody of force. The mill was in its element, literally; it was built to withstand hurricane-force winds, and Shetland knew that the power to be drawn from that wind varied with the cube of its velocity. A storm was excellent news for this mill!

And bad news for Shetland. His predicament remained.

The waves of the reservoir were now whipping up high; he dared not trust himself to that. Unless the storm scattered the throng—but this did not seem to be happening. Rather, it urged them into abandoned excitement; they might do anything.

He passed under the hoop and came up against the central tower of the windmill. Beyond this, he remembered, the escarpment dropped down into the water. He could go no farther.

The pursuers swarmed in. The intensifying storm had thinned out the gentler elements, leaving the most aggressive males. They were forging into the opposing wind, their eyes slitted, their hair flattened back. They were now beyond reason; they were governed by the blood-lust of the mob. There could be no submission; that would lead only to a quicker demise.

"I am of space!" he cried. "There will be an accounting!" But this threat, quite valid, was wasted in the howl of the wind. They could not even hear him. He *had* to fight.

Again, belatedly, he wished he had lingered for the briefing at the Station. He would surely have been warned of this type of encounter, and told how to avoid it. Perhaps they would have provided him with a better blimped route, one that did not pass high buildings or beaches or windmills.

Shetland braced his back against the stone and concrete wall and raised his hands, prepared to defend himself. He was now out of the wind, while it still half blinded his pursuers. But when they came close to the tower, they would be shielded from it too.

"Come in, Captain," a deep voice said almost behind him.

Shetland jumped, startled. His head snapped about.

A large yellow man stood in a doorway that had opened in the base of the Darrieus structure. He was pure Mongoloid, therefore another racial outcast, and he was smiling. Shetland glanced at the oncoming crowd, and decided to accept the proffered hospitality. He stepped rapidly to the door.

The yellow man closed it behind them, and the fury of the storm abruptly cut off. The host set an old-fashioned wooden bar across the inside. The door was stout, as befitted the fixtures of a hurricane-proof domicile; no one would break through it barehanded.

"The weather will now disperse them," the man said. His voice was beautiful: not merely extraordinarily low, but possessed of special tonal qualities that made it fascinating. Some deep voices Shetland had heard were coarse, but this one was almost musical, like the lowest pitch of the base strings in an orchestra. The effect was heightened by a certain subtle oriental accent; undoubtedly the man had been brought to this section of the world by one of the tremendous migratory currents spawned by the Miscegenation Act.

"Thank you. I am—Kerr Shetland," he gasped. That pursuit had become as dangerous as any threat in space! "No Captain; my level is Commander. But it is true I am of space."

He waited for the negative reaction, but it did not come. "I am Somnanda."

They shook hands gravely. It occurred to Shetland that a formal bow might be more in keeping with this man's heritage. But it would be artificial to attempt that here. "I was aware of your approach," Somnanda said.

"The whole beach was aware of it!" Shetland agreed ruefully.

"I refer to prior information." Somnanda half turned. "I have prepared a meal; you are in hunger." He showed the way to a small central compartment, more by a nod of the large head than by any perambulatory motion, for the space here was as crowded as that of a shuttleship. A compact table rising only inches off the floor was set for two.

"You really did know!" Shetland said. "Are you psychic?"

"Yes."

Shetland paused. He had spoken lightly, but the assent was completely serious. Unable to explore the ramifications of this response rapidly, he changed the subject. "Don't you have to tend to the mill during the storm? I should think there would be adjustments, and I would not wish to distract you from your business."

"I am aware of the mill." That was all the explanation a psychic needed to provide, it seemed. "I favor the oriental ways. You will master chopsticks rapidly, for you have excellent coordination."

"Yes." Coordination was another necessity of space; no psychic information was needed for that insight!

They sat crosslegged on the floor on either side of the table and picked up their bowls. Sure enough, Shetland imitated his host and quickly got the hang of the sticks. The technique was to bring the bowl close to the face and manipulate the fingers quickly so that spillage was minimal even by inexperienced hands.

The food was a mixture of vegetables, spiced. It was strange but quite good.

"How is it that you do not object to the space effort?" Shetland inquired. "You surely know how much energy it consumes."

"It is a necessary consumption, Captain. It—"

"Please, you embarrass me. I lack that status by two grades."

"I doubt that, Captain. I seldom make errors of that nature."

So much for psychic accuracy. Shetland let it go; he had

had enough of dissension, and did not wish to antagonize his mysterious host. "I regret interrupting you."

"Space is the only avenue remaining for the possible salvation of our kind," Somnanda said gravely. Oh, that melodic voice that made even obvious statements seem to have special import! "Our critical need is for energy. Only in space is there hope of discovering new sources. It is true that this search requires tremendous expenditures of resources, but we appear to have no alternative. Soon the effort may be rewarded with phenomenal success. And your own part in it—"

"I am surprised that one who is psychic should manage a windmill," Shetland said. "The task would seem to lack challenge."

"It seems I am also lethargic, Captain. Perhaps that is the root of my ability. It is easier to economize on the expenditure of energy if one is aware of the larger framework. Watchmen are needed for the comparatively dull assignments like this one, for the mill as a channel of power has considerable value to the society, and full employment is guaranteed by the government."

"The Employment Act," Shetland agreed.

"It is largely a sinecure inherent in the system that allows us to relax. I do, however, maintain the rotor in excellent operational form."

By being psychically aware of its needs? "I understand there are a number of such sinecures," Shetland said. "Many people, it seems, consider the entire Space Service to be of a similar nature."

Somnanda smiled, acknowledging the irony. He moved aside the empty bowls. "Water, Captain?"

"If you please."

They took glasses of chill water, holding them momentarily high in the manner of a toast. After the spiced vegetables, the drink was most refreshing.

"Shall we play a game of chess, Captain?"

Shetland smiled. "You certainly are aware of my foibles! Do you have a board?"

"It is not necessary. Select your opening."

A dawning hope filled Shetland's breast. What he contemplated was fully as appealing as the sex proposed by the naiad, in its special way. "White: Pawn to King Four," he said.

"Black: Pawn to Queen Four."

"Sicilian," Shetland murmured, pleased. The opening intrigued him; but more than that, he appreciated the fact that Somnanda, like himself, could play mental chess. A rare discovery! "Do you also have eidetic memory?"

"No, Captain. I merely enjoy the game. It requires no physical effort."

That was certainly true, when no board or pieces were used! Delightful.

They played out the game. Shetland knew himself to be a strong if conventional player, because he had total recall and seldom made simple errors. He could review all the principal lines of strategy from his mental chess manuals. But Somnanda, playing in less orthodox fashion, defeated him roundly. The formidable power of the man's mind manifested obliquely through his strategy; moves that had seemed superfluous showed their rationale later in the game, when it was too late to counter them. Even here, there was an economy of concept, with brilliance serving in lieu of offensive force; a lazy man's mode. Shetland was aware that he was losing from the outset, but played it through because he was fascinated by the coordinated beauty of Somnanda's technique. Every time he tried to mount an offensive, he discovered that his opponent had anticipated it and set his pieces to foil the thrust. It was a thoroughly enjoyable experience, this meeting with an original and powerful mind.

"You are a most intelligent man," Shetland said, after conceding the game. "I envy you that facility."

"Your envy, in this case, is misplaced. I am not intelligent; I merely divine your intent and counter it before it takes effect."

That seemed indeed to have been the case! "You beat me by being psychic?"

"Yes. I did not believe you would object."

"I don't object. I don't believe in the supernatural—no offense intended. I feel you are merely an excellent player. I have not had a game like this in years." And without a board—oh, marvelous!

A phone sounded. "It is for you," Somnanda said, unmoving.

Surprised, for the man had not touched the instrument, Shetland reached across and picked up the receiver. "Commander Shetland speaking."

"I shall read these orders to you verbatim," the operator said, seeming unsurprised to have her party answer on this strange number. She had a sweet voice, as they all did. "KERR SHETLAND 0–5 SPACE SERVICE, PLANET LEAVE CANCELED. REPORT TO ORBITAL STATION FOR DUTY ABOARD THE MEG II TIMESHIP AS COMMANDING OFFICER. PROMOTION TO CAPTAIN 0–7 EFFECTIVE THIS HOUR." She paused. "That is the message; please acknowledge."

Shetland sat openmouthed, unanswering.

"Acknowledged," Somnanda said loudly.

"Thank you—and congratulations, Captain," the operator said, and disconnected.

Shetland hung up the receiver and stared at Somnanda. "You really *are* psychic! I had no inkling of this!"

Somnanda nodded gravely.

"You kept calling me 'Captain,' and you knew the call was mine—yet my arrival here was random, and my garb outlandish." He glanced down at his bedraggled outfit. "*No* one could have anticipated—" He paused. "Yet the operator also knew—"

"I notified the local switchboard that you had arrived when I saw you on the beach," Somnanda explained. "I did not then know your name, for such specifics are not within my competence, but presumably there are not many space officers in this region at this moment. No mystery attaches there. It would also have been possible for me to gain notice of your new status when—"

"The Space Service does not read orders to strangers!" Shetland objected—then realized that he was arguing the case for psychic knowledge. He shook his head. "All this is entirely contrary to my mode of belief. I do not accept the supernatural as a valid force."

"Nor do I." The man smiled at Shetland's surprise. "I do not regard my psychic ability as other than natural, Captain. It is a special talent, similar to your photographic memory."

"Yes, but—I might as well place credence in a ghost!"

"Why not, Captain? *I* do."

Shetland shook his head again, but it did not clear the confusion. "I am an extremely pragmatic individual."

"This would seem to be the reason for your promotion."

Shetland, balked by the immensity of concept, focused on a detail. "You are not *sure*?"

"I know what *is*, not *why*," Somnanda explained. "And my power does not generally apply to myself, except as I relate to others, as in playing chess. I read your situation, then tailor mine to it. I do not know my own future, and I really do not know yours. I am merely aware of contemporary events as they relate to those people around me, such as your new assignment. That had been determined before we met. It seems that the message did not reach you before your leave commenced.''

"Typical red tape," Shetland agreed. He reread the message now imprinted in his memory. "Duty aboard the *Meg II* Timeship as commanding officer. So they had to promote me to the minimum grade for that office, though they bucked channels—" He frowned. "What in space is a 'timeship'?"

"That would be a ship that travels in time."

"Paradox, therefore impossible."

"I should have thought so too. It seems we were mistaken."

"We can't be mistaken. There is no way a ship can travel in time—other than straight forward at the rate we all do. Time is inflexible. Consider the anomalies if we were to go five years into our own past—" He shook his head again and rubbed his sore knees. "Paradox!"

"I agree," Somnanda said. "Yet there is no error in your orders. You are to command a timeship—and I feel this will be crucially important to the welfare of our species."

"You mentioned a ghost. What is that?"

Somnanda frowned. "You mentioned it, Captain. I only concurred."

Shetland suppressed a tinge of annoyance. "Then what ghost do you know of, that brought that concurrence?"

"I do not know. Only that it relates to you in a transcendently important manner."

Shetland stood with abrupt decision. "I must report to my new ship. I thank you for your hospitality and a fine chess game, and trust we shall meet again."

For once, Somnanda looked surprised. "Captain, you intend to have me drafted into the Space Service!"

"Oh, do I?" Shetland inquired, smiling. "If I discover that this ship, the *Meg II*, really can travel in time, or that there really *is* some kind of ghost, I am going to need the services of a really competent psychic."

Chapter 3:_____Black Hole

Shetland arrived at the orbital station after sleeping through most of the shuttle's blast up. He had had ample time to think, even so. Why had his leave been so abruptly canceled? Why had he been jumped in grade and given a new ship? He had never captained a ship before; he seemed to be the last person eligible for such command. And to be assigned to a brand-new ship, of a new type—

The *Meg II* Timeship. Shetland had heard scuttlebutt about the breakthrough in timeshipping, but had been certain it was merely one of the tall tales for which spacemen were notorious. Denied appreciation on Earth, they compensated by inventing fantastic oases in space: a planetoid shaped exactly like a woman, twin conic mountains, safe harbor for ships in the obvious place. He had never heard the distaff version of that concept; was there one? A narrow ring about Saturn composed of solidified alcohol, absolutely potable when thawed, divinely flavored. A mine on Pluto with nuggets of pure iridium—some versions said osmium—one of the most precious of metals, lying about for the taking. But also more sinister fears, such as of a ghost in space, resembling a small gaseous nebula: the ship that passed through it became haunted, a source of horrible mischief thereafter. A ghost? Suddenly he wondered . . .

The timeship rumors seemed to be fashioned of similar stuff, the futile hopes and fears of an ingrown space cadre. Once space had been a bold frontier, exciting the popular imagination. How nice it would be to take a modern spaceship back to that time, to bask in the warmth of public approval! Shetland felt that tug himself, especially after discovering the extent of the antispace antipathy that had developed. *SPACE, SPACED! WAS'E, WASTE! Go find a black hole! Prok!* Oh, that hurt, for reasons he would never speak. But he never fooled himself; reality was reality, and neither ghosts nor time travels were part of it.

And so he had slept, having settled his mind as far as feasible. He knew he would discover that the *Meg II* was a specialized refinement, perhaps containing freezing equipment for passengers so that they could endure a journey of years while aging only minutes. In that sense, for them, it was time travel. But strictly one way. There was no "time dilation" effect for ordinary space travel, because there was no way for man's present (and probably future) technology to boost a ship to that major fraction of the velocity of light in vacuum required to invoke dilation to any significant degree. Naturally the captain and crew would age the full amount, and this would make it an undesirable assignment requiring special inducement like double promotions. Most spacers lived for the time they could return to Earth, despite their low repute there. Shetland actually *liked* space—and that, he was sure, was a major element in his selection and promotion.

Who else could they prevail upon to undertake some long, difficult voyage with perhaps no return?

The orbital station was huge. It was far out from Earth, so as not to offend the delicate sensitivities of the populace aboard the home planet by being conspicuous. He smiled privately, suffering a vision of the screaming youths bumping his blimp, and of nude nymphs throwing sand. The station had a resident population of thousands. They had homes in "spinning wheels" that provided artificial gravity, and shopping and entertainment facilities. Extensive hydroponic gardens and solar energy collectors made the station largely self-sufficient in food and power.

But spacers were not permitted to take their leaves here. They had to go to Earth despite the added expense of transport. This was part of the network of regulations that had become largely nonsensical. Critically energy-short Earth still wasted its energy, as always. To this extent, the popular ire over the space effort was justified.

Well, not exactly, he had to admit. If the members of the Space Service ever became completely detached from Earth, they would have dwindling loyalty to it, and therein would sprout the seeds of disaster. In old years the armies of small nations (and sometimes large nations) could become detached, then callously conquer their own countries and rule instead of the civilians. Unified Earth intended to avoid that particular menace, for the most devastating weapons were now in space.

The shuttle docked. Shetland, experienced in free-fall as in hi-gee, cleared the locks without trouble and floated into the personal receiving station at the end of the main tube. Rotation provided half gravity here in the narrow section.

"Captain Shetland?" the desk clerk inquired, eying the Commander's insignia with disapproval. It did not matter that

Shetland had had no opportunity to revise these tokens of rank; to this functionary he was out of uniform. "Report to the Admiral at 1000." The Admiral had a name, but it seemed superfluous; no one used it.

Shetland nodded. He had almost an hour. He decided to visit Hydroponics for a bite to eat, as Somnanda's salad had been his last meal. Then he would stop by the commissary for new insignia. Strictly speaking he should attend to the latter first, but the gardens were on the way to the store. He did not like the inefficiency of retracing his steps. He liked the hydrogardens; he admitted to himself that this was part of his motivation.

At the entry a woman approached him. "Are you the officer in charge today, sir?" she inquired. She was a slightly obese Mongoloid, a considerable contrast to the sleek nymphs of Earth. She would be a likely target for mayhem, on the surface of the planet, as she obviously consumed too much food and therefore would be considered a waster. But those who worked in Hydro normally lived on the culls, and it would be as wasteful to throw them away as to eat them.

"I am not in charge," he said.

"There's a ghost in the garden, I think."

Shetland smiled; she evidently hadn't paid attention to his response. "There is no ghost."

This she heard. She was only momentarily set back. "Will you at least look, sir? It's the strangest thing, and I'm afraid it will go away before I find the—"

"I have no authority here, especially over supernatural manifestations, but if you will obtain for me some leaves of fresh lettuce, I will look at your ghost."

"Fair enough!" she exclaimed. "They happen to be in the same section." Then, in belated introduction: "I'm Tibet, sir." As had been the case with Sosthenna at the satellite station, she did not give her last name. The matter was optional, and women tended to go by their given names, while men tended to go by their surnames. He considered this distinction of address to be nonsensical, but he liked it.

"Shetland." He did not give his rank, as the mismatch with his present insignia would only cause confusion.

They entered the main tube. It widened out in a giant circular downhill slant to achieve the diameter necessary to produce one gee at present rotation. It was beautiful. Large window vents admitted sunshine so neatly they seemed to have no material at all, though of course they were completely airtight. The light crossed the hollow center to fall on the banks of plants on the opposite sides. The air was especially sweet because of the plants. In fact, this was the station's main source of oxygen. Narrow ramps traversed the rim, giving access to every part of it. There were no weeds in this garden, no waste space.

Many of the plants were in flower, and many more were fruiting. Their green boughs leaned over the ramp, making occasional arbors. Everything was grown here, from lichen to grapefruit trees. "This is very like heaven," Shetland remarked.

Tibet smiled. "I have thought that too, Commander! Especially for the plants. Here they have no disease, no droughts, no freezes—I'd like to be reincarnated as a plant right here. Nothing could ever go wrong."

"Until you were harvested," he pointed out.

"Well, perhaps. But as I see it, a plant exists to be harvested. That's its mission in life. So by being used, it is being fulfilled. Just as we fulfill ourselves by reproducing and working and finally by dying to make room for our children."

"I suppose that is true," he said. Privately he felt no similar urges; he preferred sex with companionship but without reproduction, and work as an end in itself, and he did not like to think about death.

"Haven't you ever loved, Commander?" Naturally she assumed his insignia were accurate, and he did not correct her.

She was getting very personal. "Not in the sense you mean, I'm afraid. Have you?"

She made a short exhalation, not a sigh or snort, just an expulsion of air and meaning. "No. But I would like to."

And would *he* like to? The question tapped into a long-buried artery, and it was as though blood began spouting out in a towering fountain. *To love . . .*

Hastily he blocked the wound and buried the artery under tons of indifference. In his mind's eye, a truckload of earth cascaded down, absorbing the pool of blood, covering it, concealing it. Then a paving crew came and sealed it over, leaving an asphalt highway surface. Massed bicycles rode over it. Insolent youths tramped on it, breaking wind. Nude girls danced across it, their firm young buttocks twinkling. Yet, welling up through a tiny crack appeared a drop of red that alarmed a nymph on a unicycle . . .

"Are you all right, sir?" Tibet inquired, sounding worried.

"Merely reflecting," he said quickly. Recent developments must have disturbed him more than he had realized; he kept suffering these visions. Like lava, the red pushed up through trace fractures in his paved consciousness.

"Here is the lettuce," she announced. "We are permitted to cull individual leaves, provided we select from several plants so as not to hurt any. Shall I pick you some?"

"Yes, please."

She carefully removed one firm green leaf from the nearest plant, using a little sharp knife so as not to tear or tug at the main plant. Hydroponics meant less stable root systems; no solid dirt or rocks to cling to. Then she took another leaf from its neighbor. Soon she had a dozen leaves for him, absolutely fresh but not quite crisp. That was one of the things about lettuce: it crisped most when refrigerated; therefore the crispest was not the freshest.

"Thank you," Shetland said, eating the first leaf. It was excellent.

"The ghost is right down here."

Ah, yes, the ghost! Could this be the one that Somnanda of the windmill had perceived? She led him into a section of tall sunflowers. Like so many blankly smiling faces they waved in the gently circulating air. These were nearing maturity, their nutrient seeds expanding within the large disks.

"There," she said, pointing. "Hovering above the collards—"

Shetland looked. "I'm afraid I don't see it."

"It's moving away, sir. Here, let's follow it." She hurried on. He was beginning to feel the press of time, as he had another errand to do before reporting to the Admiral, but he had made a commitment here. He kept pace with her.

"There—there!" she cried. "I can almost make out its shape now. Human—"

He followed her gaze. For an instant he thought he saw a wash of red. He blinked, and it disappeared. Eye fatigue, of course.

"Come on!" Tibet said, plunging forward. "If we can catch it—"

Shetland questioned the advisability of actually catching a ghost, but kept silent. They passed through a field of flowering sweet peas. The blossoms were exceedingly pretty—but in his hurry he disturbed the bees that were attending to them. One bee banged against his cheek and stung him just under the right eye; he brushed it away—and another stung him on the hand.

Suddenly they were getting drenched. "Oh, no!" Tibet exclaimed. "The ghost went into the shower area!"

"That should dampen its spirit somewhat," Shetland muttered.

They backed out, but it was too late. Shetland's uniform was dripping, and Tibet's dress was clinging to her torso. He saw that she was somewhat heavier than he had judged; she could not have been on Earth for some time.

"Did you see it?" she demanded eagerly. "Small, like a child, needing a mother—"

Shetland spread his hands noncommittally, his gaze still on her torso.

Tibet looked down at herself. "Yes, I know," she said ruefully. "I eat too much. My job here keeps me in too much temptation. If I had lived in the heyday of Earth's conspicuous consumption age, I'd have gorged myself on steaks and pastries and—" She paused. "Don't look so horrified, Commander! They *did* used to eat meat and sweets, you know."

"It required eight to ten pounds of feed to produce one pound of edible cow meat," he said a bit stiffly. "That was grossly wasteful."

"I know. I don't condone it. I don't mind the Vegetarian Act, really I don't. Killing the poor animals just for the flesh of their bodies—that bothers me even more than the inefficiency of it. But the sweets, now—"

"Sugar was outlawed because of its harmful effect on the human body when oversupplied," he said. "And of course nonnutritive foods are sheer waste. With ten billion world citizens to feed—"

"Yes, yes, of course, Commander. You are right. We can't justify the old ways. But when I was a child, I did like—well, never mind, it really doesn't become me. We have an immediate problem. My dress, your uniform—oh, my, what happened to your eye?''

"It seems a bee took umbrage at my intrusion."

"Oh, sir, I'm sorry! They don't sting me—they must be used to me. Here, I have some salve—"

"I really don't have the time," he said gruffly.

"And we didn't even catch our ghost."

Shetland formed the briefest of smiles. "That is the nature of ghosts."

He left her and proceeded to the Admiral's office. It was better to report in sad condition that to report late.

The Admiral, resplendent in dress uniform, affected not to notice Shetland's sodden condition or wrong insignia or swelling eye. He returned salute, then shook hands. "Captain," he said abruptly, "if you could have anything you wanted—anything at all—what would it be?"

Shetland looked at him with his good left eye, not knowing what to answer. His body itched where the soaking caused the underclothing to shift and chafe.

"The truth, now," the Admiral said. He was a hearty man who looked as if he had availed himself somewhat of the pleasures of the hydrogardens without actually putting on weight. "A lovely woman? A five-course banquet? Another promotion?"

"A dry uniform," Shetland said under his breath.

"I heard that!" the Admiral said, smiling. "Captain, take mine." And he began to strip off his jacket.

"Sir!" Shetland said, amazed.

"Come on, Captain—I know you got dunked and stung in Hydro. That's the kind of thing that happens to people who dally in the pleasures of nature." He winked. "I've been stung on occasion myself, and not merely by errant bees. Not your fault, and you did what was right without making excuses; that's all the Service ever asks of you. Let's both get comfortable. What I have to impart is too important for formality. I've got a pair of warm dry robes here.''

''Oh.'' Then, as an afterthought, he added ''sir.''

So they both changed. ''Now I am only beginning to make my point,'' the Admiral continued over their glasses of hydroponic cider. ''This is too big to say with one blurt, and you have to be prepared for it. Try again: if you could have *anything*?''

The ground under the pavement in Shetland's mind shuddered. The passing cyclists veered away, alarmed. The nymphs fled to their beach, with only the naiad glancing regretfully back. A trickle of reddish fluid appeared. ''I can't answer that, sir.''

''Then I shall have to answer it for you,'' the Admiral said. ''You were once engaged to marry—''

''Sir!'' Shetland said, spilling some of his cider. The spilled drops were like bleached blood. *The waste!*

''Very well, Captain. I will not embarrass you further. I shall wait while you review the matter in your own eidetic mind. That, incidentally, was one—only one!—of the qualifications that brought you this assignment. Do it now.''

''Sir, I—''

''I would prefer not to have to issue that kind of an order, Captain. I do have my reasons.'' The Admiral sipped his cider.

If there was one thing Shetland did well, it was to follow orders, express or implied. Obligingly he did what he most dreaded: he let the vision proceed. The pavement cracked; the earth subsided as if into a sinkhole, and the pulsing artery was revealed. The puncture reopened, and the blood gushed up. It became a frothing sea, carrying him through time: twelve years.

Black hole . . . the damned obscenity, applied to this concept, the hurt and rage . . .

She was extraordinarily pretty: long-haired, jet black, possessed of unrivaled face and figure. She had a mind, too; she lacked his trick memory, but was far more intelligent than he. He envied her that intelligence—and so he proposed to have it for his children. To his surprise and intense gratification, Maureen had agreed to marry him.

Then the Miscegenation Act had passed. It had been a sudden thing worldwide, jury-rigged amid a flurry of measures designed to abate the savage race riots then occurring. The new world government had inherited staggering regional problems, and it had to act. The haves had refused to share sufficiently with the have-nots, and the racial bomb had to be defused. Of all the ways that might have been tried, had there been leisure to work out the ideal, this was the one that by some freak of global politics attained the majority decision. No person in all the world was permitted to marry another person of his own race, or to produce offspring thereby if already married. There were complex definitions of race, and allowances for those already of mixed blood—but neither Shetland nor Maureen had any pretext of admixture. Both were as racially pure specimens of black as could be found in the white culture. In fact, Shetland privately suspected that Maureen had been attracted to him at first because he was the blackest man she knew. She was, in her fashion, an activist about such things.

"What are we going to *do*?" Maureen demanded. She was an excitable young woman who reacted with a certain flair even to a routine event—and this was hardly that.

"We must obey the law," Shetland said heavily.

"Not to marry?" she demanded.

"We can marry," he said, for of course he had memorized the entire text of the act. "Provided we—"

"Both get sterilized!" she finished accusingly. "So we can't produce any more racially pure stock! Is *that* what you want?"

He had not thought about it sufficiently, because race had not been a factor in his need for her. He did not care what color his children might be, so long as they were intelligent. "I want *you*—with or without children." But was that the whole truth?

"Well, *I* want a family!"

He spread his hands, feeling numb. Would she actually leave him—in order to have children? It was hard to imagine— yet he was unsure of the strength of her belief. He would rather not have children, if they were of low IQ; but she, accustomed to intelligence because she had always had it, had other values. She wanted her children black. Which meant she could not accept this miscegenation requirement, this deliberate mixing of races. So it seemed unlikely that she would seek to marry elsewhere. But she still insisted on her family. He had thought he knew her well, but this sudden law had changed the picture entirely.

They had gone over the issue again and again, but found no solution. He wanted her—and the law. She wanted him— and children. He saw it as a circular graph, like the old-style governmental illustrations of the use of the tax dollar: so many neat pie-slices making up the whole. One 33 percent segment was labeled FAMILY; another was LAW. The third was divided in half: HE and SHE. The situation required that their mergence comprise only two-thirds of the pie—but they could not agree on which slice to omit. He attached to LAW, she to FAMILY.

He told her of his analogy, even drawing a little diagram of it, showing how the mathematics of it made their union impossible unless one compromised.

Neither could compromise. The law was sacred to Shetland; the family was sacred to Maureen. They both knew, without ever quite saying it, that their marriage was doomed. Yet they hung on to the engagement, unable to terminate it.

One day he found a note on her door: *I have solved our problem painlessly. Love forever, Maureen.*

He didn't understand that; there was no painless solution. He banged on her door, alarmed, but had no answer. He entered the apartment, calling her name. All was silent. He felt a premonition of the sort he had once had in childhood about his dog. He searched through the rooms, knowing she was gone—but afraid to discover *how* she had gone. Finally, reluctantly, he checked the little bathroom.

Maureen reposed in the tub, the water up to her delicate chin, her dark body concealed beneath the red fluid. The color was from dilute blood. She had administered some local anesthetic to her legs and sliced open the great arteries of her inner thighs, right up near their juncture, letting the blood pulse into the warm bath water as though it were a monstrous monthly period. Painlessly she had given birth to her own death.

He had been unable even to experience proper grief. To mourn her loss would have been to imply acceptance of her view—and he would not do in her death what he had not done in her life. Had *he* been responsible for her demise—or had *the law*? Had he really loved her, would he have survived himself? Had she really loved him, would she have died? There were no acceptable answers.

He had gone to space, sealing over that tubful of blood forever, obliterating it, all traces of her, of marriage, and of racial awareness from his consciousness. The process had taken years, for his love had been great though suspect, and on occasion some chance event still could let leak a trickle of blood. But now he was reasonably secure. Time was the great healer, indeed.

Except when some chance jibe scored in a manner that the other party could not know. *Black hole*—the supposedly obscene sexual connection with such a woman, and the inescapable abyss of emotion that her denial brought him to. In space, a black hole let nothing go, by definition. In emotion— *had* he escaped, or had he merely papered over his awareness, refusing to admit that he was emotionally dead?

The Admiral was aware of the completion of Shetland's vision. "So what do you want most of all?" he asked again.

This time Shetland could answer. "To know that my course was correct," he said simply.

"Your course has been correct," the Admiral said. "You, better than any other officer in space—and I except neither myself nor my superiors—you have represented that combination of mind and law and professional detachment that we like to think epitomizes the Service. You have a very special facility—I would call it brilliance—"

"Hardly that, sir," Shetland agreed morosely. His memory vision had left him depleted; there had been no release in it, only a revival of ancient pain and doubt. "I am neither smart nor creative; that is why I go strictly by the book."

"True, Captain—but it is a good book. Your file documents an intelligence just barely sufficient to meet our minimum officer's candidate standard; only your phenomenal memory enabled you to qualify as well as you did. Your imagination—well, imagination has never been much of a virtue in the military sphere anyway, so no loss there. Yet your mind—"

"It is called eidetic memory—a literal seeing of remembered things, even the printed page."

"Precisely. You have whole volumes in your brain, don't you! If I were to ask you to read off the tenth word listed on page 1000 of, say, the Oxford English Dictionary—"

Shetland checked, flipping over the pages of the OED in his mind, finding the place. "There are only six words defined on that page, sir. Of course the numbering starts over many times, so perhaps a later volume—"

The Admiral smiled. "I should have known! I thought I was exaggerating."

"However, if you want the tenth word appearing in the text of that page—"

"No, of course not!" Then the Admiral reconsidered. "Cancel that. You've got my curiosity up. What is that word?"

"Angl."

"What?"

"The full line reads '[1483 *Cath. Angl.* 48 Burdus [Burdeus], *cinitas est, burdi-.*' The word in brackets is actually unclear; there is an obscuration on my copy. Perhaps it is 'Burdeas.' "

"What in space does it mean? Are you sure you didn't pick up the Paris French Dictionary instead?"

"It related to Bordeaux, a city in southern France, Europe. The definition begins on page 999." Shetland skimmed ahead, and smiled. "A quote from 1836, sir, if you will: 'Don't go abroad to drink sour wine, because they call it Bordeaux.' "

The Admiral emitted a snort of mirth through his nose. "They had rare humor in those days. Rare wine, too." He looked at his empty cider glass. "I must confess to missing those delicate alcoholic beverages."

"Sir!"

"Captain, don't be shocked. It is no violation of the

manual to miss the old days. Indeed, it is permissible to work arduously for their return. As I am doing now. Where was I before we drifted?''

"Commenting on the qualities of my mind."

"Ah, yes. Thank you. Captain, your mind is very special in this eidetic capacity. It enables you to know the complete Operations Manual so well you can follow it at all times. And you have the internal discipline to do exactly this. I don't believe you have ever deviated even fractionally—'' He paused. "*Have* you?"

"Yes, sir. I soiled my uniform, and reported for duty when out of uniform—''

"Prok!" the Admiral cried, making Shetland wince. "The manual didn't allow for that wetting because it never anticipated an officer encountering a ghost-chasing girl in Hydroponics. You acquitted yourself honorably, Captain. Courtesy is also part of the manual—no, don't quote me verse and line!—and in special cases judgment is necessary. As for the insignia—you are well aware that an officer is granted a full twenty-four hours to change over, and longer in special cases; you are not yet out of uniform." He peered at Shetland's eye. "However, Captain, I am not at all certain what the book says about bee stings in space. That *is* a bit irregular—''

Shetland maintained a rigid dignity.

The Admiral laughed. "Oh, posh! You have very little humor! Another prime military quality. You'll rank me one day, Captain; I laugh too much." He took a moment to sober up, not at all penitent. "At any rate, you really do go strictly by the book, in a way that few others can. That quality has become extremely important. Extremely." He paused, as though mulling over something significant. "Yet what would you do in a genuinely nonbook situation?"

"I don't know, sir."

"Well, *I* know. You'd follow what you knew the manual would say if it should be extended into that particular area. Isn't that right?"

Shetland nodded. "Yes, sir, I would."

"Mark the place; I shall have more to say on that before we close.

"Yes, sir."

"No, cancel again. I don't want to be nagged by a loose thread. What I mean to say is we are about to send you in search of a ghost—"

Shetland choked, then instantly regained his composure.

The Admiral paused momentarily, aware of his reaction, then continued. "And neither you nor your crew will be able to trust your own personal judgments, so all you will have to guide you will be the manual in your mind—and at times it will seem crazy. Understand what I mean?"

"No, sir."

"Good, you're paying attention. You'll pick it up in context in due course. Course—yes, that reminds me. I remarked that you were correct in your course with regard to your girlfriend. Let me make that quite clear."

"Sir, there is no need—"

"Quiet, Captain."

Shetland shut up.

"We face a critical energy shortage. It came upon us by stages, and relates intimately to food and population. In fact, without that limitation, our species might never have risen to civilization at all. We would still be hunter-gatherers, living in the fool's paradise of the Garden of Eden. But our population increased as we learned how to overcome the threats of our environment, and we had to stop gathering and start growing our food. By putting energy into our habitat, we increased our food supply and our population. This was the Neolithic Revolution. Do you follow me?''

"Energy, food and population interrelate," Shetland said.

"Precisely. Once we had mastered the principle, it carried us all the way into full civilization and space travel. But there are limits to all things, and now we find that no matter how ingeniously we apply ourselves, we do not have enough usable energy to make enough food on Earth to feed our monstrous population. Until we find more energy—a *lot* more energy!—we have only one route to go: conservation. You understand?''

Shetland remembered the bicycles, blimps, sailboats, solar collectors and windmills of Earth that made visceral a situation he had been aware of intellectually. "Yes."

"And what's the ultimate conservation?"

Shetland hesitated. "I believe it would be population control."

"Exactly! But you know what trouble we've had practicing that! Religious and social factors have fought it every step of the way. Some people would rather die, literally, than give up their right to—sorry, didn't mean to get personal, Captain—to procreate. So we can't just pass a law limiting babies. Now, if it were your job to reduce the birthrate abruptly, without actually telling anyone *not* to reproduce, without mentioning religion or morality, just using some other issue to effect it as if it were a by-product, diverting the public attention from the real thrust—well, how would you do it?''

Shetland considered. This was not the kind of thinking he was good at, and he could not see how this related to either the space effort generally or his own assignment specifically. "I suppose I would arrange to make reproduction inconvenient or distasteful."

"You're on the beam," the Admiral said as though complimenting a dutiful student. "Could you give me an example?"

Shetland concentrated again, but all that developed was a trickle of blood in a crack in a pavement. Then, abruptly, it exploded in his face. "The Miscegenation Act!"

"Brilliant! Didn't *that* cut the birthrate, though! Do you realize the cultural and practical problems entailed in finding a compatible mate of another race?"

"Yes," Shetland said between his teeth.

"Yes, of course you do. You were about to reproduce—and that Act stopped you cold, even though you are no bigot. As it stopped billions. Because of the really formidable geographic and cultural barriers. Most of the world's races don't even speak the same language. How could a billion orientals get out of Asia to marry blacks and whites, even if they wanted to? How could a white man from Norway court a black girl in the equatorial jungle? Where would they settle? What language would their children speak? Oh, what havoc we wrought, in the name of racial amity! Of course it hasn't worked perfectly; many people simply mated illegally and had bastards. But those offspring were stigmatized if they were too obviously purebred, and some were executed for being illicit. Some parents committed suicide when that happened. There has been a great deal of unrest. But the great majority compromised in exactly the manner intended: they accepted sterilization and married their own kind. The population of the world is definitely dropping."

"Not merely through birth reduction," Shetland muttered, seeing more blood.

"But this is just a temporary expedient. Already people are adjusting. The legitimate birthrate is rising, and the first-generation miscegenation children are nearing repro age. What will they do? Once 'miscegenation' was a pejorative term, you know. No more. So the problem is nigh on us again, and this time we won't get away with any racial dodge. We have to solve the social and political and economic problems by solving the energy problem. For once and for all. If we can't find the answer in the natural universe, we'll just have to quest for it in the supernatural universe. And that is your mission, Captain."

"The timeship?" Shetland was hardly able to keep the Admiral's words in focus; the implications of the law and the supernatural were still sinking in. Could any of this really make sense?

"The timeships. You are about to go on a quest for energy, Captain—unlimited energy, that will free us forever from the need for arbitrary controls. Find that energy, and no one, ever again, will have to suffer as you have suffered. You will know that you have done right—by abolishing the need for the law that killed your fiancée."

The hurt! "Impossible, Admiral. It is a quest for an illusion. A—a ghost." Like Tibet's ghost.

"Precisely. You are going ghost hunting—by the book. You may be the only man who can do that."

"By traveling through time? Sir, I—"

"Get this through your head, Captain. The two *Meg*s really *are* timeships. The paradoxes have been resolved. You can't travel in time on Earth, but you can do it in deep space, where your own life and the lives of others are not paradoxically affected. There are no paradoxes in that situation. You will journey into the future—and return intact. And the most beautiful thing about it is that it requires *virtually no energy*. None of Earth's precious energy, anyway. So you can go a year, or a million years, or a billion—there seems to be no upper limit, and you will not be dilated—that's always an illusion, incidentally, there never was any so-called clock paradox, the clocks only seemed to differ when they were apart, much as a ship in the distance seems small though you know it is not.''

''But they have measured the difference in the clocks!'' Shetland protested. ''Experimentally, with unmanned—''

''What they have measured is the deformation of time accomplished by sustained high acceleration. Or high gravity; same thing. Since living human beings can never be subjected to that gee, it becomes academic. But in any event, that is merely a difference in the rate of aging, not time travel. Relativity will not enable anyone to travel back in time to eliminate his grandfather, and neither will this new technique. Have no fear; that danger does not exist.''

''Sir, I can hardly be expected to believe time travel, of any nature.''

''I hardly believe it myself, Captain! But it is true, we have made the breakthrough, we have damn near perfected it, and we have two ships that can go literally to the ends of the universe, the *temporal* ends, and we shall do just that. I have been to the future and back myself, on a limited mission. Somewhere there will be energy we can tap; there just has to be, and all we have to do is find it. You will find it, and save Earth. It is that simple.''

The man was almost babbling with the excitement of his revelation. He really believed that time travel was possible.

''Sir,'' Shetland said cautiously, ''I am no theoretical expert, but there are problems about the very concept of time travel, even in distant space. There *are* paradoxes—and a paradox means, simply, that there is some fundamental error, probably in basic concept.''

''Yes, I know. You're still thinking in terms of Earth, aren't you? You heard me say that we can travel forward in time, and back, so you reason that we could travel back first, then forward, and that is true, but still there is no paradox. You want to know what happens if you do go back and kill your grandfather. And I'll tell you again: you can't do it. Because time is motion, especially when you're standing still. If you jumped back fifty years on Earth, you'd land where Earth was fifty years ago—which is somewhere in deep space, because of the cumulative vectors of the motions about the sun, galactic spin and universal expansion, among others. You'd have to use up so much energy lining up your grandfather that it wouldn't be worth it; in fact our experts' math shows the amount would become infinite. You just can't make that paradox, any more than you can exceed the speed of light in a vacuum.''

''But that's like space travel,'' Shetland objected. ''If you jump a million years into the future, you might be much farther away than light could travel in that moment, so you *have* in effect exceeded the velocity of—''

''No, no, Captain. You never exceed lightspeed. Jump a million years into the future, the physical universe will have existed for that million years, so you will have moved within the relativistic limits even if it doesn't seem that way. Jump back a million years, and as far as the universe is concerned, you never went forward; it assumes that you simply remained in place. Jump back first, then forward, same thing: the universe doesn't believe, the universe doesn't care. But you touch on a significant point: time *is* distance. To travel in time is to travel in space, because as I said, our planet, our solar system, our galaxy and our universe are moving. So you will *seem* to be moving in space—but your ship's clock will simply mark your deviation from standard time. You'll see. You will have a number of very strange concepts to master, but once you do, it will be fantastic.''

''It is already fantastic,'' Shetland said dryly.

"But also true—as once seemed to be the case with relativity itself."

Shetland still could not accept it. "Suppose the ship is already moving in space? That would add a vector—"

"That would multiply with the passage of time," the Admiral agreed. "Certainly. In this manner we have what amounts to space-time travel. We can take our two ships any*where*, any*when* in the universe—and bring them back. If what we need exists anywhere, or ever *has* existed, or ever *will* exist—"

"But the universe is—" Shetland searched for the proper expression, but it evaded him. Even when one had a literal dictionary in his head, he had to know where to look. "Large. The ship would get lost, in time *and* space. A horrible fate."

"Yes indeed, Captain. No device in our current technology can accurately guide such a ship back to its starting point in spacetime. But have you heard about psionics?" Without waiting for a reply, he continued: "Psionics is like a cross between science and magic. There have been charlatans in science and in magic, and in psionics too. But now the genuine researchers are into it, and ascertaining the core truth of it. The best that can be said for it at present is that it does seem to work. Remember the problem regular mathematicians had, accepting noneuclidian geometry? Until a real-life application was found for what had been purely theoretical. And the uncertainty principle—once anathema to established belief. But valid. Now psionics is coming of age. We are instituting a search for qualified psychics to operate what we call the beacon."

"Psychics?"

"The terminology has been cobbled from mythology as well as science. We don't mean people who hold séances and commune with the dead. We mean people who can tune in to reality in a manner that others cannot. Without depending on normal channels. Because we have particular use for them, now.''

Shetland remembered Somnanda, the psychic of the windmill. ''Am I free to make a recommendation, sir?''

''No,'' the Admiral said. ''In matters relating to your ship, the *Meg II*, you will not make any recommendations.'' He paused for effect. ''You will give directives. It is vital that a completely compatible crew be assembled, because incompatibility affects the beacon adversely. You will approve your entire crew, and work with it until you are satisfied that your ship is ready for spacetime.''

Shetland sighed to himself. When would he ever be ready for such a preposterous mission? Time travel? Psionics—the cross between science and magic? The pursuit of a ghost, indeed!

Chapter 4:____Four Dreads

"**Z**ero minus ten," the pilot's voice counted off over the intercom. "Nine, eight, seven . . ."

Captain Shetland's eyes passed to the hunched man seated across the cabin, then returned to the port. There was nothing special to see; they were in deep space, well beyond the planetoid belt. The stars were bright and still. After two years of preparations, they were abruptly on their way. *Too* abruptly. But orders were . . .

". . . three, two, one, drive," the pilot said. "Captain, the clock is moving."

It was. Shetland contemplated the twin clock faces set in the wall. Each had one hand, and the numbers went up to 23. The digits were calibrated decimally. The marker of the left dial stood on 0; that of the right was nudging off it. One-hundredth of an hour . . . two-hundredths.

"Thank you, Johns," Shetland said. His voice did not reflect the tension he was feeling.

He stood still while his stomach adjusted. There was something visceral about time travel, that wrenched the gut and fogged the brain, though the manual claimed that ship's personnel were not affected. Perhaps it was simply an emotional reaction—or maybe there were things the manual did not know. Heretical thought! Regardless, it had to be controlled.

The way to control anything was to understand it; this was fundamental to his philosophy. The restrictions of conventional physics could not be set aside with impunity. Awful things could happen when men left the normal framework of time. It was natural to feel fear—but by anticipating the threats properly he could nullify them. He clung firmly, almost desperately to that belief.

The dreads in his mind were four. As he closed his eyes a notebook appeared, a function of his eidetic memory that dramatized things unbidden. The book had an old-fashioned wire-coil binding, relic of the year when such oddities still were manufactured. On its brown cover was a picture of a small and shaggy pony and a single word: PRIVATE.

The queasiness intensified. Shetland swayed, but would not take a seat. The notebook in his mind opened, exposing a lightly ruled sheet. From offstage appeared an animated yellow pencil, freshly sharpened, faint toothmarks on the latter end. The pencil twirled, momentarily blurring the toothmarks, and wrote:

THE FOUR DEADLY DREADS OF
CAPTAIN SHETLAND

1. *Beacon, failure of*
2. *Drive, malfunction of*
3. *Personality, distortion of*
4. *Unknown, the*

It pleased him to note, as always, the alphabetic arrangement of the Dreads. But it bothered him to note the imbalance in the length of the lines. Item 4 was too short. He toyed with the notion of adding a word, so that the last entry would read:

4. Unknown, manifestation of

No, not quite accurate. The length of the line was satisfactory, but at the expense of content. Once the Unknown manifested, it would no longer be unknown. A technicality, perhaps, but nevertheless one to be reckoned with. So the modification was not made, and the distressingly short line was permitted to remain. The Unknown was unknown; no qualifications were proper.

The book closed and the pencil marched away, its pink eraser bobbing to the unheard beat of a marching band.

Most people did not comprehend the meaning of the term "eidetic"; in fact the word was not in many dictionaries, even some supposedly authoritative ones. (He kept a small collection of words like that, used to test the competence of dictionaries: "menarche," "neoteny," "parsec" and the like.) It was a literal seeing, so that he could read a printed page backward or forward with similar facility, and note the dress of the margins, as he had done when the Admiral challenged him. The page was *there*, photographed at the time he had seen it physically, manifesting in every respect except the literal. A number of children had this sort of memory, and no doubt it facilitated their learning processes, but few retained it into adulthood. Shetland knew himself to be a freak, however conventional his exterior.

At any rate, this faculty was useful now. Fears that could be outlined in an old-fashioned notebook lost some of their power. That was good, for their power was great. One of them must have taken the *Meg I* . . .

Enough! he commanded himself. Even his carelessly wandering thoughts could be dangerous when the drive was on.

His stomach was settling. He would be all right. His concern now was for the others.

Shetland's gaze returned to the seated man. This was Somnanda, mystic of the beacon, prophet of the quest for the ghost. He was a long way from the windmill now!

Somnanda sat without motion or expression, still in his adjustment phase. His forehead was high, the hair above it dark but sparse. His long ears seemed to be listening intently for something beyond the confines of the cabin, or of the ship itself; for a moment Shetland thought they twitched like the ears of an animal, orienting on distant sound. Of course they did not; that was a peril of eidetic imagination.

The man's eyes, half closed, were a curious faded gray, their color suggesting a nictitating membrane. His lips and mouth were more delicate than one would suspect in so large a man. Somnanda gave the physical impression of nobility, almost of saintliness. Shetland regretted that he had never gotten to know this sparsely communicative man well, despite two years of acquaintance during the preparation for this voyage; surely there were rich depths there.

On the little table was a small stand bearing the facsimile of a burning candle. Somnanda's unwavering gaze centered on this light. His two mighty hands rested beside it, blue-ridged veins curling over the raised tendons in back. Those tendons betrayed the impassive countenance; he was taut! But his fingers touched the table surface lightly: that tension was contained.

Somnanda moved. His head swiveled gradually, turretlike, to cover Shetland. "It is well, Captain," he said, his voice so deep and strong despite its gentleness that there almost seemed to be a staccato echo from the walls. The stone of the windmill structure had dampened that voice, diminishing its effect; the metal of the ship's chamber seemed to amplify it.

Shetland relaxed. Behind his eyes the notebook reappeared, opening to the little list. The pencil drew a neat line through Dread 1.

The beacon was functioning properly—so far.

When the drive functioned, sending the ship through time, the normal universe existed only tenuously. Relative to the ship's crew and many of its instruments, the planets, stars and even galaxies became ghostlike: visible but untouchable. Within the ship, the laws of chemistry and physics applied as always: the crew had to eat, and the *Meg II* required power for illumination, temperature control, gravity and all the other essential functions including especially the drive itself. There was plenty of food in storage, and plenty of power from the fusion plant; the ship could travel for many months, internal time. But physical communication with Earth—i.e., radio, laser or capsule—was impossible, because Earth was seconds, minutes, or years apart from the ship in time.

Thus the beacon. There was complex circuitry embedded in the table beneath Somnanda's tapering fingers. It was psionic circuitry, incomprehensible if not nonsensical to the conventional technician. The actual method of contact was largely in the operator's mind, subject to almost no tangible verification—aside from the fact that it worked.

The flickering mock candle was the crew's evidence that the beacon was functioning. It lit the way home. Time travel necessarily entailed displacement in space relative to the apparent galaxy, and though the clock accurately measured the velocity of change it could not actually direct the voyager home. Not when the time traveled, forward and back, was thousands or millions of years. Not when the universe itself pulsed and changed, real only to itself. Only this steady pseudo candle, this metaphysical elastic connection, this almost spiritual light, the beacon, could guide them back to the correct century, the proper hour and second. Only Somnanda.

"Captain."

Shetland recovered with a start. "I'm sorry, Somnanda. Was I worrying again?"

Slowly the man smiled. "No, Captain. You were not disturbing the beacon—not any more than any human mind does at such a nexus. I wished merely to remind you that your move is due."

Oh, yes! Shetland had neglected their continuing game of chess. The lonely hours of space and time made some sort of conditioning and challenging diversion essential. The manual required joint entertainment by all available crewmembers on a daily basis, and encouraged diverse individual distractions. "Of course."

Shetland closed his eyes, visualizing the checkered board. His King was in check. "White, 15, King to King Two." He smiled, knowing that Somnanda would be aware of the seeming pun, king-to, king-two.

Somnanda nodded, his face as grave as Shetland had known it would be. It would be another hour before the man replied with his own move, for he, like Shetland, was deliberate. There was time, in more sense than one; each development was to be savored, not rushed.

Shetland was hungry now, so he stopped in at the mess chamber. It was the appetite born of nervous stress, so he would have to keep the ration small. But if food helped calm him, it was certainly worthwhile.

"Toast and coffee, Captain?" Tibet inquired. She remained a large woman in her middle thirties, generous in every sense of the word. She was good at her job, which, translated from the bureaucratic terminology of the manual, amounted to "cook." She was also an engaging personality in her own right. She seemed to be fascinated with every aspect of life experience, and was always interested in what a person might say to her, however trivial.

Perhaps that was what had brought him here, Shetland reflected, more than the food. It was good to be treated like someone important, even when he knew it was just her mannerism. According to the information in the file, she was actually an extraordinarily intelligent person, far overqualified for menial service, yet this seldom showed. She preferred to be a homebody, even in deepest space. She did not appear to have been shaken by the initiation of time travel; she, like he, was a comparatively old hand at it.

She brought the food, concocted somehow from the frozen squeeze-tube rations the Space Authority insisted on stocking even in grav-normal ships, and joined him at the table. She had made similar portions for herself. It looked and smelled just about like toast and coffee: archaic but nice.

"Jam?" she inquired.

Strawberry-flavored gunk; that at least was explicable. But it was amazing what a difference it made, calling it jam! A rose by any other name was sometimes sweeter.

"How many times a day do you eat, Tibet?" he asked, biting down.

"Only when others do," she replied innocently.

"There are six others, counting me. And we all eat in rotation."

Her eyes widened as if in surprise. "That's right, isn't it!"

Shetland had to laugh. "Tibet, you're a glutton!"

"You're jealous, Captain!"

"I am at that! I envy your sheer zest for life."

"There's no secret to it, Captain. All you have to do is want."

"I fear that is too profound for me." He chewed, meditating on his toast and jam. Probably she filtered the wheat out of something else, then rebaked it on a laboratory burner. "How did you come by that name—Tibet?"

"No coincidence. I was born there. In central Asia/Tibet where the Lamas once dwelt. When the Misceg Act passed, I traveled, because if there was one experience I really wanted to have . . ." She let it fade out, shrugging.

"But you aren't married."

"The lot fell on me for military service. It was ironic: all that travel, and I would have been called anyway. I could have stayed at home with the less ambitious yellow folk."

"That's right—you're Asiatic, racially."

"Hadn't you noticed, Captain?"

"I must have at one time." He was speaking literally; he always noted the details of a person he encountered, but then the personality overwhelmed the physical format. To this day he was uncertain exactly why he had requisitioned her for this crew; perhaps it had been the coincidence of her quest for a minor ghost in the hydroponic section, at a time when he was about to be put on a mission questing for the monstrous ghost of human energy sufficiency. He had not regretted it; she was always pleasant to be with, in her deliberately mundane way. It was hard to imagine the horror of the unknown, in her cheerful, placid presence.

She shook her head. "You're a marvel, Captain. When nature put eidetic memory into your head, she must have left something else out. I should think you would be the first to notice and remember color."

He looked at her in perplexity. "Why?"

"Because you're colored yourself. Black."

"On the contrary. Black is the absence of color."

"Not in the contemporary society. I'm pure Mongoloid and you're pure—"

"Black. Tibet, I don't understand your point."

"Captain, didn't you ever live on Earth?"

"Yes, of course, in youth. What is the relevance?"

She looked at him and shook her head slowly. "If you honestly can't tell me, maybe there is none. On the other hand, you just may be the most intelligently stupid man I know."

"The makeup of the ship's complement is relevant to Earth's situation," Shetland said, not wanting to admit that he was nettled by her attitude. Normally she was not like this. "There has to be an equilibrium, a balance in personnel approximating that of the human species. That is Space Authority policy, specified in the manual. Since Earth is required to miscegenate, so must the Space Service, even though there is no actual procreation in space. It is one of the foolishnesses of appearance. So age, race and sex are—"

"That is not precisely what I meant," she said. "More toast?"

He was momentarily trapped between the polite agreement for toast and the negative reaction to her argument. The negative won. "No thank you."

"Don't be angry."

He refused to play the game of denial. "What *did* you mean?

"Oh, color—we're all aware of it, even when it's of no account by law or manual. I went through a whole series when I was small, learning to like occidental cuisine. Sound and fury, signifying nothing."

Was she trying to divert him? Well, why not? "*What* series?"

"Ice cream. You know."

Shetland felt a laugh developing. He suppressed it. "What has ice cream to do with color?"

"I liked ice cream. All kinds. But especially chocolate. Then one day I was riding in a vehicle while eating a chocolate cone, way back when private conveyances existed, and I got sick. Not violently ill, merely somewhat queasy, and I lost my appetite, which is a thing I seldom do."

"Motion sickness," he said. "Not uncommon. But what—?"

"So then I didn't like chocolate ice cream any more."

"Transference," he said. "Are you suggesting a parallel between chocolate ice cream and and brown human beings?"

She laughed, avoiding an answer. "But I still liked ice cream! Strawberry had been my second favorite, so now it was my favorite. That was only fair. It had waited a long time for its turn. But—"

"So now you prefer strawberry jam to chocolate jam!" he said, trying to make a joke of it. But she didn't react, and he realized he had failed. Evidently the Admiral had been correct: he lacked a proper sense of humor.

"But a funny thing happened—"

"Tibet, you are wandering far afield!"

"I don't think so. I found after a while that I didn't like strawberry any more, even though I never consumed it in a vehicle. My taste for it simply faded, until it became an untaste. So then the number three flavor, vanilla, moved up for its turn, becoming my favorite."

"And soon you stopped liking vanilla. I grasp the pattern." She was distracting him, all right, but he resented being distracted by something this trivial.

"And I went through all the flavors of ice cream that way, one by one, until the only kind I could eat was what I had never tasted before, and after I had had it once, I no longer—"

"There is only one end to that sequence," he observed, resigning himself to her meandering course.

"No, you're wrong, Captain. After several years something changed, I don't know exactly what or why. Maybe it was milkshakes. They were liquid, so the ice cream syndrome was not invoked, but I knew ice cream was in them, because I made them myself. Maybe, finally, the nonsense of my taste became apparent to that deep organ in me that is responsible for my preferences of palate. Maybe the imperative that drove me from familiar forms of ice cream finally exhausted itself. I really can't say. At any rate, I could eat ice cream again. Only it took several more years to complete the circuit. And it unwound in reverse. First I liked the odd flavors, like beechnut rum; then, one by one, the more common ones. Finally vanilla, then strawberry—and now I think I could even eat chocolate."

"Do you mean to say that this fantastic inconsequential course is still in process?"

"That's right, Captain. Life is forever changing. I don't *like* chocolate ice cream, but the handwriting is on the wall, and maybe in a couple more years—"

"Interesting," he said flatly. "And what did you say was the point?"

"Well, I suspect that when I finally do master chocolate ice cream again, it will mark some significant lifetime achievement or opportunity. I mean, I'll be ready."

"Ready for what?"

"That remains to be ascertained. A person cannot understand a thing until she is ready for it, and I'm not yet ready. And of course it must be mutual; the chocolate ice cream has to be ready to accept me, too. Eating is a process of mergence."

Shetland shook his head as if attempting to free his brain

of cobweb. "And how does that relate to the complement of this ship?"

She gazed at him innocently. "Why, I suspect we shall find out when the time comes, Captain."

So she wasn't telling. He suppressed his ire. He channeled it into a challenge: what was her hidden message? A childhood foible that carried on into middle age—the personnel dossier had missed that! Why had she chosen to tell him about it now? *Was* it relevant to race, or had she merely used it to evade his query? He had no answer at the moment.

"Tibet, I believe I'll have that toast after all."

She busied herself with the preparations, which became more complicated than seemed necessary. She was nervous, not aggressive; he should have recognized that before. This was her reaction to the initial stress of time travel. His developing ire abated.

"Sorry I bored you," she murmured.

"I was impatient, not bored. We are all snappish when time begins changing."

"Call it a figment of my prejudice." She paused. "Figment, illusion—no, that's unfortunate."

"Why?" But he knew why: the unease stemmed from that disorientation, and whatever concerns lay buried in her mind were thrusting out now. He had four deadly dreads; she—?

"It has connotations. Color, I mean. Look, Captain—back on Earth, did anything awful ever happen? In your mind, that is? Not a forest fire or death in the family, those are real events. Just some horrible fancy in your brain, a nightmare all your own, unique to you, like that? That makes you shudder, even today, just to remember?"

Shetland considered. The image of concrete came, with the crack in the pavement, and the blood welling up in the crevice. But that he didn't care to discuss. Tibet had something on her mind she wanted to express, something more vital than chocolate ice cream—but she needed, if not a pretext, an equivalence. An exchange. And it was his duty to provide her with that equivalence. Something he could afford to part with.

"Yes," he said. "When I was small I had a dog. A big dog. My friend. He had a name but I called him Bigdog. One day my folks took him to the vet and left him there."

She glanced about his face. Not at his eyes. "Why?"

"He was sick. Soon we had a new dog, a puppy, and I liked that too. I used to ask when Bigdog was coming back, but never got an answer, and in time I stopped being concerned about it. It wasn't until I was much older that I realized that Bigdog was dead."

She watched him, waiting for the denouement. Now her gluttony was for something horrible.

"He had been dead since the day they took him to the vet," Shetland continued. "Euthanasia. He had kidney stones— some dogs do get them—and it would have required surgery to remove them, and he was not the type to leave a wound alone. They shoot horses for similar reasons. So it was hopeless. I don't fault the decision; it would have been pointless and cruel to let him suffer. The thing was—"

"Yes . . ." she breathed. In that moment the planes of her face struck just that configuration to make her beautiful: an effect that jolted him mildly.

"The dog I expected to come home all that time was no dog at all, just a figment of my belief." He used that word, figment, advisedly. She had used it, and he was seeking liaison with her apprehension. "A ghost. In retrospect I was horrified. Of course I had *needed* that ghost; the early knowledge of Bigdog's death would have wiped me out, for he was important to me. That was part of the horror: needing an illusion. Today I realize that people *do* need illusions. *Then* the concept was novel and unkind. But the other part of it—''

She had finished her toast, but was still chewing, intent on him. Her face was back to its normal, too-rounded shape.

''The other part was: what of the *dog*? No one cared what had happened to him because no one *knew*. He was robbed of even the consolation of the grief he left behind. What unparalleled isolation! That stirred me deeply and sadly. Yet that may be the fate of all of us, for no one knows the mind of any other.''

''But some come close, Captain,'' she said. ''You *do* understand!''

He had understood only that she had need for a story relating to the pitfalls of illusion—if that was indeed the type he had told. He remembered Bigdog now with a poignancy he had not felt in years. Perhaps he had only used Tibet's need as a pretext to indulge a need of his own. But she seemed willing to accept that. Now perhaps she could give her own example, and her soul would rest quiet. He had tarried here too long already.

''Mine is the same as yours,'' she said. ''Only different, as I am different from you. I don't mean just in sex or race or appetite.'' She sighed, then took hold of herself, breathing deeply, forcing herself to divulge what had to be divulged. Shetland felt almost as if he were witnessing the birth of a baby. ''I dreamed I was walking through a haunted house with my child—she was only eighteen months, still unsteady on her little feet—and as I was leaving I realized I had forgotten her. I dashed back in, chagrined, calling through those gaunt rooms—it was getting dark and there was no electricity—and I began really to feel the dismal mood of it. If she was lost or hurt in there, so small and young and frightened—

"But I found her, standing in the center of a back room, not at all afraid, just cute and sweet and smiling, a little darling—you know how wonderful they are, at that age—"

Shetland didn't know, but he nodded.

"I picked her up gladly, all my specters vanishing. But then, as I left the house, I wondered: haunts were capable of unusual things, horrifying things. Not just spookings and frights. Golems—imitations of people. Suppose, just suppose, that while she was alone in there, a switch had been made? That what I had rescued was *not* my child—"

"Of course it was your child!" Shetland said immediately— and realized he had made a mistake.

"I woke in a cold sweat. Really, I was wet! And knew that I *had* no child. I wasn't married; I was only eighteen then." She grimaced. "I was better looking then, and snotty. Too good for the men who offered. I—I think that some vestige of racial prejudice remained, because somehow the black and white men were not appealing, and of course I could not have a yellow one—not if I wanted children. Well, if I had acted at the outset, before the law changed—but I never did marry. So the only child I ever had was lost in that nightmare—that poor, poor little girl, innocent—"

"I understand," he said.

"You *don't* understand, at the moment, but you mean well. I never will have one now. I'm thirty-five. *She* would be eighteen now, if I allow for her age at the time of the dream. No child, anymore! So the child really is gone."

"Maybe she is you?" Shetland suggested.

"Couldn't be. She was a little black girl. Brown, actually. But mine."

"When you dream, you don't stint! You honored the Misceg Act before it passed!" Then another aspect occurred to him. "A brown child—chocolate ice cream?"

"I don't stint," she agreed. "But, Captain—this voyage—it terrifies me. Something awful will happen—I know it. Keep watch, will you? Closely, carefully?"

That was his job. "I shall."

"More toast?"

Shetland stood. Obviously she could eat indefinitely, gaining weight. "No, I'm afraid I have other business. Keeping watch, you know."

"There'll be other meals," she said, her spirits somewhat restored. "I always enjoy your company, Kerr."

Apparently their interaction had been more important for her than for him, this time. That was all right.

"Captain," Somnanda's voice said on the intercom.

Shetland hurried to the beacon room, knowing what it had to be, yet hoping it was not.

"There is an imbalance in the beacon," Somnanda said.

He had braced himself for this, but still there was that cold clutch at his stomach. Immediately the candle flickered higher, an orangish, unhealthy flash.

Fear was the nemesis of the beacon: no error there! What irony if his own alarm at the news of danger to the beacon should extinguish it! He exerted control over his emotions and watched the little flame subside and become even.

"I was talking with Tibet," Shetland said. "We exchanged confidences. I believe she was disturbed, but is now reassured."

Somnanda's eyes remained on the light. "I read that tension in the flame," he said. "I knew its source. It did subside. You do your job well, Captain! But something else remains—and that is growing."

Clear warning! A mind was interfering with the functioning of the beacon, and it was not Tibet. Not Shetland. Not Somnanda himself. One of the others.

No, he could not safely make that assumption. The unconscious mind was a mystic thing, not entirely governed by reason. No one could be excluded. Tibet mourned a nightmare baby, and still could not eat chocolate ice cream; an iceberg might float under those visible tips. Shetland himself had spoken of a dog that died—but he was the only one aboard who knew of a more recent and significant demise. The immediate mission of the *Meg II* was to discover what had happened to her sister ship, the *Meg I*. A ship that had vanished in time—millions of years hence, in one framework, but only days ago in another. His own mind could harbor suppressed terror, and if Somnanda suspected—

"Somnanda," he said. The somber head rose to orient on him. "Do you know the purpose of this expedition?"

"We are not the first to travel in time," the big man said. "The mechanism has been in operation for three years. But other voyages have been brief. A few decades, a few centuries, even a few millennia. We shall pass a million years, as the name of our ship suggests. We travel far—and our limit is set only by the strength of the beacon. Once we have established that horizon, we shall have nothing to fear from time."

Shetland nodded. Somnanda's answer was consistent with his orientation. He saw the voyage as a test of the beacon, and of the feasibility of time travel when using the beacon. "But you will know and give warning before that limit is struck," he said.

"I do not believe there is a limit—through time," Somnanda said. His implication was clear: time would not hurt the beacon, but an unruly mind could.

Their conversation lapsed. The notebook reappeared in Shetland's mind. The pencil turned about and erased the lined-through Dread: *1. ~~Beacon, failure of~~* and wrote it in again unmarred. Then it sketched an arrow leading from that down to *3. Personality, distortion of*. Linked threats.

The pencil hesitated, then made subheadings under item 3, leaving a space after each. (Item 4 had to be erased and lowered accordingly, and the eraser dust blown away.) *A. Somnanda B. Shetland C. Johns D. Beeton*.

Shetland noted the inversely alphabetized listing and frowned, but let it stand. This was not the occasion to waste time and paper on a new list! Then the pencil continued: *E. Tibet F. Sosthenna G. Alice*.

And that was worse: not only reversed, but inconsistent with the first four names. Why did he use every man's surname and every woman's given name, here in his private notebook where no other could see? Personal quirk of culture—or differing status? Certainly his relationships with the sexes were not identical.

Now he remembered: Tibet had at the end called him by his first name. Was that significant?

The pencil returned to the first name, paused again, and finally wrote in modified script:

A. Somnanda—*Mongoloid, age 30. Most experienced and reliable communicator in time. Steady temper. Personal friend.*

Was he allowing friendship to influence him? This could not be tolerated. And, strictly speaking, he was presuming when he called such a man friend; he hardly knew Somnanda, really. The pencil backtracked and crossed off the last two words.

Still, Somnanda was the least likely of the suspects. He *was* the most experienced person with the beacon, having worked with it for the full two years since being drafted into the Space Service, and having made more short-hop excursions with it than any other person. He was the best. If he lost control, there would be no appeal. No one else could maintain the beacon.

B. Shetland—*Negroid, age 38. Captain. Experienced. Knowledge of danger. Can control emotion.*

But how could a man judge himself objectively? Already he had distorted the record: he only *suspected* danger. It was dangerous, actually, to assign positive knowledge to himself when he lacked it. So the pencil returned to make a correction:

Suspicion.

~~*Knowledge of danger.*~~

Did that exonerate his error, or was he rationalizing? At least he had the courage to cross out the word instead of erasing it, so that his change of mind was evident. Integrity required that a man correct but not conceal his errors.

C. Johns—*Mixed ancestry, age 26. Pilot (drive mechanic).*

The pencil stopped. The record said that Johns was competent—but Shetland had not voyaged with him before. How could he be sure of this man? Or was he allowing himself to be prejudiced because Johns had replaced the regular short-hop pilot Shetland had chosen? The original pilot had developed mild temporophobia and had had to be relieved. This was a common malady among the crewmen tested for this duty, but deadly to the performance of the beacon. Things had seemed good until almost the last moment; then the sudden change had had to be made, and Shetland could not fault it. Better a safe stranger than a dangerous friend! But a known quantity was gone, and an unknown had been introduced.

Objectivity was essential—and impossible. He would have to have a talk with Johns, but not immediately. The man had done his job in a thoroughly professional manner, instituting the time-drive, and was about to take his mandatory rest. He would sniff a four-hour sleep capsule, as required, and Shetland would not interrupt that. Lack of sleep was one of the surest routes to emotional imbalance.

D. Beeton—*Caucasian, age 21. Cartographer, apprentice.*

The pencil stalled once more. Apprentice. That did not indicate any dearth of competence in his specialty; it simply meant the man had never before had an assignment in time, other than sample hops of a day or less. No one-year to one-century training cruises. Young, inexperienced, yet in a position to comprehend both mission and hazard. A very likely suspect for the imbalance Somnanda had called out. Shetland had not really wanted him along, but his carte blanche choice of crew had turned out to have certain signficant qualifications. He had chosen the personnel, but the positions for this voyage had been determined by the bureaucracy of the Space Service, and that bureaucracy had in its perplexing wisdom assigned a cartographer. Only three candidates had been available, and on paper Beeton had seemed least objectionable, so Shetland had selected him. Certainly he would have to be interviewed—in due course. Too early a session could arouse the young man's suspicion and be disastrous. In fact, it was important that Beeton *not* be the first, that he be part of a routine procedure.

E. Tibet—*Mongoloid, age 35. Cook (dietary technician).*

He had already interviewed her, extemporaneously. She was reacting normally, considering that time travel was an abnormal situation with its unique stresses. Her fantasy of a chocolate daughter had probably lain dormant for all the seventeen years since her dream, and come out with sudden force when the time-vertigo began. Interesting that it should parallel his own memory of Bigdog—but of course he had evoked that at her behest, and perhaps similar concerns were roused in every mind in this situation. Still, neither his memory nor hers had emerged at this point during training missions.

F. Sosthenna—*Caucasian, age 28. Supplies*.

Ah, Thenna! Glorified domestic, but indispensable. The crews were meshed for social traits as much as for the listed positions, and often the job title bore little relation to the person's function within the crew. He had chosen her, really, for love, and when he retired—which would be soon—he hoped to marry her. Even the pretense of personal objectivity was pointless. Her offshade eye—somehow that had held his interest, and he had sought her out after being promoted, and they had dated during time training. She had been permitted assignment to this voyage when each of them had passed the Service's personal-objectivity examination. Each accepted the fact that while they were in the Service, no exclusivity of sexual participation existed. Accepted it totally: not even hidden jealousy of the liaisons each had with others. Because both had known that failure of that examination by either would result in prohibition of their relationship. The Service had effective ways to separate people when it chose.

G. Alice—*Negroid, age 18. Physo-chemist (framework analysis)*.

Another new crewmember, selected for availability, compatibility and technical competence. Again he had had to approve on paper the applicant possessing the best qualities for the position. Why her specialty had been required for this voyage he wasn't sure, but he had no objection, because she had not replaced a regular crewmember; she had been added. So he knew little about her—but as the youngest aboard, she was another prospect for instability. Certainly he should interview her—again, in due course.

That was the roster. One of these names on his list attached to a mind whose alarm was disturbing the beacon. That mind had to be nullified: gently, if possible.

Shetland turned about and set course for his own cabin. He was not tired, but he intended to sleep now. As Captain, he set his own schedule, and he expected to be quite busy later.

Chapter 5:_____Theories

Ship's clock said 4.57, velocity. Shetland entered the pilot's compartment and stood behind the man. "Johns," he murmured.

The pilot jumped to attention. "Sir!" He was a small, somewhat stout man, whose thin brown hair on a brown scalp made him seem prematurely bald. His features were regular except for a slightly receding chin. Shetland knew from the records that Johns was an excellent craftsman, well equipped for his position. His dislike of the man was irrational. He should not even hold the extra poundage against the pilot; those who truly adapted to Service life lost awareness of the strictures of Planetside life.

"There is no need to stand at attention," Shetland said. "I run an informal ship, and some of our crew are civilian—apart from the fact that the job comes first." In fact, in the course of a voyage like this, the crew should become a close social unit. Shetland always strove for that, and that might be one secret of his success in normal space, prior to his assignment to time. He worked to unify the crew. Thus he had endured many years in the most challenging aspects of the Service, while his higher-IQ colleagues had had to retire to less demanding commands.

Shetland lived by the manual, but knew that it required careful interpretation. Others assumed that the printed words sufficed, while he regarded them as a potent tool for achieving the best results. Crew unity was paramount, and this could only be achieved by honest and sympathetic comprehension of individual motives. Which was why his irrational dislike of Johns was a threat to the success of the mission—a threat he would have to ameliorate. He, of all people, could not afford to be irrational.

"Yes, sir," Johns said, relaxing slightly. It was a start, but not a good one. The man seemed tense, as though hiding something, and did not look as if he had had his full quota of sleep. But this could be the continuing effect of the initial disorientation. Even thoroughly experienced personnel were not immune.

"I see we stand between four and five," Shetland said, sounding inane in his own ears. But that was the problem when dealing with veiled hostility: anything sounded awkward. "That, of course, represents our velocity in time, not the internal hour. Would you care to translate our situation into something more specific?"

A patronizing smile hovered behind the quirk of Johns' lip. Now he was wondering what kind of incompetent had been placed in charge. It was known that time travel favored odd types, because of the special abilities required. "As you know, sir, the drive is designed to reflect our velocity in hours per hour, varying exponentially with the passage of conventional time. Our temporal velocity is indicated by the right-hand logarithmic dial of the ship's clock, and our actual time deviation by the left dial. Thus our present timespeed, relative to Earth-norm—''

"Your explanation seems unintelligible to the novice," Shetland said. "Assume that I'm an idiot."

"Yes, sir!" Nothing defused crew resentment of serving under a Captain who appeared to be less intelligent than others like mocking it himself. But Shetland knew that if the conquest of time had been left strictly to the intelligentsia, it would not have occurred. There were other values.

Johns tried again. "When the clock stands at zero, it means the ship's time is the same as Earth's. The universe's, actually. Ten raised to the zero power is one; the ratio is one to one. We are not moving temporally then. But when it stands at one, this is ten raised to the first power, or ten: we travel ten hours for every one Earth does. But it *seems* reversed: only one hour has passed inside the ship, but the Earth outside is ten hours older—or younger, depending on our direction. At two, or ten squared, we make a hundred hours for each standard hour. And so on up: three is a thousand, four is ten thousand. Since there are 8,760 hours in a year, at four o'clock we are traveling more than a year in each hour. At the moment we are traveling better than four years per hour. Before very long we will be covering ten, a hundred, or a thousand years in each of our hours, leaving our point of origin far behind. Too bad we can't watch Earth itself and read our future!"

"And why can't we just do that?"

"Because the world is not stationary. Earth is moving in space around the sun at perhaps eighteen miles per second; if we moved forward only one second in a second, we would be eighteen miles off. And we'll be doing days, even years per second! Apart from the fact that our Milky Way Galaxy is

traveling outward from the center of the universe at something like lightspeed. The drive is oriented on absolute rest.
So—''

"Absolute rest?"

Johns paused, suppressing annoyance. "The universe is
exploding. For the purpose of orientation, we call the calcu-
lated location of the original ball of matter the center, and it
is assumed to have been at absolute rest. It may actually have
been spinning, but we have to start *somewhere*, if we're to
get anywhere."

"Oh, yes," Shetland agreed, as if this was news to him.
He well understood the need for a reference point that was
independent of Earth; his purpose was to keep Johns talking—
until there was opportunity to test the man for fear.

"So when we travel a second per second," Johns continued, "the universe appears to move away from us at that
rate. When we travel an hour per second, the effective spatial
velocity will be thirty-six hundred times lightspeed. So we
have no chance to watch Earth—which is just as well, considering the paradox entailed in viewing our own immediate
future."

"Yes, it is intriguing how nature protects us from ourselves," Shetland said. He looked out the viewport. "It
amazes me the way we can see the stars despite our velocity
of many times the speed of light. I believe I can see the stars
shifting now."

This time there was a bark of laughter from Johns. "Captain, you've been stringing me long enough! Four point six
on the clock is forty thousand hours per hour, or forty
thousand times the speed of spatial light. We're coming up
on five light-years per hour—and many stars are separated
from each other by no more than that. You see them moving,
all right! The whole galaxy is drifting by us, because we're

standing still in absolute space. Or almost still; of course we keep our technical motion of one hour per hour, which is all the real motion we can ever do. So we don't have to worry about seeing out portholes at multiples of light; we're only seeing the stars where they will be several years from our starting time."

"Oh, yes," Shetland said. "But it is generally understood that a vessel in space-time motion does not interact with the universe at all. How, then, do we perceive light? Isn't that a physical interaction?"

"That's one of those half-truths that always confuse the novice . . . sir," Johns said. "We *do* interact, for we are a material body passing through a material universe. But we move so rapidly that such forces as gravity are normally only passing effects, too brief to affect us significantly. Even so, we can receive a hell of a lot of energy when we zip past a star or through a cluster, because we are getting what amounts to years worth of output in hours. That's why we are so heavily shielded, and why none of the portholes are direct; only a controlled fraction of the light that strikes the *Meg* is conveyed to our screens. And of course our computer compensates for the massive blue shift of that light that would otherwise put it way out of the visible spectrum. *Everything* seems to speed up exponentially, including light! It's all tied into the clock and drive." He paused. "Is that clear?"

"Clear enough, Pilot." Shetland observed the near stars edging by, while the far ones seemed stationary. But soon the view would reflect a shift not of years per hour, but of decades, centuries and millennia per hour. He had experienced this before, on a limited scale, but the wonder of it never abated. They were looking into the future and seeing it unravel. At high temporal velocity the galaxy appeared phenomenally three-dimensional. Four-dimensional, in fact!

It was a sight to give a man religion. Not only did positions shift, that motion accelerating logarithmically; distant stars aged at many times their normal rate, pulsing and flaring and expiring like living things. Shetland had watched diffuse nebulae coalesce into thick dust clouds that gave birth to bright new star clusters. He had watched those stars mature and then die of old age—all in the course of traveling to the rim of the liquidly swirling galaxy. Then, on the return trip, he had watched the process in reverse. Telescope film had clarified the details, so now he knew what he was looking for—but the mighty awe of galactic animation remained.

Yet he could not afford to ignore the personal element. "What do you deem to be the primary purpose of this voyage?"

"Why, it's obvious, sir!" Johns said enthusiastically. "We are testing the capacity of the drive. We shall be the first ship to travel a million years per hour—or a million light-years per hour, same thing. We'll be out around the range of Andromeda! That's why we're called the *Meg*."

Shetland frowned, his fingers beating little cadences on the panel below the clock. Somnanda saw the voyage as a test of the beacon; the pilot saw it as a test of the drive. What would the other male crewman, Cartographer Beeton, see?

"Mph—megayears per hour," Shetland agreed, forcing his fingers to be still. "Of course the apparent spatial distance covered is slightly below half of apparent velocity, because of the accelerative factor—but one more approximation won't hurt." Then he hit the pilot with the critical concept: a Sunday punch, unexpected, unsignaled. "What makes you assume that we are going to stop at one mph?"

Johns' eyes widened. "We're *not* stopping, sir? Not once we've set the all-time record?"

"Not then. And not at ten on the clock. We shall continue at least to fifteen, perhaps twenty."

"Fifteen or twenty!" Johns' mouth hung open after he spoke. "Do you have any idea how *fast* that is, sir?"

"Tell me, Pilot."

"Fifteen would be over a hundred billion light-years per hour," Johns said slowly, working it out in his head. "Way beyond the visible edge of the universe! Twenty—that's over ten quadrillion . . ."

"Pretty fair test of the drive, wouldn't you say?"

Johns didn't answer.

The intercom came to life. Somnanda, naturally. "Captain to the beacon as convenient."

So the beacon had flared! Yet this was not conclusive. Shetland himself had made it react when caught offguard. Every man had his moments, and he had just given Johns a staggering concept to swallow. They were going to leave the universe!

"Does velocity frighten you, Johns?"

The man licked his lips. "No, I'm used to it. I can't visualize shooting out of the universe, that's all. So how can I be frightened? I figure the drive can do it, and I'm game to try. Velocity doesn't make much difference, temporally. Set an all-time and all-space record no one will ever beat!"

Shetland did not agree with the pilot's reasoning. Most people *did* fear what they could not visualize. But it seemed that Johns had survived his crisis of information and come to terms with it. His reaction was no more extreme than the norm, and perhaps substantially less so. He could not be considered a prime suspect.

Beeton remained probable, with Alice next. The youngest, least experienced crewmember. Shetland decided to pick up Somnanda's chess move, thus implying that nothing was amiss—after all, who played chess during a crisis?—then gird himself for the more difficult interviews.

"Why fifteen—or twenty?" Johns inquired. ". . . sir."

Because that was where oblivion awaited the *Meg II* and all her racially, sexually and age-ually balanced complement.

Age-ually? His mental pencil appeared, quivering as if preparing for the effort of writing out such a term.

"Orders, Pilot."

The all-purpose answer. Orders made it right, when common sense did not. No one could argue with orders.

The key number was just over twenty-two. So far beyond the universe in space and time that nothing could exist, and certainly no physical threat to the ship.

No threat? That was where/when the *Meg I*'s beacon had failed.

The supply depot was in scrupulous order as they left the galaxy. "Yes, Captain," Sosthenna said. She was still an attractive brown-haired woman, well dressed and well deported. Of course two years was hardly enough to change that, but he tried always to view her with professional detachment. At the moment it was as if he did not love her, and was seeing her for the first time. It had been a mighty stride forward, he thought, when uniforms had been made optional for timefaring personnel. "What can I do for you?"

"I'm not sure," he said. He knew he should have gone next to Beeton's cabin, but he delayed uneasily. Was he, after all, retaining proper objectivity?

Her glance of appraisal would have been alarming in another person. Alarming in her, too, had he not known her. That faded eye . . .

"Come here, sir," she said.

He stepped up to her. Sosthenna lifted her sleek white

arms to his shoulders. There was a cleanness about her that was more than odor; every hair was in place, and her clothing fit perfectly. She was a remarkably well formed animal, fair in every physical and emotional sense. "I love you, Captain."

"Thenna, it is not necessary to—"

"I think it is, sir," she murmured, kissing him on the lips. This, too, was precisely and delightfully executed.

"I suppose it is," he agreed as she released him. "I am girding myself for a difficult—" But he had to cut himself off; no need to alarm her. "Thanks, Thenna."

She took him by the hand and led him to her bunk and began to remove her clothing, neatly, efficiently, without mussing her hair, yet with sexual élan. Phenomenal woman! If he were chocolate, she was vanilla, but with no yellow tinge. "It is all in the Standard Operations Manual, Captain. I do for you what I shall do for any man aboard this ship."

And he for any woman. "Everything is in the manual," he agreed, undressing quickly. "And nothing."

She had used the word "love," but also reminded him that she was following the manual, negating its deeper sense. She never called him by his name while on duty. True love would have been easy, perhaps inevitable, had she elected otherwise— and love seemed a fact when she did elect otherwise, between missions. But of course this was space. "The spirit must be honored as well as the letter, sir."

"That isn't what I meant." Now he sounded petulant, like Tibet.

"Of course it isn't!" she agreed warmly. "One day I may respond to you outside the manual, sir, in a professional situation—but not yet. The manual is only a guideline, though a good one; it requires people to give it life."

So she knew how he felt, and offered the hint of a promise. He had not actually proposed marriage to her yet, so the extent of his emotional commitment remained nominal. He craved so much more than the hint, but such matters could not be rushed, and they were indeed on duty. Sex was part of the manual, even passion, but not real love.

They were standing naked now, he nearly black, she all white from breast to buttock, tanned at the extremities. "How would you like me?" she inquired.

"You speak as if you were a soy steak, to be grilled just so!" he complained. "Thenna, I don't—"

She put her finger to his lips, chidingly. "Next time you may ask me how I would like you," she said, and he had to smile.

"I would like you as you would be liked," he said. He would have liked her ten times as well off the manual—but that had to wait.

"Neatly put, Captain, both levels." She rubbed close against him, forcing the masculine response. The question of whether he could love within the strictures of the Misceg Act had long since been answered: he could. "Swiftly, and a bit roughly, Captain. Make me cry out."

The prospect was tempting: punishing her for reserving her true self to herself, in compliance with the manual. Therefore he resisted it. "Thenna, you know that is not my way. There should never be pain." And suddenly the pavement was there in his mind's eye, the crack widening, the red welling up swiftly. *No pain!*

She caught behind his neck with eight fingers and jumped, pulling herself hard against him. Her lithe thighs clamped about his waist. "Hold me, sir!" she cried, letting go his neck.

He had to throw his arms around her back before she fell.

His private vision dissolved, unable to maintain itself in the face of this external emergency. Meanwhile her own hands were busy, reaching outside and around and in, guiding expertly. But her outflung weight already overbalanced him. They fell together on the bunk, his mass coming down on hers—and it was swift, and a bit rough, and she cried out.

"You are a wonder!" Shetland said as they disengaged. She was the only one who could break up one of his visions so effectively. That was one element of his feeling for her.

She handed him a tissue from the conveniently placed dispenser. "Thank you, sir."

"Everything you do is just exactly right! I wish I could organize my life similarly!" *With you*, he finished mentally.

She made the slightest nod, as though acquiescing to his thought, but her words did not betray it. "Simply a matter of pride, Captain. Anything worth doing is worth doing well."

And she would do it with Somnanda, and Johns, and even young Beeton, with similar dispatch. He felt no jealousy, having schooled himself against it, but did feel envy of her ability to be so beautifully and naturally what she had to be.

"Pride. That's the first of the Seven Deadly Sins."

"And Envy is the sixth," she said, kissing him again. Evidently some of his emotion had leaked to his face: the very failing he regretted. "But your envy feeds my pride, Captain!"

"Strange. Tibet accused me of something similar. Does it show that much?"

"Only to those who know you well. But it is not a negative thing, sir. What is envy, except the desire to improve, to have a better life? To *be* better? And how can anyone *know* what's better, unless he recognizes it in his neighbor?"

They finished dressing. "Thenna, I love you," Shetland said, hoping that it sounded the way the manual required: courtesy, rather than reality. "My sanity is deeper and stronger because of you."

She hugged him. "What a marvelous compliment!" she exclaimed.

But this time she had misunderstood. It had not been a compliment, not a polite flattery, despite the manual. It had been conviction, a completely serious observation of fact— and she had demeaned it by treating it superficially. She had honored the manual too literally. Thus the statement, though not falsified, suffered a loss of value. Like the unmeasurable property, the uncertainty principle, it was thrown into doubt by its very expression. And that was sad.

Did she, after all, truly return his love? She was so polished in her performance that it was impossible to be quite certain.

Beeton's cabin was typical of what was expected of a young spaceman, though he was only nominally such: the neat military bunk, the foot locker, the shapely pinups on the wall.

Shetland dismissed the pictures immediately. He knew that every man under thirty put them up as a matter of protocol. It was largely pointless since the ships had been integrated and sex made freely available; if the man really craved that type of woman he could call on Sosthenna at his convenience. There was really no way in which her body or her manner was inferior to any pinup. But like all traditions, this hung on past its time.

Still, after one discounted the window dressing, a man's room was often a pretty fair indication of his personality.

What showed here? Nothing. Everything in order, betraying no truly personal traits. Beeton was almost too careful to conform, when conformity was neither required nor expected. He was a man who used a social mask.

There was a chessboard on the corner desk, with the pieces set up: a game in progress. So Beeton was a chess buff! Tedium came to everyone in space despite the strenuous counter-efforts of the manual, but few took up chess seriously. Beeton seemed more promising already.

Shetland examined the game with clinical interest, noting the advantageous position held by Black. This match would soon be over.

He turned away—and paused. This was no ordinary game! This was a replica of his own match against Somnanda, complete to the last move. A game that he had thought existed only in the minds of the two men! And Somnanda was Black.

Beeton had made only one slip in his room's veneer of conformity—but what a chasm that showed! Shetland realized immediately that he was up against genius.

"What can I do for you, Captain?"

Shetland did not jump. The cartographer had come upon him by surprise, but Shetland had not been sneaking. When a room was left open, anybody could enter, so long as he did not molest anything, and the Captain had entry privileges at all times.

Beeton was a tall, blond lad, angular of limb. His face had that fresh-out-of-school look: sanguine and unlined, eyes startlingly blue and innocent.

"I was admiring your game," Shetland said.

Beeton had the grace to flush passingly. "Spectator sport, sir."

"As spectator, who would you say has the better position?"

"Well, sir, I'm sure I could win with White."

Shetland smiled faintly. "You should know that space-time career men are noted for memory, not intelligence, and that they retain comparatively few illusions. We both know who is playing this game, and who will win."

Beeton moved his hand in a circumscribed wave-away, smiling. "I'm sorry, sir. I must admit that your defense, while logical from a positional standpoint, is unsound in the present case. But it is not beyond redemption—and I do admire your ability to play without a board. I could never do that."

Shetland resisted the flattery, not entirely successfully. He was here to judge, not to be judged, and it was going to be difficult. This boy was not under pressure now—and had a mind that could outmaneuver Shetland's own so handily that there could be no contest. Except, perhaps, in space-time.

"Perhaps, in due course, you will show me how to win with White," he said. "It happens that I can see the board and pieces whether or not they are physically present. Just as I can read a book by turning the pages in my memory. Just one of the qualifications for the office."

Beeton sat on his bunk, not deigning to inquire directly the purpose of the Captain's visit. Perhaps he already knew it.

In a moment Shetland spoke again. "Going into research after this trip?"

Beeton shrugged. The records were public knowledge. "Yes. Originally those lectures on celestial mechanics and such bored me. I would sit in front of the class, my eyes fixed on the prof's desk while he gave out with the 'poop.' He used to purse his lips around that naughty word. But all that changed. I'm going to settle down, get married, and do research as long as it holds my interest."

"I'm sure you have a fine young woman waiting." Fencing, perhaps, but necessary. What was the key to Beeton's distress—assuming that he was the one distressed? So far nothing was evident.

Beeton gave him a curious glance, then made the hint of a shrug. "Woman," he remarked. "That's the word that falls between 'wolverine' and 'wombat' in the dictionary."

Shetland opened the big dictionary in his brain and skimmed the page. It was true, approximately. "Wolverine, wolves, woman, womb, wombat," he read aloud. "There does seem to be a figurative affinity."

Beeton laughed easily. "And I want to assure you, Captain, that that megalocarpous specimen on the wall is not the one."

Shetland riffled through his dictionary again and smiled when he found the word. It meant "large-fruited." New to him, but worth remembering. Megalocarpous. Beeton was playing games with him, forcing him back intellectually.

"Do you know how I met her, Captain? I was sitting in the university, studying a text on psychology, when I overheard this clip-clop, clip-clop coming up behind me. For a startled moment all I could think of was a horse. You know the sound those animals make when some rich showman takes them across a concrete street, holding up traffic, the metal-shod hooves ringing out like castanets. But in a *library*? I couldn't resist turning around in my chair to see what could make that kind of noise there. Of course it turned out to be two girls in heels. But that horse was still in my mind, and you know, their feet did resemble hooves in an attractive way. Their legs were clean and supple, rather like those of a thoroughbred racer. And one even wore a halter!

"I laughed out loud. Bad form, in a library, but I couldn't help it. I think I have something of a foot fetish, anyway. 'Now I know why they call them "fillies"!' I said. One of those girls heard that—the whole library heard it!—and she sort of changed shades and came over to ask me exactly what I meant by that crack. Severe tone, but there was a smile in her eyes or maybe in her pert nose. That was the first time I had a really good look at her, aside from her ankles. She had on a knitted green dress, form-fitting over an excellent form— might as well admit it, I was smitten by her appearance. It was a much better study than that psychology text I had, for sure. One thing led to another—''

''So that was your fiancée!''

Again that odd look. ''No. That girl was white, just like me. Couldn't marry her, thanks to Misceg. She was the other girl, the brown one. I didn't pay any attention to her at that time. She—well, it gets a little complicated. I don't suppose your records cover that sort of detail.''

Shetland got the point. The comprehensive records were illusory. They told him nothing that would enable him really to understand this too-clever young man. He was being gently told to mind his own business.

How he wished he could! But Beeton was still the prime suspect, and if fear was masked by that glib façade, the Captain had to expose it. He glanced again at Beeton's file in his mind—and saw what he had missed. Ouch!

''The records say that you are engaged to marry a member of this crew,'' Shetland said, as if he had known it all along. ''That *is* irregular—but stronger coincidences have happened in the interests of balance.''

''You needed two young ones in a hurry; there we were,'' Beeton agreed.

Shetland waited for the call from Somnanda signifying a flare of the beacon. It did not come. Odd—evidently Beeton was not sensitive about his fiancée's presence on the *Meg*.

Most young men would be. Despite the young man's belief, this placement was coincidental; Shetland had selected each as the best available representative of the specialty, considering also the advisable balance of race and age. But perhaps they had known that they were the best in each, so had applied together, knowing the sexual requirement of space. He had made the adjustment with Sosthenna, after all; the young couple could do the same. He tried again.

"You've admitted that your early scholastics were not remarkable. What caused you to change?" For here, perhaps, the record did offer a takeoff point. The shift had been abrupt, and it had been from indifferent performance to absolute brilliance. There were personal comments by several instructors: "Jumps to accurate conclusions." "Intuitive thinker: never mistaken in theory." "Too sharp to be cheating!"

Beeton's tone was flippant. "Maybe I was afraid, Captain. Afraid that the ghost of my past would come back to haunt me."

Ghost of his past . . . how strangely similar to Tibet's concern! Was Beeton mocking him, aware of that prior dialogue? Or was it that the terminology of the supernatural came readily to the fore during a voyage like this?

But Beeton continued: "These days a degree is not enough. There were too many decades of assembly-line doctorates and outright factory-degree frauds that degraded the magic."

Magic . . .

"They delve into your records," Beeton said, not seeming to notice Shetland's reactions. "As well you know. If I had left behind me a reputation for careless work—"

Was the young man still taunting him, showing the flag to the bull? He had discovered no emotional instability in Beeton, unless all this ready talk was covering it up. Was there genuine tension now?

". . . though that's an unfortunate way to put it," Beeton was saying. " 'Ghost,' I mean. I always was afraid of the supernatural. Sometimes I suspect that my whole interest in science was spurred by a lingering fear of ghosts. As though I were trying to shine a light in the dark corners, to prove that nothing nonphysical could possibly hurt me, because there was nothing there. Seems ridiculous now."

Childhood fears! Another common theme, this voyage! It did not seem ridiculous to Shetland. One of those long-buried spooks might even now be rising from its grave to menace the beacon. Was this an honest confession on Beeton's part, or was he merely playing back a tape recorded elsewhere, much as he had done with the chess game? How simple to play on the credulity of a meddling Captain. . . !

"Does the academy still teach Einstein?" Shetland inquired after a moment. Soon he would have to hit Beeton with the same concept he had tried on Johns. If that brought no flare of the beacon, Beeton was safe.

Beeton smiled, seeming to relax with the change of subject. "It still does. But of course it's a mistake to assume that time travel disproves his work. The General Theory never did limit an object to the speed of light, and we are not traveling in space anyway. We are traveling forward in time, watching the universe depart; your own velocity remains what it was at the outset: lightspeed, approximately." Familiar discourse, but Shetland did not interrupt; he wanted to get the cartographer's slant on it. ". . . As our clock passes fifteen we shall see the universe reverse its motion and go into its contraction phase, passing us again on its way to the formation of a second cosmic egg. That phenomenal implosion compresses all the matter of the universe to singularity and virtual nonexistence, which overloads the foundation of reality and triggers the counter-force. Then another explosion, another expansion universe, with all the corruption of the old universe cleared away. The purging and rebirth of matter! And so on, every hundred billion years or so—the steady cycle of the cosmos! And I shall be recording it all, mapping the geography of all space-time!''

He paused. ''By the way—what *is* our present velocity? I don't want to dally beyond—''

This time Shetland did not miss the nervous throb, the slight quiver of emotion showing in the tips of the fingers. Beeton *was* afraid—that was why he affected not to know the present position of the clock. The women might genuinely lose track of it; never the men.

''The clock stands at fifteen now,'' Shetland said. ''I have been observing the universe in such fashion as I can. It does not appear to have reversed course, or even to have slowed significantly.''

''But the hidden mass guarantees that the universe is closed!'' Beeton protested.

''Hidden mass?''

''The shadow universe. Matter that interacts with the universe we normally perceive only via the weakest of the fundamental forces, gravity. We cannot see it or feel it; we can pass through it and never be aware of it. But its gravity overlaps ours, for there can be no barrier to that. Since that force is cumulative, it becomes dominant, and acts to contain the universe. The only question is the precise degree—''

''The limits for the contractile state to be initiated have been passed; there will be no second egg.''

Beeton turned pale. His breath suddenly came in labored gasps, as if he suffered a sudden blockage of the throat. His eyes stared unblinkingly at the Captain, too much of the whites showing. The change from his former ease was striking.

The intercom blared out behind Shetland with startling volume. "Captain to beacon immediately!"

Shetland whirled, paying no more attention to the cartographer. He had learned what he needed—unfortunately.

He galloped headlong down the corridor, blood pounding in his ears. The shortness of breath, he knew, was not entirely due to exertion.

He burst into the beacon room. And stopped, appalled. He had weathered beacon crises before, on shakedown hops, but this—!

The miniature candle, symbol of Earth-contact, was a towering column of fire. Orange light flooded the chamber, flickering off the walls and illuminating Somnanda's twisted face with demoniac intensity.

Shetland knew what to do. Terror was destructive to the beacon, the effect inversely proportional to the distance of the terrified mind and directly proportional to the degree of emotion. He stood there, close by that flame, his head almost inside that cold light, suppressing every vestige of worry, quelling his own throbbing pulse with hypnotic waves of peace and security. Blood welled from the pavement in sympathetic response, but he overrode this with thoughts of imminent retirement at full pay, and of love in the arms of Sosthenna. Members of the crew had fears; these were groundless, based on ignorance and misunderstanding. Only the Captain had authority to know, and he was not afraid. Not afraid.

Secure.

Gradually he extended the aura of calm outward. Somnanda was not afraid, merely the victim of another person's fear. An unfounded fear. No one had need really to be afraid. A temporary shock, no more. To be forgotten.

The fearsome color faded. The column dwindled reluctantly, down, down, until the light returned almost to its normal pinpoint above the table. Almost.

Somnanda's countenance relaxed. A disturbance in the beacon was physical pain to him, and the energy of the climbing flame was drawn directly from the life-force of his mind. His hands remained above the table, fingers splayed, their backs an angry red. His forehead was shining, and rivulets of perspiration were draining down the side of his neck. He was a mighty man, physically and mentally, but he preferred passive existence. He had skirted the valley of the shadow of death as the flame soared.

"You have a talent," Somnanda said tightly.

"That is why I am Captain." Shetland tried not to deceive himself about that, either. He had been put in charge of a time-traveling vessel because he possessed the qualities that facilitated crew survival. Leadership was one of them, though he exerted that only with difficulty. But he could obey orders—and he could calm the beacon.

"My strength has been overextended," Somnanda said, his words slightly slurred, his voice pitched too high. "I may not be able to maintain the beacon in the face of a similar threat."

So formal, so moderate, even after this! A normal man would have been irritable, overreactive; Somnanda still controlled his inner turmoil. But that very concealment of character revealed the character of the man.

I must talk to him, Shetland thought. I must reach him, or at least reveal myself to him, for I envy and admire his composure after the ravage of his life-force. As Beeton is to me, so am I to this man of the candle. The tension is within me, and it must come out.

And when my brain has translated itself into nervous impulses, and these pulses become the atmospheric vibrations, the compressions and rarefactions that become meaningful speech sounds, and these sounds have been lost in entropy, their meaning irrelevant or forgotten—then will my concerns be ameliorated?

"I was responsible," Shetland said.

Somnanda merely looked at him, the normal color returning to his face and hands. He knew this was only a lead-in to the real situation. Technically the Captain was responsible for everything that happened aboard his ship.

"A farmer once lost a sum of money," Shetland said. "He suspected a neighbor's boy of having stolen it, but lacked proof. So the farmer went and studied the boy as he went about his chores, trying to determine by observation whether he was in fact the culprit. Though the lad performed his duties in the prescribed manner, there did appear to be something surreptitious in his attitude, as if he were trying to conceal guilt. The farmer returned home convinced, though still unable to make a documented accusation. Later he discovered the money where he had hidden it too well and forgotten it. It had never been stolen; he realized that now. What, then, of the guilty boy? He went again to look at the youth, but this time there seemed to be no guilty manner about him."

"It has happened to me, too," Somnanda admitted surprisingly. "The young cartographer looks guilty?"

"He looks guilty," Shetland agreed. "He seemed normal until I challenged his concept of space-time. He wishes to believe that there is sufficient unrecognized mass in the universe to make it closed—that is, so that gravitational attraction will slow and halt its expansion and eventually cause it to contract back into a single point. Then—this.''

"The universe is evidently open," Somnanda said. "It will never contract. But the denouement, either way, will never affect human civilization; it is too far in Earth's future. Why should that disturb him?"

"I do not know. Yet it seems that it does. But I cannot condemn a person on such circumstantial evidence. I, too, in the last analysis, am afraid. It could have been my own reaction to the appearance, rather than the actuality, of his fear.''

"Possible, but remote," Somnanda said. "You have not affected the beacon this way before."

"Still, in fairness—''

Somnanda's brow wrinkled. "I am not entirely familiar with this matter. You spoke of challenging his concept of space-time. Is there some aspect of this that affects the nature of our mission?''

Shetland smiled inwardly—a smile of comprehension, not humor. In Somnanda's view the purpose of the journey was merely to test the beacon. The validity of one theory of the universe or another would have little bearing on that, unless one theory embodied an inherent threat to the beacon.

The threat was real enough—but it seemed to stem from internal problems, not external. Had those last-moment substitutions and additions to the crew not been made, so that he could have launched with a tested and integrated complement . . .

Unless something unique had happened to the *Meg I*. What were the chances against having two ships with similar personnel problems on such a mission?

"At one time," Shetland said, "there were two major theories of cosmology: the Steady State, in which the universe was supposed to be essentially stable, changing in detail but not in nature, and the Big Bang, in which it was exploding outward from an original, primeval ball of matter and energy. The later discovery of such things as the quasars did much to turn astronomers away from the steady-state cosmos, attractive as it was. Quasar—'quasi-stellar'—an object with the apparent size of a star but the energy of a galaxy. No such objects exist in our own time; both the nature and the distribution of the quasars indicate a radical change in the nature of the universe in the course of some billions of years. Perhaps they evolved into our present galaxies. This change is inconsistent with steady state, but consistent with explosion. Of course we are now in a position to send observers back ten billion years and see directly—but the policymakers have wisely forbidden travel backward from our own time, until the true nature of the universe is better understood, for fear of some paradoxical change in our own planet's development that would eliminate man, and perhaps the entire development of Earthly life. Still, it seems there must have been a 'bang'; we have never observed a quasar in the course of forward travel in time.''

''I can accept an exploding universe,'' Somnanda said. ''I see nothing alarming in it.''

''Few do. Most are simply interested in knowing the truth, whatever it may be. That is the scientific attitude.''

''That the young scientist does not share?''

''That does seem odd,'' Shetland agreed. ''Now the question is: what type of an explosion is it? Will the galaxies and clusters slow in the course of fifty billion years because of gravitational attraction, and finally swing back into a contracting universe—or will they fling outward without limit? The evidence we have already accumulated on this voyage suggests that the latter alternative is correct, as we have already established. If there is a 'shadow' universe, as Beeton conjectures, its gravity is not sufficient to prevent our own universe from expanding indefinitely. An asymmetrical, non-cyclic universe."

Somnanda shook his head, perplexed. "Would this be reason to frighten the cartographer?"

Shetland paced the floor. "I don't understand why. That's what holds me back. The elimination of a single theory should be of no more consequence than the elimination of an invalid strategy in the course of a chess game. An inconvenience, certainly, and perhaps disturbing, for much work has gone into the opposing theories. But hardly frightening."

"Unless that game were the only one ever played," Somnanda said. "An invalid strategy would then mean irrevocable loss, unless there were a suitable alternative."

"This *is* our only universe," Shetland said. "And asymmetry is a viable alternative, if my conjecture is correct. The cartographer should understand such things better than I do. He is attempting to map the universe in space-time, and this of course would be the purpose of this voyage, by his definition. The verification of an open universe may make his task more difficult, and the resulting chart may not be esthetically pleasing—but it should not be frightening."

"Could he have additional information that suggests otherwise?"

Shetland paced the floor again, unable to relax. The beacon flickered higher, reflecting his tension. "He never mentioned asymmetry. It is as if that concept does not exist for him."

"We cannot afford to assume he has no reason for his fear. His position must be ascertained."

Yes, it had to be, Shetland knew. Danger did exist—but of what conceivable nature? What decision had the Captain of the *Meg I* made? Had he waited until the twenty-second hour to question his ''Beeton''? Or had some unthinkable menace consumed his ship and crew at the end of the endless asymmetric cosmos?

The decision of that prior Captain had been wrong. The ship's beacon had died, and ship and crew had been either destroyed or lost forever in time.

How could Shetland improve upon that course, in his ignorance?

Chapter 6:＿＿＿＿＿Ghosts

Alice was the youngest member of the crew—just eighteen. Coincidentally, the *Meg* was just coming up on clock 18 as he came to interview her. She had been assigned for this mission the same time as Beeton, by what he now realized was no coincidence.

Her hair was black, her skin brown, and she was extraordinarily pretty. Almost, she reminded him of Maureen, his lost love. But he stifled that; there were common parameters for beauty, so that those who adhered most closely to them did seem to have some affinity. It meant nothing.

Her cabin was part laboratory, part boudoir. There was a set of cages containing white mice—a breed he understood was especially sensitive to temporal changes, thus a good guide to human physiological reactions. Across from them was a frilly bed. Beside that was a lady's vanity and a supply panel set up for assorted capsules: ranging from minor medicine to painless euthanasia for specimens scheduled for the dissection machine. The mice had far more reason to fear time than did men!

Alice was seated on the bed, looking at a manual. As he saw her, Shetland's mind reread the record sheets imprinted on his memory. He had not really considered her case before, in the press and stress of other business. But he had read, and therefore memorized, the data.

Abruptly he saw the reference whose significance had bypassed him before. He had tested Beeton on it without thinking to check the other party. She was as likely to be affecting the beacon as he, and he had been remiss not to follow this up sooner.

"What can I do for you, Captain?" she inquired alertly. This seemed to have become the standard greeting: a verbal mannerism revived from past social history.

"You are a new crewmember, and new to time. You understand the rules of the ship?"

"I ought to! Otherwise I don't belong here, do I!"

"With regard to coupling," he said gravely.

She laughed, embarrassed. "Oh, I'm sorry, Captain! I didn't understand. Of course if you want to—"

He lifted a spread hand. "Sosthenna accommodated me quite adequately not so long ago. I was merely inquiring about your intellectual comprehension and social acceptance."

She had half risen; now she relaxed, but there remained a flutter about her. "Well, it's necessary, isn't it? The sex, I mean. To relieve tensions—because of the beacon. So the normal prohibitions against same-race interaction are suspended here. Anything can affect the beacon, especially frustration, and frustration knows no color barrier."

"You are engaged to marry Wayne Beeton."

"Of course! But—"

"Doesn't that make it awkward—having sexual relations with other men, with your fiancé's knowledge?"

"No. We both understand about that. We knew it before we ever went to space. To time, I mean. It's just one of the conditions of—"

"Even when you copulate with Beeton himself?"

"Captain, I can't play favorites during a voyage! And I haven't done so!" she said indignantly. "I know that as the youngest woman aboard, I can expect the most attention. Wayne knows. We have accepted that. What we have together is independent of the physical interaction."

Shetland made a sign of peace. He had tried to provoke her, and she had reacted properly; that was good. "No one has accused you of playing favorites, Alice. But how do you think your fiancé feels privately?"

"He understands," she repeated. "It's all physical—you know what I mean, not *purely* physical, but with no lasting emotion. You have to do what you can to make it nice at the time, and you can even enjoy it—but you know you aren't in love. So when Wayne and I do it in space, that's all it is. Just a pleasant one-night stand, just like the others."

With a shape and face like hers, "pleasant" was surely a gross understatement! "You have done it already?"

She looked down demurely. "No, actually. Not yet. Not with Wayne. In space. Time. But when we do, that's how it will be. And I made it a point to—to—"

"To visit another man?"

"Yes. It works both ways, you know. No one can say no unless he's busy or incapacitated, male or female. So I went to Pilot Johns—"

"Oh? He has been on duty steadily since his sleep shift—"

"He was more than courteous about cutting short his sleep."

Understandable! What man would not sacrifice sleep to accommodate the sexual behest of an extremely attractive young woman, even when that required taking a neutralizer to the sleep capsule. Yet that explained why Johns had seemed nervous and short on sleep. Alice should not have approached him at that inconvenient time, and Johns could have refused her, for he had cause. But of course he had not. Shetland himself would not have. Let it be; this young woman lacked experience in space, and had intended no infraction.

"And Wayne did know," she continued determinedly. "So you see, we—I—made the plunge, and there is no trouble. But if you think I'd let another man touch me, back on Earth—"

"I think you understand why I'm asking," Shetland said.

"Sure." She spoke more easily now that she had vindicated herself. "Something's bothering the beacon, and you want to know if it's me. Female jealous tizzy. But you can see you don't have to worry, Captain. Wayne Beeton could do it with Tibet or Thenna right now, with me watching, and that light wouldn't flicker. Not from *me*. Not much, anyway. And I'll go with you right now and do it on the beacon table, if you think—"

Shetland laughed, enjoying the image. What would Somnanda say if a display like that overlapped the candle? "That will not be necessary!" But it *would* be necessary to recheck Beeton, for there had been a severe disturbance, and what Alice had told him could account for it. A temperamental, jealous man who had just learned about his fiancée indulging in sex with another man, but who was not permitted to express any resentment. Any unrelated pretext could set him off violently. Sublimation was dangerous in a situation like this, and fear was too closely akin to anger. Something as seemingly superficial as a challenge to a pet theory of

cosmology—by denying that, could he feel that he was denying what his fiancée had done? It might not be the universe
Beeton was afraid of, but the potential loss of Alice.

"But you must understand," Shetland continued, "that
beacon deviation is a serious matter, and that many emotional
factors can cause it. Particularly fear. Is there any other thing that
might be bothering you?"

"Oh, I'm nervous, Captain. No denying it! I guess we all
are! But how can you get away from that? The fear of the
unknown—"

The unknown: dead accurate! "You lost your mother early,"
Shetland said, reading from the record.

"When I was eighteen months old, yes," she said. "Both
parents, actually. I don't remember them at all. Sometimes I
dream about a house, and I associate that with my mother
somehow, as if she were there, but of course . . ." She
trailed off with a shrug.

Another surprising connection: Tibet had dreamed of losing a girl-child that age, eighteen months—a child who would
be eighteen now. A brown child. Strange coincidence! Was
there some psychic interaction between these two women?
Such effects were not unknown, in time travel lore. Of
course the stories were far wilder than any actuality. It was as
if the tales of time were trying to make up in two years what
the tales of space had developed in two decades.

". . . so I must have been illegitimate," Alice finished,
trailing back in. "But I learned to live with that long ago,
and I'm sure it doesn't affect the beacon either."

And Tibet had never married, and had a thing about chocolate ice cream: brown, sweet. Suddenly there was a network
of potential stress, where he had thought only simple random
human relations prevailed. Was he reading things where there
really was nothing? Coincidence and supernatural fantasies—no,

better to change the subject before his own buried monsters emerged. "What is your job?"

"Why, you know that, Captain! Oh—you mean formulate it, in case there's a flicker? Sure. I'm the physo-chemist; I'm here to analyze the qualities of anything we find in space-time. Or at least to start the analysis; I don't have the lab to do a thorough job. Or the training. But if something special turns up—something that might affect our own safety—"

The other *Meg*, as he understood it, had not carried such a specialty. Did that mean that the authorities thought there could be physical or chemical danger in deep-time? Or was it merely a wild gamble? "What *could* affect us, Alice? We're traveling in time, and extremely rapidly. The universe is visible but unreal to us, literally. Or would be, if we were not now so far from the massed galaxies that their light is no more than a dim glow our eyes can differentiate. We cannot interact with the universe while the drive functions."

"I'm not certain," she admitted. "But I have a foolish female premonition."

"Premonitions are not foolish in time travel! But what matters is your own reaction to them. Are you afraid?" Tibet believed that something terrible was about to happen—and so did Shetland. Unless he could anticipate its specific nature and defuse it.

"Afraid? Why should I be?"

"It is the female reaction to ask questions!" Shetland said with mock exasperation. "But we cannot tolerate evasions; I'm sure you understand that, too."

"Yes," she said, smiling ruefully—and if she were normally pretty, she was extraordinarily attractive in that moment. Flash of rapture! Every woman had her better instants, but Alice tended to grow on one compellingly. He would have to be careful of that; she might or might not know how to use it. "I know enough not to flood the ship with methane gas or take aboard strong radioactives! I have a pretty fair working knowledge of the physics and chemistry of space, and I'm not the kind to take unnecessary risks. So, to answer your question without evasion: no, I'm not afraid. Worried, apprehensive—but not afraid."

He smiled back at her, liking her. "That is a proper attitude. What *does* move you, Alice?"

"Ambition, I suppose. Sounds funny in a girl, doesn't it—but I really want to succeed, Captain. I want money, so I'm saving all I can; I want recognition, so I'm here on the *Meg*. I want sexual equality, and racial equality—I know color means nothing to *you*, Captain, but I was raised in a low-class orphanage and I covet the respectability of—"

"Covet!" Shetland said, interrupting her. "Another deadly sin."

She glanced at him, her brow furrowed. "Did I miss something?"

"A discussion I had with Sosthenna. It's as though we can be identified by special attributes, the Seven Deadly Sins. I'm Envy, she's Pride, Tibet is Gluttony—are you Covetousness?"

"I suppose I am," she said thoughtfully. "Is there really a distinction between envy and covetousness?"

"The distinction between male and female, evidently," he said with a short laugh. "Man *does*, woman *is*; thus perhaps the man envies what the woman is, while the woman covets what the man has."

She continued to look at him, almost staring, as if just discovering something. "Envy relates to what a person is, and covetousness to what a person has," she murmured. After a moment she shook herself apologetically. "I wonder whether the others relate to the other Deadly Sins."

"Probably not. There is some of every trait in every human being, and in all the animal kingdom! It is artificial to make such associations. You're a rounded individual, for example, and—"

"Thank you."

"I was referring to your personality."

"Naturally."

He shook his head. He must have missed a nuance, and reacted boorishly rather than appropriately. He had often told himself that he didn't mind the superior intelligence of so many of the people he worked with, but that was surely the foundation of his envy. He labored constantly to understand human motivation, while others seemed to grasp it so quickly that his efforts became blunders. "I don't know what you think there is to covet! You already have what it takes."

"I don't have the intellectual honesty you do. I covet that."

"Thank you," he said, smiling. Did he have it right, this time?

"Anger," she said.

"What?"

"Wayne—he would be the Deadly Sin of Anger. He—"

"Oh." Shetland relaxed. "Does he have a temper? I hadn't noticed it."

"Not a fast temper, exactly. But he takes things so seriously, and he won't—can't—let go. So he can build up a real fury—not against people so much as against situations. He's so intelligent, he just doesn't understand stupidity—not that other people are stupid, he doesn't say that, exactly—"

"I know what you mean." Gratifying to have her say that! "But would anything about this mission make him angry?"

"I shouldn't think so. He's been eager to map the secrets

of the universe. But it's so hard to tell. His mind—who can keep up with it? I mean—"

"Yes." How well he understood!

"And Johns—he would be Lust!"

"Oh? I wasn't aware of that."

"You're not exactly in a position to, Captain," she said delicately. "To be aware, I mean."

Was she overreacting to her lone experience with the man, attributing to him an exaggerated trait to compensate for her revulsion? Had she seen Shetland with Sosthenna, she could readily have judged the one to be a satyr and the other a nymphomaniac! "It does not show on his record."

She shrugged. Her face was too brown to show a blush. "Ask one of the other girls."

He would do so. "About Beeton—wouldn't Fear be a better characterization than Anger? I have the impression—"

"Is Fear one of the Deadly Sins?"

"No. But that's only an idle game. My concern is with the real motivation of my crew. It seems that Fear is a more likely suspect."

"Suspect?"

She had thought this was all theoretical! She hadn't known about the actual stress on the beacon, or how close they all had come to being marooned in time by its failure.

"Oh, I see what you mean," she said, though he hadn't answered. "Fear and anger are related, aren't they?"

"Yes. The same adrenaline sponsors each. 'Fight or flight' reflex."

"And the man who is angry may be masking his fear . . ." She considered that, then shook it off. "Well, it would be unhealthy not to be a little afraid, on a voyage like this, wouldn't it? Leaving the whole universe behind—"

Shetland nodded. "Actually, the universe is leaving *us*

behind. But I would have to be suspicious of the person who had no alarm!"

"But there's still Somnanda. What's the seventh sin?"

"Sloth. Does that fit?"

She considered. "I don't think so. He has to watch that beacon all the time."

Shetland moved to go. "We'll talk again soon."

"My pleasure! It must be nice being Captain."

"Now don't covet me my position! There's scant joy in it," he said, only half joking. "Not a fraction the joy of being a pretty girl."

She moved to her supply panel and dialed a capsule. Sleeping potion, he realized; sleep was vital during the voyage, and it couldn't wait on insomnia. They all took the little capsules of gas: one sniff and a person was out, with no aftereffects other than the refreshment of sleep.

As the door closed, the red capsule popped into her hand. Shetland wished he could afford to sleep now. The constant and building tension of this voyage was wearing him thin. But there was a crisis in the making, and he had to abort it before relaxing. If the beacon went out—

A red capsule.

He whirled about, took two steps back to the door, and shoved it open by hooking his fingers in the corner of the iris. The overlapping panels slid across each other to widen the central hole. "One moment!" he cried.

But she had already taken it. The ruptured gel lay on the floor, already sublimating, its puff of pressurized gas expended, and Alice lay on her fancy bed.

He couldn't tell anything by the smell; the chemicals were odorless. One good sniff absorbed the contents of a capsule, and it was done. But as he watched the girl, he *knew*. She was not breathing.

The capsules were color coded: green for sleep, red for death. The reds were for laboratory euthanasia. It was some kind of nerve gas, effective in seconds—and irreversible. He had been out of the room only a moment—just time enough for her to break it open and sniff and fall back on the bed, dying.

Suicide or accident? He skimmed over their recent conversation in his mind: it was printed as on a tape, verbatim. "Is there really a distinction between envy and covetousness?" she had asked. He had replied, "The distinction between male and female, evidently," and laughed shortly, thinking himself clever. He was Envy, she Covetousness; he was male, she female. If the game were played out consistently . . .

But she had not laughed. She had looked at him strangely, staring, her mind obviously pursuing another channel, though her words continued on this one. Then she had shaken herself and gone on to a slightly different conversational line.

A minor indication—yet it was his main evidence that something was working in her mind other than the banter. Their dialogue had seemed inconsequential, no more than a game. How could any thought suggested by that have led to suicide—and not have excited the beacon?

Accident, then? Hardly. She was a chemist, and not color-blind. *He* had noted the red capsule; surely she could not have missed it. Even if she had dialed it by accident, her fingers assuming that a normal animal dissection was coming up, she would have realized her mistake before breaking it. Before sniffing. She was trained and qualified; she simply would not have made a mistake like that.

Neither suicide nor accident—yet she was dead.

But that mystery had to wait. Now he had to deal with the crisis itself. He couldn't tell the crew; the shock would wipe out the beacon. This matter had to be secret, until the beacon was not at risk. Only his own iron control prevented an emotional blast of devastating proportion. *He could not afford shock!* So he kept it rational. That was his ability; that was why he was Captain. The practical problem was to conceal the evidence—which meant disposing of the body promptly.

Which could not be done. There was no converter on the ship, and it would be extremely awkward to jettison something that size while the drive was functioning—and the matter would hardly be secret, then.

Alternative: hide it. Freeze it, put it in storage.

He knelt by the bed, reached about the body, and picked her up. She remained warm and limber and exceedingly feminine; he could tell by the distribution of avoirdupois that her proportions were even more appealing than her clothing suggested. She could have been a real vamp, this dead girl. Perhaps, on the occasion of her approach to Johns, she had been. No wonder he had reacted strongly!

All of which only intensified the mystery of her demise. No one would want to kill her, and she should not have wanted to die.

He felt a dampness on his left arm. He looked, and saw a darkening patch on the bunk. Not blood, he realized; urine. She had of course become incontinent with death, her fluid leaking out. Soon there would be an odor.

Now he had to gamble: that no one else was walking the passage. No one *should* be, but he could not be certain.

He carried her to the storage room and put her in a locker. This one contained food; much of it had already been used, and the remainder could be transferred or fitted in around the body. It was cold; the chill of intergalactic space itself was piped in to reduce it to super-hard freeze. Nevertheless, he used the projector intended for the preservation of specimens without spoilage. She would be stiff throughout in minutes, her wetted skirt too.

He locked the vault shut and added the magnetic key to his ring. The pattern of magnetism was unique to each key; no one else would get in there.

Now he would have to change her bedsheets and work out a reasonable explanation for her absence. It would be difficult to stall indefinitely—but he simply had to do it. It would hurt him to have to lie, but that was preferable to precipitating the extinction of the beacon.

Everything, he thought wryly, was hostage to the welfare of the beacon. Even his honor.

Was this what had happened aboard the *Meg I*? Had that ship's Captain refused to let its beacon be held hostage?

No matter. He could say she had been put on a special project relevant to the expedition's welfare. That was true, in a fashion.

Regardless, the heat would be on in only another hour. The mandatory group interaction session was due. Supposedly an hour of enlightenment and relaxation, it was about to become an hour of nightmare. For him, at least.

The *Meg*'s clock stood at 20. Shetland had the main table set up and a deck of playing cards out. He hardly expected this pack of plastic slips to stave off what was coming, but he had to make the attempt. He was seated, so that the sidearm he had donned did not show.

"You are nervous, Captain," Somnanda observed, reading his flame.

"I fear this coming hour."

Somnanda stood and walked to the table. He was broad

and tall, and seemed out of place away from the beacon. But of course he didn't have to be right on top of it at all times. "I understand."

Did he? Certainly Somnanda knew something momentous had happened, for the flame was responsive to every whim of every pattern of life aboard the ship. He should have been able to read the deletion of Alice's network from the whole, and would have had to compensate for that sudden gap. But he should not know how she had died, or why. "Accident," Shetland said, explaining.

"No, Captain. Self-willed."

So Somnanda *had* known! And had not advertised the flux of the flame on the intercom, deliberately. He had protected Shetland's effort in a key manner.

Then Beeton appeared and that subject had to be dropped. More than that: banished. At least he knew now: Somnanda would help keep the secret.

"What's the name of the game?" Beeton inquired cheerfully. Certainly *he* didn't know what had happened—and must not know. Her fiancé!

Shetland wondered where the young man had picked up that phrase, name of the game. "I doubt it."

"Doubt what?"

"That is the name of the game." He showed the deck. More than that, he thought, realizing that his subconscious could betray him yet. Of all the games to pick!

Sosthenna and Tibet arrived together. "Bridge or Canasta?" Sosthenna asked.

"He doubts it," Beeton said, and Somnanda smiled.

Johns came. "Sorry I'm late, folks. Hopefully I haven't missed anything rich."

"Hopefully you *hope*," Beeton said. There was such an edge of contempt to his voice that Johns glanced at him.

"What's with you, Recruit?" Johns asked.

"Your grammar. What does 'hopefully' modify?"

Johns shrugged that off without response, not seeing Beeton's point. But Shetland understood both the grammatical and the human points: Beeton, new to time, and not yet become acclimatized to the sexual code. He did resent what Alice had done with Johns—and could not admit it.

"Where's Alice?" Sosthenna inquired, looking around.

Dread question! But Shetland was braced for it. "She will not be with us this session. Something came up, so I put her on special assignment."

"*What* special assignment?" Beeton demanded instantly.

"Properties of frozen matter at extreme temporal velocity," Shetland said. "She will be given compensatory recreation time."

"Hey, I'll be glad to help with that," Johns said.

Beeton whirled about, his right fist coming up—but Sosthenna caught his arm and pinned it against her bosom, restraining him. "Oops, clumsy of me," she said.

Beeton, startled, glanced down at her, his anger fading—as any anger might in such a circumstance. If there were any woman who came close to matching Alice in overall attractiveness, that one was Sosthenna. The young man was beginning to realize that there would be compensations for him, too, abiding by the ship's code of conduct.

Shetland cut in quickly. "We'll play I Doubt It this time. I shall deal out all the cards evenly and commence by laying down one or more aces facedown. The player to my left must lay down one or more twos, and so on around the circle until one of us runs out of cards: the winner."

"But what if someone doesn't have—" Johns began.

"Then he bluffs," Shetland said. He dealt the cards. They did not go around evenly, but no one objected. "If anyone has reason to question another player's deposit, that person challenges him by saying 'I doubt it.' The cards are then exposed, and the one who is mistaken must pick up the entire stack.''

"It's a game of cheating!" Beeton exclaimed, delighted.

Shetland laid a card facedown in the center. "One ace," he announced.

The others looked, considering. "The odds are slightly in his favor," Beeton said. "Still, I doubt it."

Shetland turned over the card: the eight of diamonds. He returned it to his hand. "Your turn," he said to Sosthenna, next to him.

"Two twos," she said, putting them down. No one doubted it. There really wasn't much point, this early in the game.

Beeton was next. "Three threes!" he said.

Johns chuckled. "You think no one'll doubt a big order? *I* doubt it!"

Beeton shrugged. He turned over the cards, one by one: three threes. Chagrined, Johns picked up the stack and began assembling the cards in order.

"One four," Tibet said, putting it down.

"Hey!" Johns cried. "Where'd this jack come from?"

"What jack?" Sosthenna asked. "I put down twos."

"There're two twos, three threes and a jack in this pile I picked up."

Shetland smiled. "I am afraid you have been had. You did not call it during the turn."

Johns looked at Beeton. "You put down four cards!"

"He learns quickly," Tibet murmured.

Indeed he did, Shetland reflected. Beeton, new to the game, had just pulled a successful double-bluff, winning despite being called. At this rate, he would be an expert cheater within the hour. I Doubt It was a game of huge dishonesty potential, that some honest people were suspiciously good at.

Now was an upbeat moment for the young man. The time to broach the major concern. "You play well already," Shetland said. "Not like someone whose fear affects the beacon."

Suddenly every person was alert. More than one surely thought this was the Captain's folly. But Shetland knew he had to resolve this conflict now, rather than letting it resolve itself—at the twenty-second hour.

Johns, with assumed nonchalance, put down a card. "One five."

"Beeton, beacon," Beeton murmured as if arranging a pun. Then he met Shetland with a steady gaze in which there was not a trace of fear. It was not bluff, for the Captain's peripheral gaze covered the candle, and it remained quiescent. "May I speak frankly, sir?"

When a crewman felt it necessary to address that question to the Captain, the message was unlikely to be pleasant. But Shetland had deliberately provoked it. "Yes, certainly, this is the occasion for candor," he said. "There will be no offense taken, by any present."

"I would like to rephrase the question," Beeton said, dropping the "sir." For him, it had always been an affectation. He seemed to have anticipated this session, though not its public nature. But Shetland wanted it public: there must be no equivocation about what ensued. "I think I am afraid of the same thing you are. Will you admit that much?"

"I am afraid of many things—but particularly of fear itself. Continue."

The card game was lagging for the moment, understandably. But most eyes remained on their own hands.

"We fear a very real danger, and it has little to do with the beacon. You and I know that there is death waiting for us at the fringe of the asymmetric universe. One ship has already been taken, perhaps others. They may have lied to you too, Captain. To the authorities the end always justifies the means."

Somnanda looked up but held his peace. To an extent the beacon served as a lie detector, for a conscious lie included the fear of being caught. The flame was higher, but reasonably steady. Somnanda had not been told of the loss of the *Meg I*; now he must suspect. Curse the brilliant leap to an accurate conclusion the cartographer had made!

But Somnanda showed no concern, and the others held their faces straight. "One six," Somnanda said, laying down his card.

"The important thing to realize is that this was no freak accident," Beeton continued. "We face the same demise, unless we reverse the drive. Soon."

"No," Shetland said simply. Then: "One seven." He laid down his card.

"I doubt it," Sosthenna said, sounding as if the seven was the least of her doubts.

Shetland turned over his seven, and she groaned and picked up the pile. He wished that bluffs of time travel could be called with as little risk. He was playing a larger game of I Doubt It, and had already had to account for Alice on a bluff. The moment someone called that one—

"Beeton believes that our course leads to danger," Shetland said. "I submit that there is more danger in the fact of his belief than there can possibly be in the external universe. So I call his bluff: he must explain his reason for his request that the *Meg*'s drive be prematurely reversed.

"Prematurely. . . !" Johns muttered. "Over twenty on the clock!"

Then there was silence. Was the beacon flickering now?

Whose tension was responsible? Shetland had acted to prevent Beeton from calling the Alice bluff, by calling the time-velocity bluff first. Would it work? Or would he wind up with a doubled threat to the beacon?

It was the Captain's duty to be decisive in a crisis. Shetland had decided to gamble, rather than allow his mission to be compromised. "Go on, Beeton," he said firmly. "You have expressed the desire for frank speaking, and you have suggested that there is an external menace in time. Because of the apparent asymmetry of the universe. Surely you can be more specific. Turn over your card."

The cartographer swallowed, a nervous young man now that the challenge was upon him. The flame *was* brighter; Shetland watched it without looking directly at it. "You are familiar with the 'oscillating universe' theory," Beeton said. This much was rhetorical. "I had expected this theory to be confirmed by our findings. I had—hoped."

Now Beeton himself glanced at the rising flame, then averted his gaze. "To most people, there is scant difference between one concept of the universe and another. After all, in all the prior history of man it has had no discernible bearing on our daily lives. But now, to those of us who venture into the extraordinary reaches of time, it becomes a matter of life and death. Particularly death."

"Say what you mean," Shetland growled. The card game had stalled again while Sosthenna made a show of sorting her few new cards.

"In the oscillating universe, matter never exceeds the age of the cycle. Before the galaxies can age completely they are drawn back into the primeval ball and restructured. There is a continual renewal, every hundred billion years or so. But in this alternate, open-end universe, the galaxies are not terminated by the end of the cycle. They become old. After several hundred billion years—'' He paused in the yellow light. ''After that amount of time, they die.''

He looked at each of the others and met only bafflement. No one else had followed his intuitive leap. ''Don't you see?'' Beeton said, half pleading and half angry. ''They pass on. There is no longer any dust or gas to fuel the stars; even the planets are consumed in energy. Those galaxies are at the opposite end of the scale from quasars. Instead of being brilliantly alive—they are dead.''

Again he glanced about, and again encountered only confusion. ''Only their ghosts live on,'' he said earnestly. ''The malignant spirits of once-living nebulae.''

Ghosts of galaxies?

''Five eights,'' Sosthenna announced, laying down six cards. No one challenged her.

Shetland looked at Somnanda, who shook his head negatively. He looked at Johns, whose mouth was hanging slightly open.

''One nine,'' Beeton said.

''You're crazy!'' Johns exclaimed.

It was Beeton's chance to turn over the card and show a nine. But his control snapped. He jumped up, and the flame leaped with him. ''No, no!'' he cried. ''You have to understand, all of you. We are entering the time of ghosts. Within an hour or two. We have to stop the ship before it's too late!''

''The supernatural is no threat to the natural,'' Shetland snapped.

''Captain!'' Somnanda's voice was urgent as he strode to the beacon.

Shetland whipped around. The flame had burst into an inferno, its star gone nova.

"Stop the ship!" Beeton screamed, standing behind Sosthenna. "The ghost is out there—"

In a moment he would realize that the ghost was not *out there*, but *in here*—in the food locker. Suddenly Shetland's sidearm was in his hand, above the table. The tableau seemed to freeze at that moment: Somnanda in the corner, half standing, the sweat of agony reflecting orange on his face. Johns, staring at the young cartographer, confusion and incredulity distorting his own features. Tibet, grim and mute, her eyes on the cards scattered without order. Beeton, one hand clutching Sosthenna's shoulder, four fingers indenting the upper contour of her breast; the other hand in the air, clenched into a fist; mouth insanely wide, lips pulled back from teeth.

One word from the Captain would ease this threat. He had only to agree to reverse the drive. To set aside his orders.

Then Beeton was falling, his head engulfed in a sparkling cloud. The gas from the capsule Shetland had fired was dissipating already; with the sure aim that was another prerequisite of captaincy he had placed it high enough to leave Sosthenna unaffected. But Beeton would be in a deep coma for several hours. Long enough to carry him beyond the crisis point.

Sosthenna twisted around and managed to half catch the falling man, preventing him from crashing into the deck. She was a smart woman, Shetland thought idly as his own inertia held him still. She always reacted properly, doing what was necessary at the time, sparing others much discomfort.

"Captain"—Somnanda's low voice cut through his reverie, as it always did—"there is little doubt that the young man's terror was the cause of the disturbance. But it should have abated, had you agreed to reverse the drive."

"Yes!" Sosthenna gasped as she laid Beeton flat and disengaged.

The beacon flame was almost normal. "I could not do that," Shetland said.

Johns made a sound. "You knew how simple it was to stop the trouble—and you cooled him anyway?"

"Yes." Shetland still held the sidearm.

Johns stared at him with the same expression he had turned on Beeton before. "Captain—now I'm not so sure Beeton was the crazy one. Maybe he was *right*. You never let him make his point."

"That's right," Sosthenna said. Her blouse was torn where Beeton's fingers had involuntarily clawed it; she would show a bruise later.

Shetland looked at the unconscious form, so peaceful in body and mind now. Like Alice—except that Beeton's state was not permanent. It was not safe to admit this to Johns, but it had been necessary to put Beeton away on one pretext or another, before he comprehended what had happened to his fiancée. That bomb had now been defused. "If I had verified his suspicion, Pilot, his terror would certainly have extinguished the beacon."

"Verified his—" Johns was shocked. "You admit it! There *is* a ghost out there!"

"Not a ghost, precisely. A derelict. A ship that severed contact suddenly for an unknown reason. My orders are to duplicate its course and investigate. That is why this voyage was organized so abruptly; it was deemed best not to wait. I shall carry out those orders."

"By heading into the same trap?"

"Those are my orders."

"Orders!" The flame was rising again. "Captain, I can't agree to that!"

Shetland studied him sourly. "*You* can't agree, Pilot?"

"No, I can't. The ghost will eat us too. We've got to turn back."

Behind the growing flame, Somnanda's head turned to bear on Johns.

"Now look, men—" Tibet said. "Let's not—"

"I see it now," the pilot said. "Beeton was right. After the galaxies die, they are ghosts. And they hate the living things." He looked around, saw the flame. "Don't you understand? We must reverse the drive—and I'm going to do that right now!"

"This is mutiny," Shetland said.

Johns started to go, ignoring him. There was the flash, the sparkle—and the pilot joined the cartographer.

Sosthenna was not in time to catch this one. She looked, then shook her head grimly. Tibet took her arm and they walked silently out of the chamber. They were not going to doubt the Captain openly . . .

The flame subsided. Somnanda and Shetland gazed at each other. "I believe we have halted the contagion," Shetland said.

Chapter 7:_____Revelation

"**Y**our move, Captain," Somnanda said gravely.

The chess game! The man could think of that at this juncture! But it was his way of acceding to the Captain's course.

"I only hope that my personal situation is better than that of my pieces," Shetland said. "I will have to reconsider my move."

"Your situation is not adverse," Somnanda said.

Shetland hauled the two unconscious men to the side of the chamber. "It may seem unreasonable to sacrifice two human beings in this fashion, rather than accede to their seeming reasonable request. But I can delegate their functions as necessary, while I could neither humor their fancies nor allow their emotional stress to destroy the beacon. I am the Captain." Yet he felt the need to justify himself to Somnanda, though he cursed his own frailty.

"You seem unreasonable." From this man this was an observation, not an insult.

"I *am* unreasonable. Sometimes that is the only course—just as an apparently illogical sacrifice is at times required in order to win at chess." The chess analogy kept running through his mind now, as chocolate ice cream had before; was it valid? He was tempted to doubt it.

Somnanda waited.

"Extended trips through time have been rare so far," Shetland continued. "Evidence is therefore inconclusive. But there appears to be a certain—a certain distortion in many personalities as temporal velocity is increased. The initial disorientation may be an aspect of this—but not the whole. Perhaps it is a side effect of the drive, or simply an emotional reaction to isolation from the normal universe."

"This also manifests in the beacon," Somnanda agreed. "I have conjectured that it resembles the disorientation experienced when a person travels quickly to a part of the world in a different time zone. Here there are no zones; time is always changing, ever more rapidly. We try to maintain the established ship schedule, but still there is an effect. So such reaction is not surprising."

"Possibly," Shetland said, appreciating the analogy. "There is much we do not understand about our own biological mechanisms. But it is one of my dreads, and I always watch for it. That's why I am careful about revealing my orders prematurely. Individual judgment cannot be trusted in time travel. Normal people are not aware of this distortion, and I cannot be certain I am aware of it myself. It is more fundamental than a state of intoxication or drug expansion. It is futile to point out such aberrations to the victims; to them, they are *not* aberrations. The crewmen are, in effect, mental patients. I think we have seen this, now."

Somnanda nodded gravely. "In all of us."

"The Captain is not excluded," Shetland agreed, smiling

wearily. "To me, my course is the correct one. To you it may seem otherwise. But you are subject to the distortion. There are only two safeguards against it. The first of these is the balance of viewpoints. That is the major reason for the selection of a mixed and balanced crew: two of each major race, the seventh a mixture of all three. Four males, three females. Age spread from eighteen to thirty-eight, with the median at twenty-eight. The sum of these viewpoints will normally be in approximate balance, it is conjectured, for personalities distort outward from the center. For every pull there must be a counter-pull, only the center remaining constant."

"The assumed absolute rest of the microcosm," Somnanda said. "Something to orient on."

"Yes, exactly! Even an inaccurate reference point is vital."

"But two of the crew have been temporarily eliminated," Somnanda pointed out. "The factor of youth has been reduced."

Counting Alice, three were out. The three youngest. That *was* bad. "Yes. Perhaps I made a mistake; I was not thinking of it quite that way." Shetland considered a moment more, then returned to his original thought. "I *know* my judgment is suspect. I have preoccupations and I entertain doubts. I question the wisdom of this voyage, its apparent expandability, the attitude of certain crewmen, the evidence of the supernatural. I do not believe, at this moment, in the beacon—that is, that it represents any valid connection with Earth. I think it is an ability within your mind that brings us home, like my eidetic memory. I think the circuitry of your table is irrelevant, or perhaps only a minor aid for you. Since I doubt the beacon, I must investigate the possibility that I am wrong. But if the beacon is real—why not the ghost of a galaxy? How can I choose between these doubts and possibilities?"

Somnanda nodded. "I appreciate the problem, though I differ on details. It is true that I can maintain the beacon without external circuitry. Yet I would think that if all aspects suggest danger—Beeton, the loss of the prior ship, the premonitions of the crew, even suicide—"

"There your own thinking is suspect. I do anticipate extinction at the critical hour—very soon!—but I will not reverse the drive."

Somnanda shrugged as if his own life were not in the balance. "Yes, there we differ. I would reverse the drive."

"Because even this seemingly rational perception of the threat may be distorted," Shetland said. "I can rely now on the only remaining objectivity: my orders. These were presented to me before the voyage began and seemed reasonable then; they must therefore be reasonable now. If I desire to modify them, it is because my present insight is biased, not my earlier one. I must therefore uphold what seems to be unreasonable, even suicidal, to me now—and I shall."

The clock read 21.2 hours. Better than a hundred quadrillion years per hour. Eight-tenths of an hour until the termination of the voyage—one way or another.

Shetland found himself in Beeton's cabin, looking at the chess game. Why had he come? Because there was a lingering uncertainty as the critical hour approached? Or simple guilt for overriding that uncertainty, at any cost?

No, he was still seeking to achieve alignment with the net consensus. It might seem academic now, but if he could somehow pick up some clue, something to bring the dichotomy between his orders and his intellect into—

He saw a picture of Alice, smiling for the man who would never see her again. That picture had not been there before.

Beeton must have set it out recently. Now she was cold in the freezer, and Beeton himself was unconscious. A gloomy consensus of youth! Were they victims of the stresses of time—or of the unknown?

He looked about the room. Nothing was out of order. His eyes returned to the picture. Alice was looking at something to the side; had she been that way before? Shetland felt a little chill, but suppressed it immediately; he could not afford to let his imagination deceive him. His memory said she had looked straight ahead before, that her eyes had moved. His memory was normally infallible, so this was one of his few tangible evidences of distortion. One time or the other he had perceived the picture wrong.

Still, he glanced the way she was looking. The chess set was there. It was uncanny, the way in which the young man had divined the moves and kept up with a game the Captain had never advertised.

No, this was not that game; the configuration was different. It—yes, it *was* his game, two moves later. White had undertaken a highly questionable Queen sacrifice, forcing an unorthodox line of play. An accelerated defeat.

Shetland swept the pieces into the box and folded the board. The young cartographer had no right to tease him by making such a suggestion! It was a private game.

He started to leave—and saw the picture again. The eyes were staring straight ahead.

"Now damn it!" he exclaimed, exasperated. It was possible that he had been mistaken the first time—though highly improbable!—but now he was certain there had been a change. In the picture.

Yet it could not be. The image was inanimate. So it had to be in his perception. Only he and Somnanda knew that Alice was dead; was this information preying on his mind, giving Alice a seeming animation?

What was a ghost, after all, except an apparition, a vision of something that was not really present? Returning to haunt the guilty person, a figment of conscience, visible to no other—because the guilt was in the mind of no other? The personality distortion engendered by travel through time, perhaps an analog of the physical and temporal distortions inherent in near-lightspeed travel through space—was it actually a facilitation of guilt manifestations?

But he had no guilt regarding Alice! He had not killed her, and certainly had not desired her death. He had only concealed her demise from the others, so that it would not by its very shock value wipe out the beacon and doom them all. His deception was a necessary function of his office, to salvage what could be salvaged.

Yet he did feel something, and it was important to clarify it now. He had to narrow it down, to comprehend the source of his perceptual bias, to reduce his own distortion. Alice had been a pretty girl, and he still felt the impact. He had thought he was over his shock at the loss of Maureen, and the sight of this similarly pretty creature had jolted him—but he was sure that wasn't it either.

He lay down on Beeton's bunk and contemplated the picture. Alice's eyes had moved to fasten on him—no, that was merely the nature of any picture. The eyes that viewed the spectator straight ahead also viewed the one at the side. Shetland looked into those lovely eyes and let his control relax slightly. If the horror of her untimely death affected him too strongly, there would be a warning from the beacon.

But she did not seem dead now. As his gaze fixed on her, she seemed to animate, to manifest living hues and shadows.

Then he realized: this was no ordinary photograph, but a

holographic image: a representation of three-dimensional scope, a true window on the subject. Double or triple phased, so that not only was she rounded in perspective, but her representation had alternate aspects. Her eyes moved, her expression changed, depending on the angle and perhaps the mood of the viewer. Expensive technique, but neither magic nor madness!

So young, so beautiful! He recalled the perfect heft of her body as he carried her to the freezer. She had been no artificial creature, no construct of enhancements and artful apparel. She had been a genuine functioning being, as the leakage of her defunct body had demonstrated. It would have been pleasant to make love to her, in the living state. More than pleasant.

No, that was not quite right. Something jarred. It would have been easy to *love* her. Sex was not to be confused with love, in space. Perhaps he had taken a step in that direction, after finding himself balked by Sosthenna's completely proper behavior: passion without commitment. Yet Alice was Beeton's fiancée. So there was guilt. It was not his place to entertain romantic inclinations toward that young woman, quite apart from the twenty-year differential in age. Sex was free on the ship; love was not. He had perhaps in his secret heart been tempted to transgress, and so felt guilt.

That still did not explain her suicide. He had given her no signal of his feeling; indeed, had not been aware of it himself then. He had not voiced anything untoward. He had merely done the job required of him as Captain. And she had understood that.

That chess game: that disturbing sacrifice Beeton had set up. Shetland viewed the board in his mind, his thoughts passing rapidly from the mystery of Beeton's fiancée to the mystery of his game strategy, irrationally suspecting that both were linked to the mission of the *Meg II*. He played through that combination again, studying the possibilities as the powerful Queen piece fell, as if it were a suicide . . .

Suicide, sacrifice—two faces of the same strategy? Appalling concept! Yet—

He lay on the bunk and closed his eyes, studying that game. The sacrifice led into a line of play that was radically different from his normal style, just as Alice's death had forced him into difficult moves as Captain. This was not positional chess, for his position seemed hopeless. It was a dynamic, oddball spinoff. Black's obvious response was *this*; White then had to do *that*. Black—Black had the advantage, of course, but there were awkward aspects. White was forcing the play, as a drowning man might clutch his rescuer and pull him under too. Then—

Then it opened out into a King-Queen split, giving White the abrupt and decisive advantage. There was no way for Black to break the sequence; it was determined by that initial sacrifice on the eighteenth move. Black would face mate by the twenty-second move. The series violated many of the tenets of good positional play—yet it was quite valid.

He would not use the sacrifice play, of course. The genius that had conceived that strategy was not his own, but Beeton's. But he would show this interesting lesson to Somnanda: how independent and bold foresight could convert a potential loss into victory. Book play was not always valid.

Sacrifice at move 18 . . . termination at move 22.

Coincidence?

He looked up at the picture of Alice, into her eyes. Eighteen years old when she died—for no reason he understood. And it had been the twenty-second hour when the *Meg I* had mysteriously faded out.

Shetland found himself shaking. This was lunacy!

Yet who was to say, at this moment, how lunacy might be defined? Perhaps it was only common sense, and his distorted mind misread the cues. Suppose this were a message that Shetland's own stupidity or bias had prevented Beeton from delivering? Beeton had been alert and sharp right into the I Doubt It card game. Irked at Johns, but by no means unbalanced. Was it reasonable that Beeton had suddenly lost control? That such a brilliant mind had been mistaken in the one case that counted? Or had the cartographer's terrible fear been based on fact, not fancy—while the distortion merely prevented him from making himself sufficiently clear?

Had Johns, also, finally responded to the actual message, grasping its validity?

Ghosts in space and time? The malignant spirits of bygone galaxies?

Shetland shook his head: more shudder than motion. Was it possible that his firm disbelief in the supernatural was mere prejudice?

Yet there was Alice's picture, with its shifting eyes. If ghosts existed, why not her ghost, too?

Assume, for the sake of argument, that Beeton had been correct. That his cosmology, like his chess game, was accurate: based on sound though unconventional logic. That a ghost of some kind did wait at the twenty-second move/hour. That the situation was hopeless only because the man in charge refused to deviate from the book, from his orders, even though the Queen sacrifice had already been made.

Shetland looked at his watch, synchronized with the ship's clock. 21.5.

In chess, the answer had been a total revision of strategy. The book had had to be discarded. In life—

No! His orders were the only certainty he retained! He could not allow them to be compromised. He would not reverse the drive. He would remain right here for the next half hour, no matter what contortions of rationalization his mind undertook. As Ulysses had tied himself to the mast, refusing to yield to the sirens' call, Shetland would hold firm until the letter of his orders had been discharged.

His body tried to move, his mouth tried to speak, but self-control was the Captain's strength. He stayed on the bed. The present course continued.

The chessboard image in his mind faded into a figurative map of the universe. Plasma of the asymmetrical, indeterminate explosion hurtled outward at virtually the speed of light, never slowing, never reversing, never returning its energy and substance to the great cosmic egg that was now known as the beginning but not the end. No oscillations! Now the fragments were born in the center as brightly shining Pawns (quasars), matured as Knights and Bishops and Castles (galaxies), and died of old age at the rim as fading Kings (ghosts).

Then, as it were, the pieces came to life. The Pawns were babies, the Kings old men. The board, which was the universe, became a city without buildings. Babies were born spontaneously in the center, hatched explosively from that great egg, and they crawled at lightspeed in all directions. As they made their way outward they formed into children, stars with the energy of galaxies, and some of these beings had bishop's hats and some had horse's heads. Farther out they developed into galactic men and women, and the men were Castles and the women Queens.

A billion years were as one year. Finally the century-old Kings staggered to the rim to die. The size of this city was determined by the age of the inhabitants. When they became too old to function, it ended. The rim was a desolate grave. There was no way to bury the bodies; where they died, they lay, they rotted, they gave up all their lingering fractional vitality, and at last the leached bones guarded the memory of what had been.

But lo! There were no babies anymore, no children, no young men and women. All had been born together, and now all died together, and there was nothing to follow. The center was almost as vast a desolation as the rim. The game was over.

Except, amazingly, a mote appeared at the rim. By some freak a child had bypassed age and entered the domain of death long before its schedule. A child called "Meg."

The ancient bones quivered with outrage. No living thing was permitted to desecrate the mighty graveyard. The angry spirits gathered their forces, concentrated their ghastly energies, opened their ponderous jaws and cried:

"Captain! Captain!"

Alice's voice! Shetland vaulted to his feet and stood looking about, hand on his sidearm. But there was only the pinup picture: the megalocarpous nude.

Had he ever seen Alice's portrait? Or was that, too, a ghost?

Then he was pounding down the passage to the beacon chamber. Somnanda was there, stiffening in seeming agony, unable to speak. The yellow light was rampaging, and this time Shetland himself was the cause.

Shetland turned and lurched on toward the pilot's compartment. He found the drive control and shoved the emergency handle from FORWARD to REVERSE.

The clock stood at 21.7.

Now the velocity dial began nudging down and the *Meg*'s temporal motion abated logarithmically. And the beacon, Shetland knew, was subsiding.

*   *   *

Now the clock was coming down on 10—a bare one million years per hour. The two gassed crewmen had slept out their human hours as the velocity wound down at the same rate it had increased, one clock hour per human hour.

They were not returning to their own time, however. The reversal of the drive merely slowed their thrust into the future, much as a breaking action in physical space would operate. The second face of the clock continued to mark off the cumulative time traveled. At zero on the right-hand clock, the *Meg* would be stationary in time—moving forward at the precise rate of Earth-normal. But the ship and crew would be sitting several quadrillion years in the future. Then the acceleration backward could commence, followed by deceleration backward, until at last the *Meg II* guided in along the beacon to the precise time spot it should have occupied had its human hours been taken straight. Thus no paradox, no misalignment with normal Earth.

They were still moving toward that rendezvous with oblivion: what they should have passed at the twenty-second hour of acceleration. They had not intersected it yet because of the tremendous difference the logarithmic scale made, where the last three-tenths of an hour from 21.7 to 22.0 amounted to more actual travel than in all the first twenty hours.

Shetland stood behind the pilot, pretending that nothing had happened. Of course Shetland himself had reversed the drive, after shooting down the pilot for urging that very action—but that was the Captain's prerogative.

"Captain," Johns said, not looking around. There was nothing that required his immediate attention; the drive ran itself, and the pilot was on duty merely to watch the gauges and make sure there was no hitch developing. "Captain—I request permission to say something."

What was there for this man to say? That he resented having been gassed for voicing an opinion less than two hours before its time?

"Speak," Shetland said.

"Captain, I just wanted to apologize. I don't know what came over me. I never lost my head like that before. I don't believe in ghosts. I just—somehow I couldn't—what I mean is, you did the only thing you could do, when you faced something—something very like—" He swallowed. "Like mutiny. And I can see that you were right all the time. I'm sorry I forgot."

Johns was apologizing for his own disorientation, engendered by temporal velocity. That effect had not been his fault—and Shetland himself had suffered from it similarly.

"We were all a little on edge," Shetland said, discovering that his dislike of the pilot was becoming tenuous. Was there any point in trying to explain? "There is no record of anything like mutiny."

"Yes, sir." This time those ordinary words carried a freighting of extraordinary gratitude.

He looked at the main clock. 9.88, going down. Almost twelve hours of deceleration; almost ten more to go. Then what? Things had settled in so quietly, after the excitement of the acceleration.

9.85. Only when they came to a dead halt relative to their starting point could they safely release the drive and rest in space. The drive had to complete its cycle; an incomplete cycle could strand the ship in some limbo of no return. Time travel was not precisely like space travel.

Hell broke loose.

The ship bucked violently through it did not move, fling-

ing Shetland to the far wall. Shooting pains went through his
left shoulder as another upheaval bounced him on the floor.
He tried to right himself—and was hurled about again. An
agonized keening sounded in his ears, and some insubstantial
yet effective fog clouded his vision above a seemingly hori-
zontal line. Dimly he saw the pilot's legs wrapped around the
bolted-down stool; Johns, more alert than his Captain, had
held his position. There was the beginning odor of burning
insulation. The power gauges were fluctuating wildly.

"Cut the drive!" Shetland roared. He tried to stand, but
the heaving room that did not move brushed him aside. The
clamor of the suit-alert began; the *Meg*'s hull had been
pierced. Another impossibility.

"Captain." Johns' voice drifted back from a far distance.
"We're in temporal motion. We can't—"

"CUT THE DRIVE!"

Johns moved his hand, and miraculously the ship was
quiet. Shetland lurched to his feet, heedless of the pain.

"Somebody was firing on us—through time!" Johns exclaimed. "Some alien—"

"Shut up!"

The alarm had stopped. Someone must have slapped a
patch on the leak—Sosthenna, probably. Shetland's hands, of
their own volition, groped for and found the archaic regula-
tion fire extinguisher, not obsolete after all, as smoke curled
up from the drive panel. Suddenly the unit was blasting
noxious foam all over his boots. He turned it, already feeling
the biting cold; crystals of ice flew off like broken glass as he
tramped toward the panel.

"Stop, Captain!" Johns cried. "No need, no need! The
power is off. I'll replace the blown unit before turning it on
again."

Shetland lowered the extinguisher. True: the smoke was

already dissipating. Now he had time to assess his own injuries. Pain, for the moment, was masked; it was there, but the enormity of it would be felt only later—by which time he would have taken medication to alleviate it. He was surprised to discover no blood.

"But how could any ship get a line on us—" Johns began.

"There is no other ship," Shetland snapped. "The effect was natural." He felt along his left arm, realizing that the trouble with the extinguisher had been due to his one-handed control. The left hand was useless for the moment, though there were no visible breaks. Nerve damage?

"We're in nulltime," Johns exclaimed, appalled. "We'll never return—"

"Pay attention to your job!"

Automatically, Johns looked at his dials. "Nothing to check, with the drive off. Power only goes to—" He started. "Captain!" His voice was ragged with his shock. "Captain— the instruments are registering!"

"That's what they're for," Shetland said shortly.

"I mean the perceptors. The matter spotters. They're self-powered. They—" He did not finish.

Shetland knew what was coming, but wanted the pilot to come to it himself. "So?"

"But we're in null!" Johns, so capable in the crisis, was now falling apart. "The drive is off, but we're still traveling in time. We're sealed off from the realtime framework until we start the drive again and phase back in with—"

"Nonsense. We can still receive external energy. Otherwise our voyage would be pointless."

"We're a ghost! But why aren't we dead?"

This wasn't getting anywhere. Johns was preoccupied with an assortment of fears, most of them invalid.

Shetland had understood the situation the moment the ship

bucked. Such movement was impossible when traveling in time—and of course the ship had not actually moved in space. When the shock came, *he* had moved—and thrown himself about as though his timing were seriously off. And that was the key: the *Meg* had been undergoing fluctuations in time! The muscular exertion Shetland attempted for normal motion of two or three seconds was either condensed into a fraction of a second or stretched into minutes. Naturally he had felt it as an external force, never having experienced this effect before. Johns, seated, had had less difficulty, as he did not have the same problem of balance.

The seemingly simple act of walking was dependent on a consistent time scale. Change that scale erratically, and a man was soon flat on his face! They were passing through a timestorm—the storm that must have wiped out the first *Meg*. Better to cut adrift entirely, floating with the waves of it, than to be racked on the fluxes of an invisible, unfeelable holocaust that nevertheless was destroying the drive!

Probably Shetland's action in cutting the drive had only postponed the demise of the ship. But their situation was not hopeless. Ordinarily the drive would have been destroyed by such severance during operation, but in this unique current they had saved the drive by disengaging it. Re-engaging it after the storm passed would be difficult, perhaps impossible, but there was a chance. Meanwhile, they had to chart the storm. What could have caused it, here in complete vacuum?

Shetland's eyes passed over the bank of dials. He held back his reaction. The thing he had seen before, and tried to get Johns to verify, was still there. "Do you believe in ghosts?" he inquired.

Johns stiffened, thinking he was being chided or mocked. He had already taken pains to deny his earlier remarks about ghosts in space. Shetland understood, and sympathized—but this was necessary.

"No, sir," the pilot said.

"Look at your instruments again," Shetland commanded. "Tell me what's out there."

Johns looked. "In null I don't know what—" He paused. "We're approaching a system of galactic scope at an apparent rate of six thousand light-years per hour. At that rate we'll intersect it in about five hours human time—" His head jerked up. "But we're drifting at a million years per hour! No galaxy could stay that close for more than a few of our minutes, and—"

"Do not theorize," Shetland said. "Just read the dials."

Johns swallowed like an adolescent and read the dials. "Approximate mass of the system—" He faltered.

"Go on, Pilot."

"Sir, I think the instrument is broken. That surge could have scorched the sensor leads—"

Shetland responded with deliberate cruelty. "Do I have to instruct you in elementary navigation? Where are the warning lights? You know the instrument is not broken!"

"But what it says can't be—"

"It is what we think of as a temporal storm—something we have only conjectured before. No man has studied one and returned to report on it. We are in the process of clarifying that mystery, for we are at the fringe of it and drifting in its framework. What does your instrument say?"

Johns seemed to shrink inside himself. His lips stretched to form the words his mind rejected. "It says—it says the system we're approaching has the scope of a galaxy—but no mass."

Shetland smiled grimly. That was what he had seen. His perception could have been distorted, but Johns' perception should not have been distorted the same way. "A galaxy with no mass. I ask you again, Pilot—do you believe in ghosts?"

"Yes, there *is* a ghost," Shetland said to the gathering in the beacon chamber. He flexed the fingers of his left hand, glad to feel its reawakening; his injury had been minor after all. He thought of Alice, the ghost he still had to conceal. He was pretending that the majority of their problems had been solved, when actually the worst ones were only hidden.

"All of us had some hint of it," he continued. "But we were blinded by our separate conceptions of the mission, and by our mutual dread of the unknown. We tried to exclude the supernatural—not appreciating that when the supernatural is understood, it becomes natural. Cartographer Beeton was closest to it—"

"But I wasn't able to face emotionally what my intellect showed me," Beeton said. "The thing is so incredible—"

"Oh, I don't know," Tibet said. "Alice told me—"

"One thing at a time!" Shetland said, interrupting her. He had hoped to keep Alice out of this conversation. He could not stall very much longer about her whereabouts.

"I still don't follow you," Johns protested. "We're alive when we shouldn't be, and there's a—a thing out there. I'll admit that much. But nothing in the universe is solid enough to rock a ship in high velocity temporal travel, and we are frozen at almost ten on the clock—almost three thousand years per second! But we were battered so badly that a crate of beans or something broke loose and tried to shove itself through the hull!"

That break, Shetland realized—it should not have occurred. The shaking had been temporal, not physical.

"Crate of beans!" Tibet exclaimed indignantly. "There are no beans aboard this ship! Our food is all processed—"

"It was a food freezer," Sosthenna said. "I got a patch on the break before it aggravated. Couldn't find the key to the freezer, though—"

"I have that key," Shetland said, feeling a chill as of that locker's depths. *Alice's coffin!* How could it have moved—unless something were struggling inside it, causing it to shift about? "The unit was empty, so I locked it up and—"

"It is not empty," Sosthenna corrected him. "I had to shove it aside. There's at least a hundred pounds in there."

Did she suspect?

Johns laughed. "Wouldn't *that* be an epitaph for a lost ship: torpedoed by an empty freezer during time travel!"

"I, too, am perplexed," Somnanda said. "I had understood that it was certain destruction to cut out the drive while temporal motion was—"

"We phased in with the ghost," Shetland said. "Sosthenna must have pushed the freezer just as the time flux began, her strength exaggerated by the effect so that it shot through the hull." She might not believe that, of course—and he would not push the matter.

"I *was* trying to move it," Sosthenna agreed. "The time flux—that must have been why it seemed so heavy! First my push had no strength—then it had way too much strength!"

"The ghost's framework differs," Shetland agreed, greatly relieved by her ready acceptance, though she had a detail wrong. "What was a timestorm to us while the drive operated, became the ghost when—well, Beeton, make your own explanation."

Beeton plunged in happily. "As I was trying to say on an earlier occasion, but somehow couldn't quite put into sensible words: at the center of things, near the beginning, the galaxies are young. First they are blobs of radiation and plasma and gas; then they are quasars; then they develop into the various forms of galaxies that we observe, which are really the progressive stages of galactic evolution, depending on mass, rotation, and local fluxes. But in the course of several tens of billions of years, the typical galaxy ages, and like an aging man, it changes. It puts on weight, becomes sluggish. A galaxy in its late prime is an amazingly massive thing—so dense that its surface gravity prevents its own light from escaping into space. All its energies are now reserved for itself, which is why it appears to fade out. It cannot be detected from a distance directly. In fact, it is one gigantic black hole. Never before has man had opportunity to study the interior of such an artifact. Quite possibly it is much like that of a normal galaxy, with most of its mass in the form of shadow matter that we can hardly even perceive, and—"

"Black hole!" Johns exclaimed, alarmed. "Nothing can escape from a black hole in space! Nothing!"

"That's true—initially," Beeton said. "But remember, we are not traveling in space, but in time, and temporally we should be able to escape it, simply by retreating to the time before it existed. We have never had experience with a galaxy-sized black hole—and we don't know what develops in the course of a trillion years. I am conjecturing that within it, nevertheless, breakdown continues, its lingering gas and dust forming into nebulae and then into stars that convert more matter into energy—which is imprisoned by that colossal gravity of the system as a whole. A galactic pressure cooker! That energy incites continued transformations at the expense of the dwindling matter available—because much of that matter may be compressed into singularity. That is, infinite density in zero volume. All that would be left would be its all-powerful gravitational field. Maybe that matter even pops through to some other universe.

"So let's assume that eventually all matter is gone, one way or another. Still there is no escape for that phenomenal complex of energy. We are left with a galaxy whose material portion has passed away, but which still exists as an entity. A ghost."

"The ghost of a galaxy!" Johns said. "Yes, I see that now! In the beginning it's a quasar, all radiation out through the rest of the universe, and at the end it's a ghost, no radiation! But that doesn't explain its virtually matching our present apparent spatial velocity, or its interfering with our drive. Why did we have to cut adrift, and how did we survive—"

"The ghost is largely timeless," Beeton said. "Maybe it attained this state after the first hundred billion years—and will maintain it for eternity. Maybe the universe we know was merely the momentary transition from the cosmic egg to the galactic ghost state. The cosmic egg, containing all the matter of the universe as we know it, was, it seems, too massive to maintain the state of singularity, so it exploded. But a galaxy is smaller, so may be stable. Or maybe this entity will gradually lose cohesion and dissipate in the course of a few trillion years. It could even be an element of a much larger formation, like an electron in an atom—a blob of energy as the ultimate component of matter. All we know for certain is that it is here, on the order of a trillion years old. Our temporal travel becomes irrelevant in the face of longevity like that. It is not an unreasonable coincidence that our course should approximately match that of a ghost. There must be many billions of ghosts. And we *were* tracing the course of the first ship to intersect it."

"But still, we should have passed by it or through it

without effect," Sosthenna said. "We must have passed through many galaxies on our way here."

"Not so many," Johns said, working it out. "Our exploding universe is not infinite. After we left the cluster of galaxies surrounding our own Milky Way, we would be left in largely empty space. There would be no way for a galaxy to come back to us—unless the universe oscillates after all." He paused. "Oscillation doesn't make much sense at this point—but I don't see what else—"

"There's the key!" Beeton said. "This colossal system of unique energy, this timestorm—it has to come from—"

"Another universe!" Sosthenna exclaimed.

Beeton looked at her appreciatively. "Yes. Or at least another cosmic explosion. We don't know how many of them there are—but we now have the proof that ours is not the only one of its kind. Our own explosion has long since spread far beyond this region of space. The ghost is a galaxy flung out from some neighboring explosion, that only now has intersected our region. Technically, we have entered another universe."

But she was less impressed by the conceptual significance than the practical aspect. "Does this mean we can never go beyond this point in time? Because the ghost will stop us?"

"Surely not!" Shetland said. "It merely represents a new challenge! We have to reorient on the absolute rest of *this* universe instead of our own, in order to travel within it. That was why the drive was affected: you can't make it operate when it isn't oriented on absolute rest—of whatever universe it occupies! The *Meg I* must have perished before its crew had a chance to appreciate the changed situation."

He paused, but no one else spoke. "Now it is our task to come to understand the ghost."

"Captain." It was Somnanda, smiling. "Your move, Captain."

Chapter 8:_____Committee

"I'm throwing it open to majority decision," Shetland said.

"Why?" Johns asked. "You're the Captain—and you've been right when all the rest of us were wrong."

Shetland knew that to be untrue. He had been wrong when the majority had been right. At the last moment, thanks to the death of one crewman and the message of another via the chess game, he had reversed himself. That switch from orders to group opinion had saved the ship. But it was hard to confess his error openly.

"Because this is no longer a Captain's matter," Shetland explained with his best semblance of sincerity. He was speaking a half-truth, because of his infernal pride—and because the full truth would bring out the matter of Alice. "We're virtually at rest with respect to the ghost. If we enter it we'll be doing the equivalent of making landfall. The rules of space and time may no longer apply."

Beeton looked up sharply. "That's right!" He could as readily have argued the reverse, for a galaxy was not Earth. But he was thinking of the sexual code. In a moment he would inquire about Alice.

"No such thing," Sosthenna said. "We're still in time, about as far from home as we can get. The fact that we have discovered a remarkable—and dangerous!—item, an object with no apparent mass, doesn't change anything."

"It's not an object if it has no mass," Johns said.

"Don't quibble, Pilot," Sosthenna said, flashing him a smile to defuse the sentiment. With her beauty, her sexual talent, and her courage under stress, she was emerging as perhaps the dominant cohesive force amid the crew. It was a pleasure to see her operate. "It's an identifiable construction in an identifiable universe, whose spatial velocity just happens to almost match that of our own galaxy a trillion years ago. And—"

"Some coincidence!" Tibet interjected. Shetland was reminded that she was standing up well, too. "The odds against—"

Beeton shook his head. "The universe is large. Multiple universes must be infinite. Time is eternal. It was inevitable that some other universe infringe on our territory at some time, whether a trillion or a quadrillion years later. Probably this ghost is traveling spatially at a rate similar to that of our own ghosts, whenever they are—but its absolute rest differs from ours, so that its velocity of perhaps one light-year per year relative to its own framework is equivalent to about fifty-two million light-years per year relative to ours. So it seems to be approaching us at that speed—six thousand light-years per hour. Of course, since we are traveling a million light-years per hour, our own galaxy would seem to be moving a million light-years per hour—if we could see it now. So it isn't such a—"

"Hold it, Einstein!" Tibet squawked. "I can't keep track of all those figures! What's the ghost's motion relative to us—if you assume we're stationary in our own universe?"

Beeton waved his hand negligently. "It would be approaching us at about fifty-two times the speed of light. So, considering the time it has taken to intersect, it must have originated about twenty trillion light-years from our own galaxy. Practically next door! Which leads to intriguing speculation, because if that universe is on collision course with ours—"

"Nuclear fission!" Johns said. "One universe sets off another—"

"Nonsense!" Beeton returned. "They would simply pass right through each other, because there is so much space between galaxies at this range. Probably they have already done it in a manner, with interacting secants. Which means I should recalculate the point of origin—"

"*As* I was saying before you men started gibbering irrelevancies," Sosthenna said firmly, "we are still at space, and the Captain's word is law."

"*He* says it isn't," Beeton pointed out. "So the law says there is no law."

"There *is* law!" Shetland protested. "The law of majority decision."

Tibet glanced at him. "Do you really want this, Captain? I mean, for us to decide?"

"I do. I feel a group decision will be more accurate than an individual one. My orders do not cover this contingency, so the group picture is our best guide. We have evidence that the ghost is dangerous to a ship under power—that is, one accelerating or decelerating in the temporal sense—but we cannot be certain of the consequences of reorientation. Perhaps that will ameliorate the threat here—but perhaps it will ease only one threat of several. So we must either risk destruction of the drive by engaging it within the field of this alien system—or allow ourselves to drift right through the ghost proper. That, too, might destroy us.''

"Obviously we should—'' Johns began.

"We don't dare—'' Beeton started.

"There is no way to avoid decision,'' Sosthenna said.

"But we could argue all month!'' Tibet cried, showing some strain now. "And we only have three hours until we're *in* the ghost!''

"Suppose we take the easiest legislative route,'' Somnanda said. "Secret ballot.''

"Sloth . . .'' Alice muttered.

Shetland's head snapped up. It had not been Alice, of course. No one else had reacted—though they had no reason to, not knowing she was dead. Someone else had spoken, sounding like her, awakening a guilty response in him.

Strange, though, that there was not more objection to her continued absence. He had expected to have to fend off persistent queries and suspicions. Instead the others acted as if Alice were still with them, in the next room. Or was that only Shetland's distorted impression? A ghost walking the ship, real to every person except him?

Ridiculous! He *needed* to step down! He was not so far gone as not to be aware of the signs of his own breakdown under stress. But that, too, he had to conceal—for the sake of the beacon.

They cast ballots. The vote was two in favor of starting the drive immediately, two in favor of drifting through the ghost, and two abstentions. Shetland himself had not voted.

He stared at the six bits of paper. There should be only

five. No one had cheated; he had watched, though he knew the "I doubt it" syndrome did not extend to this. The members of his crew were honest. More so than the Captain.

Had he absent-mindedly voted after all? No, he had torn the paper into six sections and set aside the extra deliberately. Now it was marked.

Could Alice the ghost have voted?

There would come a point when he had to admit what he was hearing and seeing. Whom should he appoint to relieve him as Captain, after he confessed his insanity? Not Somnanda, who was bound to the beacon; not Beeton, too young and volatile. It would have to be Johns. Unpleasant necessity. Wait a while longer . . .

"Very well," he said with a sigh. "It's deadlocked. Reveal yourselves, if you're amenable, and we'll discuss it further—for half an hour. If we still can't find a majority, I'll make the decision then."

"Let me see those ballots," Tibet said, taking them from his hand. "I can tell everyone's handwriting. I used to enjoy graphoanalysis."

She looked at the first. "Somnanda voted to start the drive now." She shuffled it to the bottom and read the next. "I voted to drift through the ghost. Funny—I would have expected him to vote the way I did, and vice versa!"

Only Johns smiled. She was trying to ease the burden of tension, but it was beyond her ability. "Beeton abstained," she continued. "Johns wants the drive. Alice wants a sample of ghost-substance for testing. Thenna abstained."

Were they conspiring to taunt him about Alice? Did they suspect what he had done, so they were trying to trick him into confessing it? He dared not ask! All he could do was play along, ignoring the references, until he discovered the rationale behind this mystery. There had to be one—and he was not yet ready to attribute it to his developing insanity!

"As I make it," Shetland said slowly, "Somnanda voted to start the drive because he avoids any potential threat to the beacon. Failure of the drive would not directly affect the beacon. The ghost *might*." Somnanda nodded. "Yet our reaction to the complete failure of the drive would quickly extinguish the beacon—so that course represents a balancing threat that may force Somnanda into neutrality." He turned to Johns. "You don't like hanging around one place too long—even when drifting at a million years per hour! You want the drive functioning; you don't feel secure while it's off." And Johns nodded. "Yet it was the subject of severe stress while in operation before, and there is no stress on it now. Why should the ghost affect it—so long as it remains off? We might readily pass through that entire complex in a few hours and get far enough beyond it so as to be free of the peripheral effects and make reinstitution of the drive that much safer. Remember, the ghost probably cannot hold us, in time; we are not in danger of getting crushed to singularity."

Now he turned to Tibet. "You want experience—and the ghost should be a terrific experience! Alice wants a sample. Are the two of you eager enough for these things to risk oblivion in that vortex, if I have misjudged it?"

"Yes," Tibet said.

He turned to Sosthenna. "You are perhaps our most objective individual. And Beeton is our most intelligent. Why did you abstain?"

Beeton shrugged. "I'm afraid of ghosts. But I think it's too late anyway. Either way."

Sosthenna said: "Funny things are going on. Our judgment is suspect."

They knew! he thought. They knew Alice was gone—and that Tibet refused to know it. So they were moving carefully, not committing themselves.

But Beeton would hardly accept the death of his fiancée with such equanimity! Unless he had lost interest . . .

Shetland glanced at the two, sitting side by side. Handsome vanilla man, attractive vanilla woman. Forbidden love, back on Earth, but legitimate here. Strong temptation? Or was it his own jealousy manifesting? Maybe nothing serious developing there. Bright young man could get tired of bright young woman, for a while—or might reconcile himself to her death. A mature woman combined attributes of parent and paramour, increasingly rewarding in continuing crises. Where did that leave the older man who wanted to marry her? No, that was paranoia!

"As you know," Shetland continued, finding it necessary to move on to some other subject, "we are not the first mission to this time. It seems obvious that this ghost galaxy eliminated the *Meg I* . . ." He continued, summarizing the ground they had been over before, partly to show the inevitability of the course he had suggested, partly to convince himself that he retained intellectual and emotional control over the situation. He tried not to think about Beeton and Sosthenna, their evidently deepening relationship; tried not to feel isolated, discarded. It was all in his mind, for there were no permanent liaisons in space. And his mind had far more serious things to concern itself about, including a ghost aboard the ship as well as beyond it. ". . . but we are in a position to ascertain the nature of this obstacle, so that if we survive it and return, no further losses of this nature will occur. There is risk no matter what we do—but investigation of the ghost seems to me to be the most profitable avenue, considering not just ourselves but the future of time travel.''

"Precisely," Sosthenna agreed.

No one else offered further comment.

Slowly they entered the fringe. Six thousand light-years per hour relative velocity; one hundred light-years per minute; one point six per second. About 7.7 on the corrected clock—two hours less than the home-oriented figure.

The projected intersection was slight, only three thousand light-years—the skin of an onion a hundred thousand light-years through. But quite enough to survey the nature of the mighty entity. Even one inch inside the event horizon of a black hole was far, far more than had ever been attempted before—because there had been no escape, before time travel. If death were awaiting them in the ghost, perhaps this peripheral encounter would amount to no more than a warning illness.

Perhaps . . .

There was no external gravity, for that was a function of mass, and the instruments claimed that the ghost was massless. What held it together, then? For the instruments defined a clear band of energy, an invisible demarcation that established the magnitude of the system. Perhaps the horrendous mass of the singularity within the ghost would manifest the moment they intersected the event horizon, and they would be instantly crushed into oblivion. A black hole so intense that not even gravity waves could escape its fringe!

Meanwhile, nothing physical distorted the course of the *Meg*. No timestorm, no stars. It was as if they cruised through simple space and time. But Somnanda's flame quivered blue.

It was, indeed, ghostly.

All hands maintained their business stations. There was a kind of vertigo, but this was neither excessive nor unpleasant. No worse than the initial stages of the drive, and not really dissimilar. Under Shetland's direction the *Meg*'s sampling scoops took in measured quantities of whatever existed or failed to exist externally, and its recorders recorded the energy patterns that could or could not be recorded. Nothing else happened. The ghost was . . . nothing.

It seemed ironic to Shetland that the first really scientific documentation of a genuine ghost should be accomplished by a semi-military expedition into the far depths of time. And that the ghost should be alien: not even the product of man's own universe.

In half an hour they were out of it, unscathed. "All in order?" Shetland inquired over the intercom, knowing that it was. One by one the affirmatives came in: Somnanda, Tibet, Johns, Alice, Beeton, Sosthenna.

He shook off the vision of the freezer. It needed no rechecking; she was surely there! The voice was either an auditory hallucination or someone's imitation. If someone thought Shetland had murdered Alice, and was trying to provoke his guilty reaction—

" 'The play's the thing,' " Shetland repeated to himself softly, " 'Wherein I'll catch the conscience of the king.' " Hamlet—who was mad. For Hamlet had seen a ghost.

But there was a mission to complete. "It appears to have been a false alarm," Shetland said. "We have observed no threat to the ship or crew. We were not trapped within the ghost. But I distrust the simple answer." No one commented, so he continued. "Volunteer to check the samples."

"That's my job," Alice said.

The play's the thing . . .

"Very well. Seal yourself into the specimen chamber and

report as convenient," he said, making sure there was no quaver in his voice. "There will be a general rest shift for the remainder of the crew. We shall not attempt to activate the drive until we are at least twelve hours' distance from the ghost. Drifting at present velocity."

He waited for further response, but there was none. What had the others thought of his dialogue with ghost-Alice? They might not have heard *her*, but they had certainly heard *him*! Those who knew she was dead—how long would they toy with an insane Captain?

How long it was in human time he was not certain, but in due course he was roused by Alice's voice on the intercom. "Captain, this stuff is fantastic! Can you come here and—?"

And meet the ghost directly? "Sorry, I'm tied up at the moment." Tied up hanging on to sanity—or foiling a frame-up for murder. "Why don't you just describe it—for all of us?"

"Well, it's energy, of course," she said. Her voice seemed absolutely normal. Shetland tried to concentrate, but he was haunted now by Tibet's nightmare: the child that might be a phantasm, a mockup that looked and sounded just like the original, but wasn't. This voice sounded just like Alice. Soon he hoped to ascertain just how much of Alice's mind was behind that voice. If Tibet were doing the mimicry, she would not fool him for long. She lacked the technical expertise that Alice would have had.

". . . divorced from matter and extremely concentrated," Alice's voice continued. "For the sake of convenience, I'll call it plasma, though obviously it can't be that—I think. We've never had occasion to know what really happens inside a black hole, especially not one of this magnitude that continues for hundreds of billions of years until all solid matter is gone. This stuff—I can hold it, shape it, toss it about—but it doesn't *do* anything! It's as if it's bent around itself—a tiny curved universe, each fragment—and simply doesn't respond to outside stimulus. If this were a human being, I'd say it had completely retreated from reality."

Human being retreated from reality—another half-veiled message from the play? "It's ghost-substance," Shetland said. "Ectoplasm."

"Ectoplasm—the outer layer of a cell," she said. "Are you suggesting we should have taken a deeper sample?"

He had forgotten: there was a scientific meaning for the term, and she had taken it biologically. Exactly the kind of response a biologist would make. Tibet would immediately have responded to the supernatural meaning. "Ectoplasm: the substance evoked by a medium in trance," he clarified. "Have you tried exorcising it?"

"That isn't funny, Captain!" she said severely. "I'm sure there is incalculable potential locked up in this ecto—this plasma—especially considering that we have an entire galaxy full of it to draw on. If we could only find an application. We shouldn't think of it as only a toy, the way the ancients did mercury—something to roll about on the hands, quicksilver. This—"

"I apologize," he said. This certainly seemed to be Alice's mind!

He looked up as someone entered. "Yes?" he said to Tibet.

"I just wanted to suggest—" she began. "I mean, I'm no scientist, but—"

Shetland froze. If Tibet was here—who was mimicking Alice's voice?

"In a moment," he said to Tibet with sudden resolve. "Suppose you tell everyone to meet here. No, make it in the beacon room."

"Of course," she said, her brow furrowing.

"Alice?" he said to the intercom.

"Yes, Captain."

"Can you bring that sample to the beacon room?"

"Oh, yes. I'll be happy to. It seems to be perfectly inert. Of course, I can't be *sure*—"

"Excellent. All of us are gathering there, and Tibet has a suggestion that I think relates to the sample. Perhaps we can figure it out. I'll see you in a few minutes."

"Certainly," she said.

Shetland leaned against the wall. His heart was pounding. Was he half as clever as he supposed, or was he blundering? If the voice were not Tibet, it must be Sosthenna. If not her, some kind of recording. Not a straight one, but a composite of speech sounds, phonemes, assembled to make relevant combinations in her manner. A complex procedure. In any event, the device would be exposed when they all gathered in the beacon room. Alice would not appear, of course—but no one else could manage her voice while he had the entire crew in sight. Not without paying obvious attention to a voice synthesizer. Once the mask was off, he would proceed to business.

Yet what if he should actually *see* her?

Well, there was something to be said for crossing bridges when the occasion arose.

They gathered in the beacon room. All but Alice. Shetland took a deep breath, trying to attain the sensation of relief. He was not successful. He had made it impossible for anyone to continue the masquerade for the moment—but he had not isolated the specific person responsible.

Who could it be? Not Tibet; he had eliminated her before. Sosthenna? She had handled the freezer, and could have estimated the mass of its contents, and realized that Alice was missing. She did seem to know. But she was not the kind to act on incomplete information. She would not assume that Alice had been killed without first establishing the motive and most likely suspect. And she would not play games with voices: she would expose the matter forthrightly. If she suspected Shetland, she would come to him first.

Beeton actually had motive. He would be the first to note Alice's absence, and might for once have jumped to an inaccurate conclusion, and try to clinch the case by extraordinary procedures. But surely he would have attacked more specifically. A voice over the intercom could emanate from anywhere in the ship, and would be heard everywhere; every other crewmember was subject to the same pressure Shetland was. That would be no good to a man seeking to smoke out the murderer—unless he had no suspect in mind.

This assembly had been a mistake. It would prove nothing. He should have checked out all the other crewmembers while keeping "Alice" in conversation. Four suspects remained: Sosthenna, Beeton, Johns and Somnanda. He should not be duped into thinking that a male could not arrange it.

But Somnanda *did* know about the death—and that it had been self-inflicted. And Sosthenna would not proceed this way. That narrowed it to Beeton and Johns.

"What's holding up Alice?" Tibet inquired.

Naïveté! "Go ahead with your suggestion," Shetland said.

"This ghost-substance—it can't be affected by anything physical," she said. "Except to move it about. I thought— maybe it's mental. Maybe Alice could move it around because she was *willing* it to move. She only *thought* her hands were doing it. But machinery has no willpower, so machines couldn't analyze it or . . ."

"Terrific!!" Sosthenna exclaimed. "We've been thinking conventionally, when we all know nothing conventional could affect the drive the way the ghost did! A changed absolute rest might foul up navigation—but complete *elimination*? Space and time might be meaningless for this stuff, because it isn't physical and its energy has no focus. But minds, a shipful of minds—maybe our thoughts are the key!''

Johns and Beeton looked dubious, but Somnanda nodded. "My mind controls the beacon," he said. "The ghost could be a galactic-sized beacon. The principle is not extraordinary by my definition.''

"All right, I'll try it!" Beeton said. "I was afraid of the ghost when I wasn't sure it existed; now I find it fascinating. As soon as Alice comes with the sample—"

Parable of the guilty-looking farmer's boy: was Beeton the one? On the surface his words were innocuous.

"I'll go see what's holding her up," Tibet said, standing.

"Use the intercom," Sosthenna said. Then, following her own advice: "Need any help, Alice?"

Shetland's muscles tightened involuntarily, though he knew there would be no response. After this session he would set about making the truth known. But carefully, so as not to stimulate beacon-destroying reactions. The situation was becoming untenable.

"Yes, I do," Alice's voice replied. "I can't get this stuff to come with me down the hall.''

Shetland clamped a block on his emotion. *All the other members of the crew were here.* They had no machinery, their faces were in sight, and their hands were still. Sleight-of-hand seemed out of the question. A straight recording would not do, because her reply had been responsive. No one could be talking except Alice herself.

That meant the other explanation was now the most logical one. That Shetland was no longer able to distinguish between fantasy and reality, and only *thought* he heard—

No! The others heard it too! *There was a voice.*

There simply was no other reasonable explanation. An actual, speaking ghost was aboard the ship. A poltergeist.

Unless they had all carefully rehearsed their lines answering to silence—but no, there still had to be a voice for *him* to hear. So he might be the victim of a campaign, but he wasn't insane.

"Try willing it along," Tibet said. "You stand there, and I'll stand here, and you sort of mentally throw it to me—it should pass through the walls, shouldn't it? I mean, ghosts do—"

"Then why did the scoops work?" Johns demanded.

"Because we *willed* them to!" Sosthenna said.

Johns and Beeton exchanged lifted eyebrows. That explanation would do for almost anything.

"All right," Alice said doubtfully. "Ready, heave!"

"Ready, catch!" Tibet cried, holding up her hand as if ready to snag a beach ball.

Ludicrous!

In Tibet's hands appeared a cloud of something. It was transparent, but refracted the light slightly so that its location was evident by the shimmer and distortion. Vapor of some sort—or ghost-substance. Ectoplasm.

Beeton stepped up to it. "Now I *know* I'm seeing things," he said. "But if this stuff really is plasma, controlled by the mind . . ." He concentrated.

The cloud slid over to him. "It doesn't even tingle," he remarked. "I wonder whether it can be shaped?"

Then it was a perfect cube. And a pyramid. And a sphere. "God almighty!" Beeton breathed, showing his awe without shame.

"Let me see that," Johns said.

The sphere sailed over to him like a hydrogen balloon.

Johns poked it with his finger, tentatively. "No sensation," he remarked.

Shetland, forced to the verge of believing in human ghosts, found this new manifestation less shocking. *This* ghost could be tested, one way or another! He could see that the others were as amazed as he, despite the seeming flippancy of their reactions. Flippancy could be a fair defense in the face of the incomprehensible.

"What good is it?" Tibet demanded, perhaps nettled because her part in the substance's acquisition had been forgotten.

"Can it be rendered solid?" Somnanda inquired.

"Dunno." Johns concentrated, then touched it again. "God almighty!" he echoed.

Shetland strode over and touched the ball. It was solid, with a metallic surface. "Energy transformed to matter?" he inquired.

"If matter transforms to energy, why not energy to matter?" Beeton asked. "It occurred at the time of the origin of our universe, and it can happen at the termination of it. Plasma—the ideal intermediate state, capable of going either way. All it requires is guidance. There must be fantastic potential in this entity—a galaxy of matter and energy, a trillion years of time. It—"

"Plasm," Sosthenna said. "Neither matter nor energy, neither plasma nor ectoplasm, partaking of aspects of both."

"Just as a real live ghost can transform," Tibet said.

Sosthenna laughed shortly. "A real live ghost!"

Tibet smiled. "You know what I mean. The genuine article, instead of a made-up spook."

"Spooky!" Sosthenna agreed, smiling.

Shetland listened, not smiling.

"This stuff's dangerous!" Johns warned. "I turned it into

hard plastic—but suppose somebody made it into mustard gas or something?''

"How about bubonic plague germs?" Tibet suggested.

"We'd better find out what its potential *is*!" Beeton said. "Germs are living organisms, and if it could do *that*—"

"Better test it outside the ship," Sosthenna warned. "Better laboratory there, anyway—a whole galaxy. All the ghost-glow we can ever use."

"Turn it into chocolate ice cream!" Tibet said.

"That's like lighting a match in an ammunition dump just to see your way!" Johns protested. "God only knows what might happen if we started animating that whole galaxy!"

"What harm would chocolate ice cream do?" Tibet demanded.

"A mass of it the size of a galaxy?" Johns shook his head as if contemplating idiocy.

"If that could happen—or any of this—why hasn't it happened before?" Sosthenna asked.

"Perhaps it could have happened before," Beeton replied. "But not without guidance. If it requires the catalyst of conscious thought—then we are the first to make such change possible."

"Sure, like a computer," Johns said. "It can do anything, but you have to tell it what to do; it doesn't initiate commands. But with potential like that, you better not give it the *wrong* command!"

"What do you think, Captain?" Sosthenna asked.

Shetland, amazed at the proceedings but also concerned about the Alice matter, was uncertain what to do. Alice, perhaps by no coincidence, had become silent after the ghost-blob—the plasm—had been transferred. He had a vision of a galaxy of chocolate ice cream, roiling and tossing like an infinite ocean, finally forming an ectoplasmic head, whose brown lips moved and spoke of hitherto unimagined horrors. Why had Tibet chosen the flavor she didn't like? "Continue the discussion," he said. "But do not attempt anything rash."

"What about a controlled experiment?" Sosthenna said. "With this one blob. We can set the limits before we start it."

Beeton nodded agreeably. "This is fascinating stuff. No interaction on any level but the mental, except to the extent we force a physical semblance upon it. But harmless in the absence of the human mind."

"One ship died!" Johns reminded him.

"Traveling at speed, with human minds aboard! Who can say what monster they might inadvertently have conjured up? The devil himself, possibly!"

That, Shetland realized, was no joke. "What sort of experiment did you have in mind?" he asked Sosthenna.

"Something simple. We—oh, we might re-create an animal. A model. And take a picture of it, to show back home."

"They'd think it was taken back on Earth," Johns said. "Talk about an international game of I Doubt It . . ."

"What about a unique animal? A unicorn—"

"Why be conventional?" Tibet asked. "We could invent something completely strange—something never seen before! Or imagined! And take yards of holographic tape on it, images from every angle, so they'd know it couldn't be faked. What an exhibit!"

"It *could* be faked," Johns said. "A genuine picture of a statue of an imaginary animal doesn't prove a thing about the animal."

"A living animal?" she asked.

All heads turned to Tibet. *"Living?"* Johns demanded.

"We won't know till we try, will we?" she said.

"But the complications!" Beeton exclaimed. "What if we

succeeded halfway, and had a stinking corpse on our hands? Or—''

"No, we can do it outside the ship, as we agreed before," she explained. "An animation that looks alive, but couldn't possibly exist. So that they'd know that we really had seen it, but that it could never have been set up on Earth, or anywhere except in a ghost galaxy."

"I think she's got something," Johns said. "We *do* want to test the potential of this ghost-substance, and we *are* going to face a galaxy-sized credulity gap when we carry word back. If we don't want to wind up in psychiatric wards ourselves, we'd better have convincing evidence! We can't just blab about ghosts in space-time; Wayne and I tried that before, and I don't blame the Captain for—''

"The proposal makes sense," Shetland said gruffly. "We do need to test the propensities of the ghost, and we will need to present unimpeachable evidence for our claims. Suppose we design a completely novel animal first, then attempt to activate an image of it outside the ship when we pass through the ghost on way back to our own time. If we succeed—*when* we succeed in cutting in the drive again, we can accelerate to our present velocity and coast through it safely in the other direction. But what kind of animal do we want?"

"Something truly different," Beeton said, taking hold of the notion with boyish enthusiasm. "But we still have to watch it, because anything any one of us might come up with might be a rehash of forgotten stories or myths read in childhood. We have to find a way to prevent that."

"No problem," Sosthenna said. "Make a committee animal."

"A what?" Tibet asked.

"A committee animal. You know how a committee design is always such a compromise with so many viewpoints that the overall result is nonsensical. Since in this case we *want* a nonsensical creation—"

"Yes, I see now!" Tibet agreed. "We can parcel all the parts of it out for design, then assemble it together for ghost-protoplasm. Someone take the head, someone else the feet—"

Shetland had to call a halt. "This is a serious mission, not a parlor game! To what purpose—"

"That's the point!" Tibet exclaimed happily. "We don't dare fool about with anything serious! But with a joke animal we can test our thesis in microcosm, harmlessly. And produce evidence for the doubters back home! This really is the ideal compromise!"

Shetland shrugged. He had elected to throw the decision into group discussion. Foolishness was the risk taken. Meanwhile, Alice was forgotten and the beacon burned steadily. "As you wish."

"You're too permissive, Captain," Sosthenna said. "You should be assigning the parts."

He glanced at her, wondering whether she was now mocking him, though that was not her way. She was wearing shorts that showed off her well-formed legs to advantage, and he felt a momentary pang at her seeming alienation from him. Her feet were angled down before Beeton, who was contemplating them when not watching the ghost-ball. Beeton had said he was something of a foot fetishist . . .

"I assign you the legs," Shetland said to Sosthenna. "Beeton, take the feet." Nothing like lining it up appropriately! Then he went after the rest: "Tibet, the trunk. Johns, the reproductive anatomy." Or was that unkind? Tibet was a bit thick in the trunk, and Alice had thought Johns oversexed. "Somnanda, the tail." For that was the lazy part of the animal.

He paused. "That leaves the head for—"

"For Alice!" Tibet said.

Oh, no! He had intended the head to go to the Captain, having forgotten Alice for the moment.

"Hey, where *is* Alice?" Johns demanded. "She never did show up!"

Past time to make a clean breast of it, hoping the moment was propitious. He had to tell them *sometime,* and there was no way to avoid some peril to the beacon. Far better to have a careful presentation than an accidental revelation. Then they could consider just where Alice's voice was coming from, assuming that this was not some kind of setup. "I am afraid I have to tell you that Alice—"

"Oh, I'm here," Alice interrupted him on the intercom. "I got distracted with another mass of the massless stuff, but I've been listening. I'll be glad to take the head!"

Once more Shetland had to clamp control on his emotions. That remark could not have been prerecorded; no one could have known where the discussion was to lead! But an actual ghost—how could he accept that? If his revelation of her death did not set up a reaction that extinguished the beacon, what about her constant manifestation as an undead voice? He *had* to solve this mystery, however difficult the truth might be to accept.

Play along! he told himself fiercely. One way or another he would run this down—eventually. If it was a mass hallucination, so be it—just so long as he *knew.*

Still his mind set up a gruesome picture: the lock breaking on the freezer, the lid lifting, the corpse rising . . .

"But there is nothing left for you!" Sosthenna protested.

Shetland thought a moment, focusing with difficulty on her concern. "It needs an environment. I will handle the locale." He looked around, still not quite believing that they were serious, his vision on split-level: smiling people above, opening freezer below.

But they *were* serious. Sosthenna had hit upon something they all could focus on, a way to comprehend an aspect of the ghost, a way to test it safely and render it commonplace. That was of paramount importance! Fear remained a greater danger than the sheer immensity of the unknown that was the ghost. "All of us will work out our parts individually, consulting no other," Shetland said. "When we're ready, we'll assimilate them into one composite picture—"

"Or one sculpture," Sosthenna said. "Nanda can do it."

Did Somnanda have artistic talent? Shetland had never thought to inquire. New horizons continued to open! He looked at the man, who nodded slowly. When had Sosthenna learned about that? When she learned to call the man by a nickname?

"All right," Shetland said. "Fifteen minutes to design the parts. Then we'll assemble a model—in ship material. We'll send our ghost-blob back to Alice so our concentration won't animate it disastrously. Later, when we're sure of our figure, we'll try it in ghost-substance. In plasm."

They passed around paper for those who needed it. Beeton fell to work immediately, making what looked like stress diagrams and jotting computations in the margin. Sosthenna studied her own legs, pinching the muscle between thumb and fingers, checking the articulation of the joints. When she began on the thighs Shetland looked away; this was not the appropriate occasion for the thoughts that aroused in him. Johns looked ceilingward, smiling. Tibet made a slow, clumsy sketch, tore it up and tried again. Somnanda remained staring into his flame.

Meanwhile, Shetland had his own homework to do! Where, he wondered, was the *least* likely locale for a living animal on Earth? For it had to be on Earth to be impossible, ironically; if the animal were set on some other planet it just might turn out to be possible. Who could prove it wasn't? But the animals of Earth, past and present, were known. It would thus be obvious that there had never been a creature like this!

It would also be smart to set it in a ridiculous time. Millions of years in the past—civilized man's past. What were those ages called? He imagined a text on geology and opened it as far as he had read: to the chart showing the names of such ages. He picked one at random: Oligocene.

"All right," Shetland said in due course. "Time's up. If anyone isn't finished, we'll use what he has. That will do for an impossible animal." He looked about. "What do we have for modeling it?"

"Plastic caulk," Sosthenna said. "Normally used for patching leaks. Hardens in about two minutes after removal from the tube. I'll fetch some." And she did.

"Very well," Shetland said when she returned. "Model the torso first. Tibet?"

"Solid," she said, patting her own middle. "Strong backbone, buttressed like that on an elephant—"

"Stop it!" Sosthenna cried, laughing. "In one week of dieting you could bring your figure into line and you know it! And the men know it, too."

Tibet laughed too, a trifle awkwardly. "Heavy in front, weak behind. Big—six or seven feet long. It eats well."

"Uh-uh!" Johns warned. "You can't define its eating habits! That's part of its living—its environment."

The others were protecting Tibet from her own self-ridicule! And it was true: Tibet was only moderately overweight, and the men *did* know it. She would have it that no one appreciated her, but she was in fact the mundane, homey element that unified the crew in a fundamental way.

Somnanda shaped the torso in caulk: a stout animal body with a strong back ridge and substantial belly. No doubt about it: the man was a skilled sculptor whose strong yet sensitive fingers shaped even the crudest outlines exquisitely. Artistic expression—beacon communication: not surprising in retrospect that they were found together.

"Put on your tail while you're at it," Shetland said.

Somnanda added a tiny tail, no more than a ratlike thread covering the square posterior. Obviously it had been designed for a smaller beast. Now it only accentuated the oddity of the torso, so strong before and so inadequate behind.

"Now Alice's head."

"Long," she said over the intercom. "On a flexible neck— about a yard from shoulder to tip of snout. With a proboscis and tusks—like the elephant before the crocodile stretched its nose out long. I always did like that story!"

The analogy of the elephant again. True to form, for many people saw the elephant as a fantastic beast.

Somnanda modeled it, making a grotesquely elongated head with a bulging snout that stopped short just beyond the upper lip. He set in two tusks pointing down.

"Elephantine tusks point up," Tibet said. "Or at least forward."

He started to change them, but Johns objected. "I heard of one with down-tusks."

"*Deinotherium*," Shetland said, finding the picture and caption in a book of monsters he had read as a child.

Somnanda paused, waiting for the consensus. "Put them in both ways," Alice called out. "Up and down."

So it had four small tusks, and cowlike lips. Somnanda

added little ears and eyes. The thing now looked like an exaggerated pig without legs, yet obviously wasn't porcine.

"Legs," Shetland said.

"Four," Sosthenna said. "Like—well, any animal's, but reversed. The strong ones in front, the weak ones in back."

"It will collapse when it tries to run!" Tibet exclaimed.

"I just didn't want anyone making a man out of it," Sosthenna explained. "It has to *stay* on all fours."

"And feet," Shetland added as Somnanda worked on the legs.

"I have made a diagram of the bone structure," Beeton said, showing his sketches. "Nothing has feet like this!"

Indeed nothing did! Shetland was no naturalist, but he could see that the front feet did not match the back ones. The toes of the fronts radiated out in the better part of a circle, and the ends of them were flattened, so that round bones attached to flat ones. Pointless for locomotion. There was some webbing between, but not in the fashion of duck's feet.

"They can fold up, you see, like little umbrellas," Beeton explained proudly. "How's that for a unique design?"

Shetland wondered if he had been wrong to assign a foot fetishist to the feet. This animal was not being given a fair chance.

"How can it walk?" Tibet demanded.

"I thought it might swim."

"With that heavy head and those legs? Those are *walking* legs!" she said.

Beeton shrugged. "I designed my part." His eyes flicked over to Sosthenna's legs, her human ones. "Legs, like other parts of anatomy, can be dual purpose."

Time to break this off. "And the, ah, organs," Shetland said.

Johns was ready. "Like those of a stallion. Telescoping penis—"

"Haven't we had enough of self-description?" Tibet inquired maliciously.

At last the model stood complete: a four-tusked, heavy-snouted, dome-headed, strong-bodied, small-legged, splay-footed animal whose sexual apparatus dwarfed its own tail and whose aggregate resembled nothing that could have evolved naturally.

"A definite success!" Tibet said.

"But where does it live, Captain?" Sosthenna asked.

"Patagonia," Shetland said. "In the Oligocene epoch."

"Isn't that South America—far south—where it's cold?" Alice asked. "I don't think our animal would be comfortable there."

Shetland was tempted to ask her how comfortable *she* was in the cold freezer. "No doubt it has wool," he said.

"No, it doesn't," Tibet said. "Short hair."

"Don't interfere with his specs," Beeton cautioned her. "Patagonia was warmer then. And wetter. So our monster could have—" He paused, evincing mock horror. "Hey—we forgot to name it!"

"Oh, don't get in a pother," Tibet said. "Name it George."

Sosthenna's brow furrowed. "No, that wouldn't be proper. We need a good Latin technical name. What about something to do with space? Nova, astra—"

Beeton began laughing.

"What's the joke?" Alice's voice demanded. "I can't see what you're doing—"

"We're a bunch of astronauts in a pother," he said, chuckling. "So our committee animal has to be an Astra-pother!"

Tibet glared—then looked thoughtful. "Well, why not?" she asked. "It is descriptive. Add a Latin ending—"

"Magnum," Sosthenna said. "That means large."

"A large mistake!" Johns put in.

"Astra-pother-magnum?" Shetland asked. "Cumbersome."

"Break it up," Beeton said. "Latinize the first part, with the second part descriptive. That's how it's done. And put it in italics. *Astrapotherium magnum.* Spaceman's big bother. Pother, I mean. Couldn't ask for a better name than that!"

The others nodded, smiling. Shetland knew it to be a foolishness verging on the hysterical—but at least it was keeping them occupied and calm. "Now let's model it in our ghost-sample," he said. "Inanimate, small—a statue in glass. We won't try for a living edition until we re-enter the ghost galaxy."

To that they all agreed.

Chapter 9:_____Puzzle

They rested and slept and talked and relaxed in the various ways possible to the human state. In the course of that they reviewed the situation of the drive and agreed that in the absence of other effects even within the main body of the ghost galaxy, the alternate-absolute-rest theory must be correct. There really was no such thing as absolute rest; only rest relative to a particular universe. The *Meg*'s clock was now oriented on the universe of the ghost, and could safely travel here; but once they re-entered their own universe, the clock would have to be changed again, and the drive integrated accordingly.

Then, with trepidation, they matched the drive to the clock and cut it in.

It functioned. There was no violence in time, no overheating of the controls. They had gambled and won—but still had to decelerate, reverse and pass through the ghost again. There was no way to avoid it, for it was between them and home, on the timeline.

Shetland suppressed his foreboding and used the time to try to catch the local ghost, Alice, alive. But the specimen chamber was empty; her voice always emanated from elsewhere in the ship.

And what would happen if he did find her? Better to leave well enough alone, to wait until the ship got home. Then, at least, the truth could safely be had.

Now the clock said 4. Four more hours until deceleration was complete and the drive could be reset for the return trip. Shetland was rested and reassured, as far as was reasonable in the circumstances, but bored. Somnanda was pondering his chess move, for they had agreed to begin a fresh game. Sosthenna was closeted with Beeton, and he did not feel like chatting with Johns or Tibet at the moment.

He went to the freezer and unlocked it. Alice's corpse was there, stiff, beautiful and undisturbed. That was a kind of relief.

So the voice could not have issued from the physical Alice. No corpse walked the ship.

It was the occasion for simplistic mental diversion. Shetland went to the game cubby and took down *Flopsy Mopsy*—a two-sided jigsaw puzzle. One side was the nude front, the other the nude rear.

He opened the box and began sorting pieces on the table. He had been in space many times before, and in time often enough during the past two years, and had become an expert puzzler. This was a new one, but enjoyable, and promised to occupy him the necessary time. There was a special compulsion about a good puzzle that was invaluable at a time like this.

First he picked out every edge piece and made a pile. The others he sorted into sections for "dark," "light," "straw," "shadow" and "contrast."

The edge built up rapidly, as it was basically linear: twenty-seven segments of the interlocking rim. After that he tackled the similar contrast pieces: where a sharp line divided black from color or shade from shade. He had no trouble telling which side was up because despite its name this was not really a jigsaw puzzle; it had been pressed out of plastiboard, and the top edges of such pieces were rounded while the bottoms were more sharply cornered. In fact, the two-sidedness of it was a tactical advantage for the puzzler, because when he was in doubt about the location of a given piece he could look at the underside and get a notion from that.

By the time the clock said 2 he had completed all the edge except two pieces that refused to show up; possibly they had been lost by a prior puzzler. He also had the head, one arm and the highlighted right side of Mopsy's body, except for a few gaps. Soon her excellent primary and secondary characteristics would manifest.

Actually a puzzle like this was a serviceable example of negative entropy. It took energy to gather the scattered pieces into an ordered whole. Energy and intelligence. Nature would not assemble Mopsy properly, for all that nature had done the original; it required a man to complete the picture puzzle.

"What are you doing?" Alice's voice inquired over the intercom.

Shetland sighed. That was one of the things he had hoped to put out of his mind! "Are you addressing me?"

"Of course, Captain! The others are busy or asleep."

Busy . . . well, why not ask her? "Alice—are you aware of what Beeton is doing?"

"Sleeping," she said. "He finished with Thenna an hour ago. She's asleep too. They make a nice couple."

No jealous ghost! "Yes, it can be beautiful in time and space," he said carefully. "I regret that I did not have occasion to interact similarly with you, before you became indisposed.''

She was silent for several minutes. He completed Mopsy's left breast—the right side of the puzzle—and found one of the missing edge pieces. It had a very narrow border side, easily overlooked.

''I wish you had not said that, Captain,'' she said at last.

''It's only sex. Has no bearing on private life.''

''Don't say that!'' she exclaimed. ''It's unthinkable.''

Odd remark for a ghost, particularly one who had in life sought a sexual liaison with a man she did not love, just to prove she could do it. But perhaps he could learn something, one way or another. ''Your indisposition—was it accidental?'' Somnanda had said it was self-willed, but a person attempting to haunt a man for murder would have a different version.

''No, Captain. I did it deliberately.''

There went the last bastion of third-party accusation! No one but the ghost would say what she had said.

He kept his eye on the black hole in the puzzle that was Mopsy's pubic region, and picked out a shaded piece that might fit. The backside was brightly flesh colored: probably a highlighted buttock. But his concern this time was with the front; a person could not do Flopsy both ways up simultaneously.

Black hole? That could be taken in at least three contexts: puzzle, woman, space . . . and a gap in reality, such as occurred when a man conversed with a ghost.

''You intended to have it happen as it did?'' he asked. He would not refer directly to her death, because someone else might be paying attention.

''Yes.''

The piece in his hand began to shake, and he had to quell

that. Real or pretended, this ghost was speaking to the point!
"If it is not too personal, I should like to inquire why."

"It is personal," she agreed. "I realized suddenly that I
was in an impossible situation, and there was really no way
out. No acceptable way. I could not go on—so I stopped."

It was ridiculous, but he was coming to believe her. Which
had to mean that he accepted her as a geunine ghost. Knowing the implications for his own sanity.

"I think we should continue this conversation privately,"
he said. "Why don't you come to the game room and help
me with my puzzle?"

She paused. "I'm afraid it might disturb you, sir."

Not half as much as the present situation did! "Forget that!
I want details on—on what happened. It put me in a rather
awkward position, you know."

"I know," she agreed. "And I'm sorry, believe me I am!
But you see, I'm not—I mean, there could be trouble."

"Let me be the judge of that! Come here."

"All right," she said.

The puzzle-piece began to shake again. He had not expected her to agree! He had merely wanted to force the
supposed spirit to deny him, admitting that it could not face
him directly. That would put the perpetrator on notice that
Shetland was not being fooled. Except that he had already
decided there *was* no perpetrator.

He put his hands on the table to steady them. But this time
the tremor was so violent that the table moved, skewing the
partially formed picture.

"Hierarchy!" he muttered. The puzzle, symbolic of so
many things, was also an example of hierarchial organiza-
tion: when two pieces interlocked they formed a new unit,
inseparable in the normal course, that could be integrated into
a larger section. If this were not so, he could just now have

destroyed all his prior work! Man himself was organized similarly, hierarchically, his cells built into organs and the organs into the whole, and the whole individual integrated into his larger society. Piece by piece—anything could be assembled. So long as it had an in-process cohesion. Even the true picture of a ghost.

"Maybe if you turned out the light . . ." Alice's voice said. "It would be easier."

Shetland stood and turned out the light at the same time as he disconnected the intercom. He was ready to compromise, for the sake of getting to the root of this. He sat down again and waited.

"Thank you, Captain," Alice said.

She was in the room with him! He could tell by the location of her voice and the faint smell of her perfume. An elaborate charade indeed!

"Your conversation prior to the event in no wise suggested your state of mind," he said. "What was it that compelled you to do it—right then?"

"It is private now," she said. "No one can overhear us. You don't have to be oblique."

"Why did you kill yourself? You had so much to live for—and the mission needed your service, and your fiancé—"

"I—" She paused again. "I thought I could tell you, but I find I can't, Captain. Any more than I could then. You will have to figure it out for yourself."

Ever thus! "It makes it difficult for me to accept your validity in your present incarnation if you will not speak to the point!"

"I know," she admitted. "And I don't blame you for being upset. I really do want to tell you, really! I am a foolish girl."

"You're certainly an unsophisticated haunt. If I have done

anything that requires retribution, you should be more than ready to acquaint me with it. That is the conventional purpose in such manifestations, as I understand it.''

''Oh, no, no, no, Captain! You have not done anything wrong!''

''I am not much for mysteries,'' he said firmly. ''And I can't complete my puzzle this way. I am about to turn on the light. If you wish to continue speaking with me, you will do so in my sight.''

''I shouldn't . . .'' she whispered.

He stood, reaching for the switch in the dark.

''Promise me you won't react,'' she said as he touched it.

The light flared on. For a moment he was blinded. When his eyes adjusted, the room was empty. As he had expected, though he found himself disappointed. At this point, a living ghost was one of the less objectionable alternatives.

''There just isn't anything to see,'' Alice said from mid air.

Shetland strode forward and swept his hand through the space from which the sound emanated. There was nothing.

''Maybe it's easier if you don't believe . . .'' she said in his ear.

He turned and cupped the air at the level of her head. ''Speak,'' he said.

From between his hands her voice came again. ''I shouldn't be doing this.''

''Come with me,'' he said abruptly, and led the way out of the room.

He went to the freezer and opened it again. Alice still lay there, quite cold and physical. ''How do you explain this?'' he demanded.

''It looks so cold, so very cold!'' she said behind him. ''I wish I had kept my body. If I had known—but I can't take it back now, can I?"

He closed the freezer. "You are an invisible spirit?"

"I must be."

"I will thaw your body, if you wish to reanimate it."

She gave a little scream of horror. "Oh, no! It's dead! It would spoil! I could never—!"

"How do you speak, without lungs, vocal cords, tongue?"

"I can't explain that, sir."

"You seem to be getting even less communicative, rather than more!"

"Well, I haven't been a ghost very long . . ."

"Will you be getting better at it after you've had more practice?"

She missed the sarcasm. "I hope so. It took me a while to learn to talk."

He led the way back to the puzzle. He could not discern any mechanism to the illusion. Alice did seem to be a ghost. "What do you do when not talking with us? Do you have to sleep or eat?"

"I don't think so. When no one's thinking of me, I just sort of fade out. Maybe that's the same as sleeping. And I've been playing with that ghost-material, the plasm. Tibet is right: it does respond to mental impulses."

So they had ascertained. "Even yours?"

"Yes. Usually."

He shook his head and returned to Mopsy. The shadowed pieces were fitting into place very slowly now; he had done the easy parts. "Well, suppose you continue your activities as before, and we'll talk again as convenient."

"All right," she said. "Thank you for accepting me, Captain."

He hadn't accepted her. He had merely been unable to

refute her. But it seemed unkind to bring that up. "I face a phenomenal crisis aboard this ship if the others discover in the wrong fashion that you are dead. Cartographer Beeton especially; his grief would surely extinguish the beacon, and doom us all to a similar fate as yours. As long as you are able and willing to manifest, so that you seem to be alive, I must cooperate. But I would much prefer to have had you alive."

"Thank you, Captain," she whispered in his left ear. He felt the merest suggestion of a touch there, as of a kiss. Then her presence faded.

If he was to believe the evidence of his ears, Alice lived though she was dead—and could never reanimate her body. She did not blame him for her condition. As a manifestation of his own guilt, this seemed ineffective, even pointless. What, then, was the explanation?

If he assumed that she was exactly as represented, could she animate a suitable quantity of the ghost-plasm and assume a living form? Before he suggested that, he wanted to see how their upcoming attempt to animate *Astrapotherium* succeeded.

In three hours from his starting time he had completed virtually all Mopsy's body except for three pieces in the left side shade. Three black holes in a black region. As the ship's velocity clock came to zero he had made some progress in the gray-brown background, establishing bridges from body to edges.

If only he could establish similar bridges spanning the reality gap between a logical ghost galaxy and the illogical ghost girl! Surely they were connected.

Black holes . . . like three ghost galaxies in a foreign universe. But in a universe a black hole was a lost piece, forever beyond recovery. The portion of the picture unfortunate enough to be on that piece was doomed to be incomplete.

Black hole. By definition, a region from which nothing could escape, spatially. The ghost was a black hole. Quite possibly it retained its original matter; they had merely guessed at what happened to matter after it achieved the state of singularity. More correctly, Beeton had guessed, glibly as always.

Beeton. There was something odd about the young cartographer. About his reactions to the absence of Alice, and the presence of the ghost galaxy. As though the genius didn't comprehend the significance of either.

Which was laughable. Beeton should have comprehended both matters first, and surely *had*. More likely he was playing dumb, to cover up the awful truths he knew. To hide the inevitable from the others. Paying attention to Sosthenna, and explaining that the ghost galaxy was harmless.

Shetland reread his mental tape of one significant conversation, at the time of their vote to enter the ghost. Shetland had inquired why Beeton had abstained, and Beeton had replied, "I'm afraid of ghosts. But I think it's too late, anyway. Either way."

Afraid of ghosts: of Alice's and the dead galaxy's. Too late: for Alice and the *Meg*?

Black hole—from which there was no escape, if its original matter remained. Except temporally.

But was that a true exception? Or could it be that a black hole exerted the same effect on time also? Time and matter interrelated, and the effects were most extreme at a black hole, where the velocity of light became zero and time became infinite. Had Shetland made an error of assumption?

Beeton had known—and perhaps, now, Shetland knew also. If Shetland had a secret to conceal, so also had Beeton. They had already entered the event horizon, that rim from which nothing departed. There was no guarantee that it lay at the visible fringe of the ghost galaxy; it could lie far beyond it. In fact, that could have been what they had taken to be the timestorm. Their passage through the event horizon. *Could* they pass back out of it?

Pointless to make an issue of his realization—because there was no way to alleviate that doom.

Could this be true?

Shetland was not as quick to grasp such realities as Beeton was, but now the Captain had caught up. He was the master of this ship; it was his responsibility. But what could he do more positive than simply keeping the grim secret?

So he would carry on, tight-lipped, hoping Beeton was wrong—until the end. That probably would not be burdensomely long.

Yet there was a store of energy available here equivalent to the total output of a full galaxy for hundreds of billions of years. They could draw on it for minor effects, such as creating a four-dimensional vision of an invented committee animal. Why not draw on it for escape?

But how? That energy was not propulsive, and even it if were, infinite propulsion could not remove them from this abyss of gravity. Beeton must have thought of that, too.

Shetland broke for a conference with Johns. They decided to start the return trip immediately. Did Johns also know the futility? The drive engaged and the clock nudged up again.

Pray that Beeton was wrong!

He returned to the puzzle. Now the only way to progress was to sort out pieces by shape and keep trying given configurations until the right item was located. At least there was a solution to *this* puzzle—provided none of the pieces was missing.

As he worked, his thoughts drifted across other subjects, less pressing at present. What was the real purpose of this expedition? To discover what had happened to the *Meg I,* of course. That had been accomplished, in sufficient fashion. But more broadly, it was to locate an energy source for energy-starved Earth. That, too, seemed to have been accomplished. There was more energy in the ghost than Earth could use in all eternity, probably, no matter how wastefully expended. But that energy was *here* while Earth was *there.* How could the two be joined? He had no idea.

Still, if they solved the riddle of their personal survival, and managed to return to Earth, then it seemed likely that some transfer of energy could be arranged. If a physical body like a ship could cross the void between the two, it was not too great a stretch of belief to assume that energy could cross too. Perhaps a cargoful of plasm. So if this crew could save itself, it might also save the world. A monstrous pair of ifs, but they would suffice for now.

He thought of Alice, so attractive when alive, and of Sosthenna, sleeping off her liaison with the cartographer. He envied Beeton at the moment, but not critically. He, Shetland, had had his turn, and would surely have his turn again, while what would Beeton have, once the truth about Alice was known?

Shetland knew that what he most desired was not really sex, but love. Sosthenna had given him the former, and it seemed not the latter. In that sense perhaps his loss was greater than Beeton's, for perhaps Sosthenna would grant the young man her love. Maybe Alice would have done the same for Shetland, had she lived. Now, no chance.

Why *had* Alice died? That was the single most disturbing thing about this voyage. He might die here; they all might die here. But their deaths would be involuntary. Alice's death had been voluntary, and it just didn't make sense. *Why* had she done it? Somehow it seemed that if he could know that, he could accept the rest of the situation.

But what man could truly know the mind of another? Or of any woman? He had never really understood Maureen's suicide, either. Was he doomed to live and die in such ignorance?

In just over six hours of working time the sunny-side-up view of Flopsy Mopsy was complete. She was not megalocarpous, but she was adequate.

With that rather limited satisfaction he had to be satisfied.

Chapter 10:_____Parodies

They drifted again at just under 8 on the clock, relative to the ghost, traveling backward in time but not accelerating. The *Meg* re-entered the apparent fringe of the galaxy, which Shetland now feared was merely a fluctuation in its imponderable gravitic well.

Shetland passed Beeton in the hall as they assumed their stations. "In space we cannot escape," he said. "But we're not moving through space, but through time. Why can't we just—"

Beeton shook his head negatively. "The tide," he muttered, and moved on.

What did he mean? Shetland did not have a chance to work it out; he had to assume his station for the activation of the vision. But it seemed to him that they should theoretically be able to escape the ghost, merely by traveling back to the time before it existed in this region of space. Time might be infinite, but so was their ability to travel through it.

Yet Beeton believed they were doomed, and Beeton had been right every time so far.

"Now concentrate on *Astrapotherium magnum*," Shetland said on the intercom. "We will be permitted to return to time travel after this experiment has been completed." Was that foolish optimism, or painful irony? "Form the image outside the ship; the automatic cameras will photograph anything that manifests, and your own vision screens will keep you informed. But each of you must develop his own portion of the creature, and the images must be unified. Center on the torso that Tibet will project."

Would it work? He doubted it. Did it matter? He doubted that also. But their experiments with the sample had been impressive, and other strange things had become commonplace on this voyage. It was certainly an excellent diversion.

The tide, the tide. What did that mean? Not that of the oceans of Earth, obviously. Of course tide was a universal phenomenon; wherever bodies orbited each other in space, there was tide. But the effect on a spaceship was normally far too small to measure, let alone to distort the ship's progress.

He watched the screen himself. And saw something forming outside, where nothing had been visible before. Swirls of white, of color, fluxes in space. Then—

The torso formed. Quickly the legs and feet appeared, then the tail and the huge genitalia. Headless, it faced them.

"Alice?" Shetland prompted. And wondered: did her presence portend the death of all the crew? Was that the real reason, perhaps unknown to her, that the supernatural had intruded into this natural setting? The notion did not seem fantastic now.

"Help me . . ." she said behind him. "I can't project that far. Not without physical brain power."

Shetland visualized the strange head and concentrated. Slowly the head formed, and the animal was complete.

The tide. There was something about it—

"Don't forget the environment, Captain!" Johns said.

Damn! The key thought was gone—if it mattered.

To the business at hand. Shetland had named the time and place, but had not thought it out properly beyond that. Now, with the creature manifest before them, the land and background were needed, certainly. Beeton had said Patagonia was warmer and wetter during the Oligocene, and he had to trust that, for his own information did not extend that far. He wished he had read the entire paleontology text, way back when, but then he had lacked sufficient interest. What use did a space officer have for information about ancient plants and creatures of Earth?

Astrapotherium magnum walked through the marshy terrain. His proboscis snuffled near the ground, searching out edibles. For a moment he stood still, sleek in his corpulence, muscular in his odd proportioning, actually a splendid figure of an animal. The large head no longer seemed grotesque, the body no longer mismatched. He stretched, his proboscis quivering to the odors of the swamp.

"He's handsome and he knows it!" Johns said. "That's a real masculine specimen!"

"Pride," Sosthenna said. "Justified."

"Odd how well our committee design works out in practice!" Beeton remarked. "We make a better team than I thought. Poth certainly seems to be at home."

"I hope the cameras are seeing it the same way we are," Shetland said. "They are mounted permanently, pointing out; there is no way we could deceive them." Assuming that the Captain was right, the cartographer wrong, about who would ever view those pictures. An insecure assumption!

"Even if it's a mass hallucination," Tibet said warmly, "it's a good one!"

The animal turned his head, orienting on the ship. Tibet gasped—but it was a false alarm. The head carried on, the nose searching out some new smell within the framework of the vision, the ears twitching to some sound. The small eyes peered, never having seen the ship.

The scene expanded to show the surrounding marshes. Shetland wasn't sure who was doing it; he doubted it was himself.

A second animal came into view. This one was smaller than Poth, but of the same species. A female. Beyond her a third creature grazed, her mate, tusking out succulent swatches of edible swamp root. Poth stood still, eying the corpulent lady *Astrapotherium*.

"Thou shalt not covet thy neighbor's wife . . ." Alice said, amused.

"Thy neighbor's ass, more like it!" Johns said, laughing coarsely.

"Poth is not related to the horse," Sosthenna said, a trifle primly. "Maybe she's a cow."

Whatever the appropriate terminology, Poth *did* covet. He snorted with a curious hornlike sound and plunged toward the fair female. Sound, Shetland realized with a little shock: sound was now part of the vision! Who was responsible for that?

"Covet, hell!" Johns exclaimed. "That's plain lust!"

Indeed it was. The lady wiggled her delicate snout and lifted her tail in a definite come-on, and Poth redoubled his effort to reach her.

"But if she's in heat, why isn't her regular mate taking care of it?" Tibet wanted to know.

"Her mate's upwind," Johns explained. "She just came

into heat—it happens suddenly with Potheriums—and Poth's the first male downwind. Who put in that third animal, anyway?''

"Who put in the *second*?" Tibet demanded in return. "We were only going to make one creature!"

Shetland nodded to himself. So the vision, like certain other group efforts, was following its own inclinations. Probably two or three crewmen had thought passingly of the possibility, and the combination had been enough for it to happen. In similar fashion artists talked of paintings designing themselves, and novelists of characters with wills of their own. He had once read a Spanish or Italian play concerning six characters in search of an author . . .

Poth's progress was surprisingly rapid. His four legs carried him along as if he were paddling, and his stout body forged through the clustered reeds. His torso undulated, pushing serpentlike against the vegetation and the muck that buoyed him. Shetland realized that the complex feet, now sunk far into the swamp, were well adapted to this motion: their peculiar structure splayed them into cuplike pads on the downthrust, and folded them narrowly as they lifted. Clumsy on land and ineffective in water because of the vertical positioning of the legs—but ideal for muck! The committee design was functioning far better than anyone had expected.

Poth reached the female and proceeded to essentials. She was deep in mud now, her belly resting against the surface while she munched her cud. A romantic setting! Poth struggled to lift his foresection, but could not free it vertically from the thick substance. Finally he scrambled onto her back, foot over foot, hauling his telescoping anatomy into position. She was willing; her small tail was lifted straight up, out of the way. A tail, Shetland realized, could be a considerable barrier to activity of this nature; some animals possessed their own chastity mechanisms.

"Oh-oh," Beeton said. "Hubby just caught on—and he's angry!"

Shetland shook his head wonderingly. Were these intelligent people parodying themselves deliberately, or were they actually blind to the nature of the dramatizations they were announcing? Johns talking of copulation with another male's mate; Beeton talking of the mate's discovery of that act and his anger . . .

The other male, though upwind, was hardly deaf or blind, and obviously recognized copulation when he saw it or smelled it. He charged upon the two.

Poth, prevented by swamp resistance from achieving a hasty culmination, had to disengage with bad grace. He spun to face the aggressor, snorting warningly. This was a special situation, he seemed to be announcing; he had smelled her first, and the other had no complaint coming.

The two reared up, now finding the muck to be no impediment, batting at each other with their front feet. But they were not efficient fighters, and this was obviously ritual. They tried to gore each other with their short tusks, with no better success. A tooth that was good for excavating a tasty root was not necessarily good for combat.

They broke for a moment, and the affronted male took this opportunity to swing a tusk at his mate. She was culpable too! Her tail had been up, hadn't it? Affrighted, she absented herself.

Shetland felt another qualm. That strike at the female—why hadn't he thought of that before? It was natural for the male to be as furious at his female as at her lover; perhaps more so, for it was the nature of males to wander. *She* should have behaved!

Had Beeton somehow killed Alice? And her ghost was unwilling to admit that he had been the cause of her demise? A touching if awkward loyalty!

But Shetland himself had seen her take the red capsule. No one had forced it on her. She was not color-blind or ignorant of its nature. So the mystery remained.

In time, mutually disgruntled, the two males desisted. The wind had shifted. Poth returned to his home stamping ground.

"Who did that?" Johns demanded. "Why break up the romance? Some prude—"

No one would admit to the crime. "Poth is a composite," Shetland reminded them. "He acts in accordance with the compromise of all our wills; no one person controls him now." And one of those wills was that of a ghost!

The scene was not over. Poth happened upon an exceedingly lush nest of vegetation. "Plushweed," Tibet said, inventing a name for an invented plant.

Poth plunged his snout into it, rooting out the succulent tubers and biting away the attached stems and roots. He swallowed them only half chewed, intent on new mouthfuls despite the warning rumbles of his bloated stomach. Soon his belly bulged visibly with tuber and gas.

"Gluttony!" Tibet said. "My, that stuff looks good!"

They had agreed upon an animation for the cameras, but it was obviously much more than that. Every playwright was stepping up on stage himself.

But the plushweed tubers, like all good things, finally came to an end. Poth lifted his handsome ugly head as he masticated the last root and peered across at his neighbor—who was contentedly rooting in an even larger nest of succulents.

Poth's proboscis quivered. He opened and closed his mouth and rotated his ears restlessly. "Envy!" Shetland said, aware that he could not eschew the game of self-expression, humiliating as this particular type of it was. Actually this was not a perfect definition for the term, but it was close enough for the moment. "Why should that other one have both female and food? We didn't even create that one!"

Poth considered moving back into his neighbor's territory. But the other snorted warningly, and the notion lost appeal. So he aimed his rump at a favored bush and defecated.

Johns uttered a four-letter expletive appropriate to the occasion. "Look at it fly! Gas-powered!"

Gas did seem to be providing some propulsion, but it was more than that. "The tail does it," Tibet said, evidently conversant with many aspects of digestion. "Hippopotamuses do the same thing. Waggling the tail back and forth while dunging so as to spread it over a wide area. Excellent way to spread the smell across the territory and start the material composting."

"Who needs a fan!" Johns said with admiration.

Had Somnanda actually designed that function into Poth's tail? If so, the man had an earthy sense of humor that had never manifested before. Back in the Oligocene the saying would have gone "Then the dung hit the tail." Same effect.

His toilet completed, Poth slewed over to his favorite mud slick and settled down for a nap.

Light faded. Poth rolled over, sniffed the air, broke wind with another feculent blast, and flopped luxuriously back into the mud for the continuation of his repose.

He slept through the night—indicated by a blackout of a few seconds—and on into the next day, stomach burbling.

It rained, drenching the marsh with inches of water. Poth snoozed on, shifting position only to facilitate the rinsing of burrs and insects from all sides of his hide. The swamp became covered with a sheen of clear liquid as the runoff from neighboring highlands filled the reedy slough. Still Poth did not move.

"Sloth," Somnanda said.

"Too easy a life," Beeton said. "He should be more alert against predators. See—here comes one now."

It was a crocodile, or a related reptile. Its snout was long and high in front, instead of depressed like that of other varieties, but it was well toothed and the creature was about fifteen feet long overall. It forged silently through the marsh, swimming in the shallow covering of water. It did not move swiftly, for the weeds and mud still inhibited the process. But they also offered concealment as it picked up the waterborne taste of mammal and centered on the sleeping *Astrapotherium*.

"Wake up, Poth!" Alice cried, alarmed.

Poth woke. He sniffed, and caught a whiff of reptile. He splashed hastily into the deeper muck.

"Fool!" Johns cried. "Get out on dry land where you can outrun it!"

"Not with those feet!" Tibet reminded him.

The crocodilian, discovered, accelerated. Its sinuous body flexed through the reeds as its powerful tail churned the water. It was, after all, capable of fair velocity, now that noise and visibility were no longer factors.

Still, it followed the water scent, going toward the place Poth had been, not cutting across to where he was headed. "Fathead!" Johns exclaimed. "You'll never catch him that way!"

"Hey, which side are you on?" Tibet demanded.

"Poth's, of course—but that doesn't alter the sebaceous content of the croc's cranium! No wonder that skull bulges so!"

"Sebaceous?" Thenna asked.

"It means 'fatty matter,'" Beeton said. "Call him *Sebacus*—the fathead."

"Sebecus," she said.

"Close enough."

Sebecus abruptly changed course, orienting more accurately on the refugee. "He heard you!" Tibet cried. "Now see what you've done!"

They were really getting into it, Shetland realized. Just as if this were not an impossible animation for the sake of the cameras.

"He just got up to where he could see Poth through the reeds," Johns said. "Fathead wouldn't understand me if he did hear me!"

The terrain still favored Poth. He forged into the thickest reeds, and there made better time despite his larger and less streamlined girth. The very muck his plunging passage stirred up interfered with the crocodilian's progress. The longer the chase continued, the slower Sebecus became, until he gave up in disgust. Poth had weathered the threat.

"But what about the dry season?" Sosthenna asked. As she spoke, the rain abated and the swamp's water level dropped. Poth returned to his caked mud slick and snoozed, oblivious.

"Oh, come on, let's be fair!" Johns cried. "Sloth is bad, but Poth isn't *that* bad!"

Poth dutifully roused himself and looked about. Now the swamp was almost dry, and the mud was sere: brick-hard and cracked. The reeds were dessicate stalks, stiff and brown. It was almost impossible to root out the plushweed tubers, and the tubers themselves were shriveled.

Poth was no longer fat. His torso was lean, his last joyful bubbles of flatulence expended, and he was hungry. He ranged the awful swamp-desert, his feet hurting from the heat and hardness, his inadequate hind legs tired from the constant brunt of his full weight.

A predator appeared—a huge saber-toothed cat weighing perhaps two hundred pounds. Not a lion, not a tiger, not a leopard, but definitely feline. It, too, was hungry—and now it could walk with ease across the dehydrated swamp. For the first time since the rains, it could reach Poth.

Poth let out a bleat of sheer terror and ran. But his best velocity was no match for that of the predator. Normally the big cat would hide and pounce, as it could maintain speed for only a short time compared to the doglike carnivores of the period. But this was a special circumstance.

Poth stumbled, fell, rolled, and scrambled painfully to his tender feet. The cat overhauled him and sprang upon his back as he rose, digging claws into Poth's unprotected shoulders and hips while its teeth took hold of the extended neck.

"Do something!" Tibet shrieked.

"*You* designed that vulnerable body!" Johns snapped. "No armor—"

"Maybe I could put horns on the head," Alice cried. "Sharp, backward-curving horns, like those of some deer, to stab anything on its back—"

Poth stumbled while the cat clung. The saber teeth lifted, dropped, spiking into the vertebrae of the neck, seeking some critical nerve or vessel. Poth's hide was tough, and his backbone was ridged, interfering with such an attack, but if a tooth penetrated into the spinal column—

"No time for that!" Beeton said, sounding choked.

Thus vision became nightmare, Shetland thought.

"There is a waterhole just ahead," Sosthenna said. "Isn't there, Captain?"

Bless her! "Yes, yes, there is!" Shetland agreed. "A big spring, deep, that never dries, all the thirsty animals come to it—"

The waterhole appeared, responsive to the description of

the mind in charge of locale. Poth plunged into it with a thankful and perhaps somewhat surprised squeal. He splashed and rolled over, letting his whole body sink except for the tip of his snout, which he now elevated for breathing. Naturally the feline was dunked too, and had to let go before it drowned.

Poth splashed up a storm, his splaying front feet excellent for that if not for running or swimming. The cat clawed at the bank and scrambled out, furious. It prowled around the hole several times, compelled by the odor of blood spreading into the water from Poth's gouged neck and shoulders. But obviously Poth was not about to move away from that respite. The cat finally moved on, after snarling some very unkind snarls.

"Hey!" Beeton exclaimed. "I just remembered! Patagonia is the southern tip of South America—and the continent was separated from North America for most of the Cenozoic era. Many of the more advanced placentals didn't reach there until comparatively recently."

"What has that got to do with us?" Johns asked sourly.

"There weren't any of the dog or cat carnivores," Beeton said. "So that sabertooth couldn't have attacked Poth!"

Tibet groaned. "*Now* he tells us!"

"Oh, let's not rerun that scene!" Sosthenna cried. "Poth did beautifully!"

Beeton shrugged. "As you wish. Pit an animal that wasn't there against one that never existed at all—why not? Actually most of the exotic forms in South America became extinct once the continents rejoined, so it remains an excellent setting."

"Still, after allowing for paleontological error, *Astrapotherium*'s habitat is restricted," Somnanda said, making one of his rare comments. "He resides in swamp—not too wet, not too dry, or the water predators or land predators intrude.

There can't have been many periods when such swamp was extensive—and it would have been hard for him to migrate when local climatic conditions changed. He could not have lasted long, geologically, back on Earth.''

Trust Somnanda to put the vision into perspective! They had not, after all, invented a viable creature. But that, of course, was the point: to show an impossible animal in operation, so that there could be no question of any prior recording.

"*We* haven't lasted long, geologically,'' Alice protested. "We designed Poth; we could have given him a long tenure—personally and geologically. We have no right to make him what he is, then condemn him for it!''

Was this really a ghost speaking? It sounded just like the living Alice!

"Poth is us,'' Sosthenna murmured, almost inaudibly.

"Maybe we should uninvent him and put him out of his misery,'' Beeton said. "The cameras must have plenty of film by now, and soon we'll be passing out of the ghost—''

But Beeton believed there was no escape, Shetland thought. Because of the tide . . .

"Don't you dare,'' Tibet exclaimed.

"No! That's not fair either,'' Alice said warmly, agreeing with Tibet. Had that reference to "ghost'' set her off? "We performed an act of creation when we made him—but that doesn't give us the right to practice genocide!''

Beeton laughed, but it sounded forced. "Come on now, Al. Genocide? On an imaginary species?''

"He's not imaginary!'' she retorted. "Poth is *created*. There's a distinction.''

Something began to shape in Shetland's mind, like one irregular section of puzzle fitting into another and completing a formerly unfathomable picture. If an invented creature could become real by the act of creation—

"She's right," Sosthenna said. "We can make babies too—but once we've done it, they're not imaginary, and it's murder to kill them."

Making babies . . . Tibet had made a baby, long ago. Not with her body, but with her mind, in a dream. A brown baby girl, who would have been Alice's age by this time. Alice had lost her parents at the same time Tibet had dreamed, remembering only a lonely house. Had she been created—and lived on, until returning abruptly to ghost status? Had that been her preordained fate? Had that been what she had suddenly realized just before inhaling the red death capsule?

But Beeton was talking: "All right, girls! You can make babies—with maybe a little help from men. And we'll let *Astrapotherium magnum* go to hell in his own fashion. Geologically."

The image-Poth and the ghost-Alice—something surely linked them, Shetland thought. Was it coincidence that these manifestations were occurring at the same time the *Meg* was associated with the galaxy ghost? Not just their use of the ghost-material to form Poth's image, but the very notion of animating animals or evoking spirits?

Beeton figured in all of it, directly or deviously. He had no compunction about wiping out what had been wrought . . .

That was it! To Beeton, a failure should be abolished. And by one kind of reckoning his engagement to Alice had been a failure, for she had lain with another man. Beeton could not protest directly, for he knew he had no legal or moral cause in this situation, and he had said he understood—but he could let the entire group associated with that failure "go to hell in its own fashion." That, by his definition, made it right.

Wayne Beeton, consciously or unconsciously, wanted them

all to die within the ghost galaxy. And he knew they would, if something wasn't done—because of the tide.

There must, then, be an escape. If Shetland could only fathom it.

But first he had to fathom the danger. What had the tide to do with the ghost?

Meanwhile, someone was accelerating geology. They watched it happen, there in space, now a living scene just beyond the ship.

The contours of Patagonia changed; the swamps filled in and dried. And in the epoch following the Oligocene, the Miocene, *Astrapotherium magnum* became extinct. Nature had no mercy—assuming nature was really the driving force of this vision. Shetland had growing doubt.

"Poth is us," Sosthenna had said. Now Poth was gone. The animal had, as it were, strutted and fretted his hour upon the stage, and was seen no more.

With the extinction of the viewpoint character the framework sundered. The ground split into shuddering cracks that extended right up into the clouding sky, as though a picture were being torn. There was no lava, no smoke, only a whirling chaos.

Shetland felt vertigo, and reached for an emergency hand-hold beside the screen, relic of the years when crewmen had to survive the colossal chemical thrusts of actual space travel. For a moment it seemed that the bar did not exist, that there was nothing but the crumbling manifestation of Poth's doomed existence. Then he found it, caught it, grasped it hard, inordinately relieved—and felt it begin to give.

The tide!

He looked—and saw a crack extending into the ship itself. It was too close to the ghost-image, and the very real forces that were acting on the one were now acting on the other.

The focused energies of a galaxy could rapidly fragment a mere ship! That was the significance of the tide. The peculiar aspect of gravitation that could destroy even an orbiting body. Unless he beat it back, controlled it as he controlled the beacon, somehow reorganizing that devastating force and channeling it constructively—

"Captain! Captain!"

The cry of anguish from the beacon-master! Shetland whirled about, ready to rush to Somnanda's side—and saw a ghostly mist infusing into the hall from the broadening crack. The ghost-substance was taking over the *Meg*!

He charged through it, but the vapor thickened, clouding his sight, dissolving the reality of the ship. His feet found no purchase and he began to fall through fog. Now he could make out nothing beyond the swirling mist except for the land of Miocene Earth dwindling on either side, melting, evaporating, fading along with the ship, until there was nothing but the swirling mist, the mist . . .

"And God said, Let there be Chaos," Shetland remarked as philosophically as he could. They had activated the ghost, converting much of its substance to mass, and now the tide associated with that mass was deactivating the ship. Always better to let a sleeping monster lie. How long had they been within it this time? Thirty minutes? Soon the others would catch on that the *Meg* was not going to pass on out of it . . .

Or were there even such things as minutes now? They had oriented on the ghost, an entity of appallingly vast spatial and temporal reaches. A black hole—from which the puzzle-piece called *Meg* would never emerge. Time had become no more relevant than space.

They might swing about the central singularity of the ghost, passing through the apparent fringe—but the *Meg* would inevitably be drawn deeper inside with each orbit, never to depart the compelling radius of the event horizon. There would be no time, literally, no momentum. They would stay here forever, at one with an alien eternity.

Beeton had known it. Had they made the return pass the same way as the forward pass, drifting through time, activating nothing, they might have escaped the ghost unscathed. But they had wanted proof of their discovery—and in that pride of accomplishment lay their joint doom. Too late to cancel the vision now; the tide had already struck.

Yet he had to fight, however futilely! To restart the drive and get back on the logarithmic progression, accelerating in a fashion even the ghost might not be able to handle, now that the vision was gone. The thrust might tear the weakened ship the rest of the way apart—but it might also wrench them free of this morass of energy. Maybe, just maybe, the *Meg* was still at the fringe of the event horizon, unable to extricate herself spatially, but able temporally. Faint, desperate hope! But if the attempt failed, they would be no worse off than now.

"Johns! Johns!" he cried, flailing in the vague translucence.

The pilot's face phased in, bodiless: a true apparition. "Sure I've had problems," it said. "Last leave on Earth was an explendiferous mess, I kid you not. Listen—"

"Johns, connect the drive! Connect the drive!" Shetland shouted.

The face ignored him. ". . . the local shuttle to Port York was a full fifteen seconds late! Damn near collided with the incoming Moon commutery, and that bushleague pilot had the effrontery to 'nounce over the 'com that ev'thing was AOK! He was a Marsie. Ask me, ought to put a complete stop to immigration; Earth already has too stinking many people without those buggers sneaking in to take jobs while our own kind go on welfare. Too damn many foreigners— how we going to feed the entire solar system?"

"Johns—connect the drive!" Shetland cried again. "This is no time for reminiscing! This may be our only chance to get back to that world you're criticizing!" Futile, futile—the ship was already gone! But necessary, if only as a last gesture of human defiance.

Johns' disembodied face looked through him. "On the jaunt itself I took up the slack by graphing my petition for another offspring. Zero-gee office's been giving me flak about my quota, 'sif I wasn't 'titled to at least one girl-baby to match my trio males. Damn bastard bureaucrats—who the hell they think pays 'em? 'Sif the Miseg's not bad enough! My taxes come to a good eighteen percent, not even counting the hidden levies! That ain't henfeed, as the colloquials say; that's enough to buy and sell the deskman who thinks he can veto my petition out of hand!"

Shetland took stock. Was this a true representation of Johns' character? If so, the pilot was an incredible egocentric and a disastrously shallow individual. An unfeeling hypocrite who rationalized the necessary restraints imposed by a stressed society as personal affronts to his convenience. This was a side of Johns he had not known, but perhaps of no more substance than the visible face. He would have to reach the man physically before he could reach him intellectually. He could not allow a specter to be the prime character witness.

"Saw a flight of bald eagles as we came down," the face continued. "Port's right adjacent to the endangered species range. Man, if I'd had a good rifle I'd have bagged me one, they were that close! Get at least a nominal return on the taxpayers' wasted cash . . ."

Shetland tuned it out and struggled with concept. The seven members of the crew had become identified with the animation of *Astrapotherium magnum,* and thereby merged his extinction with their own. But it was not yet complete oblivion; rather it was a chaosity of form and mind. A literal nightmare. As long as the *Meg* remained within the ghost, the phantoms of the activated substance would surround them, suffusing body and mind and parodying both. There would be no awakening from this abyss—unless he found some way to isolate the real from the replica.

Nothing could escape a black hole. But never before had there been intelligence within one. Mind that could shape its content into a completely unnatural effort. Suppose that mind formed that entire energy into the thrust of a supernova—and channeled that thrust in one narrow direction? To carry one small ship back out along its timeline?

But there had to be unity of purpose. Right now there were six or seven separate identities pulling discordantly at the ghost-substance. They needed to reunify, to pull together on the one essential thing: getting out of the ghost!

He had had the right idea before, but the wrong person. He might collect the members of his crew, but he had to start with the broadest, most stable personalities. Johns was self-interested and superficially inclined: probably not as bad as the apparition-parody made him, but tending in that direction. Too narrow a base for crew unity. But a broad man like Somnanda—

"Somnanda!" he cried. "Here to me!"

For a long moment there was nothing. Then, faintly, came Somnanda's response. "Where?"

"Here! We must unify, and draw the others in, and get the ship moving out: How stands the beacon?"

"Captain, I can't find you . . ." the voice said, as from a distance. And the swirling gases of nothingness blocked the impulses of the optic nerves, blinding the two men to each other. Shetland knew he might now be in the beacon room, having blundered there in the course of his mist-struggles, but it made no difference.

He had an inspiration. "We'll meet on White King Four!"

"Too far," Somnanda protested. "I'm on Black's Rook One . . ."

"Then I will come to you!" Shetland cried. He concentrated, visualizing the chessboard, willing the malleable ghost-plasm into actuality. His body might be prey to its mass, but its substance was subject to his mind!

Slowly the board took shape about him, large red and black tiles extending into infinity. He imagined the border, and that formed too, delineating eight squares on a side. Not so very long ago he had dreamed a chess analogy, and been horrified by the vision that resulted, and so had taken the action that had spared the *Meg* from whatever fate would have resulted from striking the ghost under temporal power. Now he returned to chess, hoping to prevail over the same enemy again.

He stood on King One. "I am King!" he thought. But he knew that every man was king to himself, in his private vanity. Even Johns. Now he had to travel to Black's Rook One.

"Which Rook?" he called, belatedly remembering that there were two Black Rooks. He should have used the algebraic system of notation, to prevent such confusion. Now he was too late; there was no answer.

He did not want to guess, as there were surely many dangers on a living chessboard and he could not afford to waste time. At what point did the tidal effect become irreversible? The King could not move directly into check, but careless exposure could lead him into disadvantage and rapid loss of the game. So he concentrated, willing it to be King's Rook Eight—White's nomenclature of the Black King's Rook

One—and knew then that it was. In imagery of this nature Shetland was superior; no other crewman could match his eidetic vision.

He stepped forward a square, and stopped. He had not intended to stop; he just did. After a moment of frustration he realized that this was because he was now limited by the King's move in chess: one step in any direction, no more. "But I can't wait seven moves to get there!" he protested. "This is no game, just a geography!"

He had said it, and so it was so. He was no longer bound by the rules of chess; he merely walked its board. He strode across the tiles to King's Rook Eight.

And wondered whether that abridgment of available rules also freed the inanimate opponent, the ghost itself, for the development of its own frontiers. The ghost had monstrous capabilities, powers barely touched upon so far. Perhaps he should have taken the time for chess, and thus confined it to familiar rules.

He encountered a castle. The Rook in chess was like a little tower, and the piece was alternately called a Castle. Indeed, his mental dictionary defined a rook as a castle, in that connection. So—

But this was no miniature representation. This was a *real* castle! Its turrets towered fifty feet, and its ramparts were powerful bulwarks against penetration. Tiny embrasures showed high up: slits from which bowmen could fire their arrows, secure against return fire. In addition there was a formidable moat.

What quirk of nomenclature had conjured forth this edifice? Shetland intended only to meet with Somnanda, not to joust with him!

But he had abridged the rules, and already the consequence was upon him. He should have known that the ghost would not readily give up any part of its prey. The first apparition had been Johns, and Shetland had merely dismissed him. That could have been a mistake! Now he was up against a more formidable personality.

If it remained his intent to recover his crew, he had forfeited Johns. Score: one to nothing, favor of the ghost. He could not afford to give up any more!

The castle was not defended, however. The massive drawbridge was not only down, it was overgrown by weeds. No guards paced the walls. How like Somnanda: to develop a splendid physical framework, then neglect it! (But all this had been conjured only minutes ago; how could two months worth of weeds have encroached? Beware too glib a theory!)

Shetland pondered, and saw fit to conjure himself some light armor: a crash helmet, bulletproof vest, metal codpiece and iron-soled boots. The last thing he had anticipated was a medieval stage, but until he comprehended its ramification he would play reasonably safe. As an afterthought he also equipped himself with a small concealed blaster. Whether such a thing could operate in a fantasy stage he wasn't certain, but until he grasped the limits he would assume that everything worked the way it was supposed to.

He stepped boldly across the drawbridge—a greater boldness than he felt!—noting the scum on the surface of the moat. Stagnant.

The inner passages and courts of the castle were labyrinthine; he could never find his way unguided. But that was readily solved: he conjured a thin thread to spin out behind him, so that like Theseus he could follow it back out. Then he commanded the appearance of a castle servant.

"Yes, sir," the servant said, appearing—literally—from air. He was an absolutely nondescript young man whose face and clothing tended to fuzz out when inspected closely. A cardboard character.

"Take me to your leader," Shetland said, suppressing a smile.

The servant bowed and showed the way, little realizing that Shetland had just substantiated a formidable concept: a living human person *could* be fashioned from the energies of the ghost. Not merely a vision of one, but an entity that responded responsively to human directive. This was the galaxy of literal magic.

No, he still could not be certain of that, he realized on further consideration. This could be a mere simulacrum, a golem existing in shape only, guided by the will of the master. Or one of the other crewmen, his identity masked by plasm, playing the part. Nothing was certain, here!

The ghost of Alice had manifested in the vicinity of the ghost galaxy. Certainly a ghost was easier to create than a complete being. Such a ghost could be guided in much the manner this servant-manifestation was. So though Shetland had not yet satisfied himself about the reality of either Alice's ghost or the servant before him, he was reassured about another aspect of the present reality. He could indeed be experiencing what he seemed to be experiencing—without having to question his own sanity. That was important.

In a moment they entered a tremendous hall, elegantly designed but now littered with refuse. The housekeeper here was evidently lazy. In the center, on a giant feather bed, lay Somnanda.

"Nanda, what *is* this?" Shetland demanded.

The man looked at him and shrugged with minimal effort. "It just materialized," he said.

"An entire centuries-old unkempt castle? What happened to the beacon?"

Somnanda gestured indifferently. There at the foot of the bed, perched precariously on a bedpost, guttered the candle. Its wax dripped wastefully down the post and to the floor as the flame neared the base. If this were truly the beacon, its time was short! "There was a crisis that was overwhelming the beacon," Somnanda explained. "You did not come, so I had to pursue whatever course would most readily preserve it. Thus I find myself here."

"We have a ship to extricate!" Shetland said. "You'll have to orient on home, so we can—"

"Tomorrow," Somnanda said, closing his eyes.

"Tomorrow! There *is* no tomorrow, if we don't get moving! Not even any end to this day, this hour! We're trapped inside the ghost!"

"Is that unfortunate?" Somnanda asked carelessly.

"Unfortunate! It's *fatal*—if we don't—" Then he realized: Somnanda was now the embodiment of Sloth, one of the Seven Deadly Sins. There was little hope of rousing him to action by conventional means.

Shetland turned and followed his thread out of the castle. He crossed the drawbridge. Then he turned again and contemplated the edifice thoughtfully.

He needed to do something about this—but what? Conjure a cannon to fire at it? No, that could hurt Somnanda himself while demolishing the castle and extinguishing the beacon. Any mechanical violence would.

How could a man be jolted out of a seemingly impregnable bastion? Without danger to his person or mind?

Shetland smiled. Such a man could be evicted by the proper use of ridicule. Few bastions were proof against the ludicrous. In his youth Shetland had much enjoyed tales of magic, and had read (and therefore could recall eidetically) the complete works of Grimm, Lang, Andersen and Bulfinch as well as sundry more recent authors in the fantasy genre. He concentrated.

The outlines of the castle quivered. The color of the stone changed, turning brown.

Then he focused on the moat. It sparkled like soda water, and from it rose a grotesque head: a cartoon sea monster. The monster reared high, exhibiting delicately tinted underplates. It sniffed. It salivated. It took a bite of the castle. The stonework crumbled like gingerbread. This was hardly surprising, since now it *was* gingerbread.

Shetland sat on a cool grassy knoll, under the shade of a giant toadstool, and sipped a sundae that appeared in his hand. He frowned: his beverage contained chocolate ice cream. He abolished it and conjured a new one: vanilla. That didn't suit him either, so he let it vanish, closed his eyes and followed the demolition with nose and ears.

The monster slurped loudly as it consumed huge chunks of pungent wall and turret. But Somnanda was safe, for the monster had a giant sweet tooth and ate only gingerbread. It was strictly cake-ivorous.

"Captain." It was Somnanda, of course.

Shetland stretched lazily. "What is it, friend?"

"There appears to be a structural flaw in my residence."

"Oh, is there? I hadn't noticed." Shetland yawned. "That certainly is unfortunate." He leaned back against the stem of the toadstool and closed his eyes.

"Perhaps the flaw was in my philosophy . . ."

"No, I suspect the flour wasn't fresh."

"At any rate," Somnanda said with what gravity he could muster, "I believe you have made your point. Would you mind surveying the situation?"

"Tomorrow," Shetland said, hunching down more comfortably. But he could not resist peeking.

The castle had dissolved into a stinking mountain of gingerbread debris. Chunks had fallen into the moat and absorbed soda water, conducting the moisture up through the whole with much fizzle. The sea monster, satiated, had formed a nest in the dough and foam and was now peacefully snoozing. Only Somnanda's bed remained dry; he had conjured pontoon supports for it so as to cause it to rise partially out of the mess.

"Your point being," Somnanda continued gravely, "that if we do not actively attack our problems now, they may soon become rather more sticky. There is no place for sloth in the current scheme."

"You were never truly slothful," Shetland said. "This was merely a gross exaggeration of a trait that has both positive and negative aspects. Man's constant desire to accomplish his aims with the least effort has contributed greatly to his enormous progress. Perhaps your facility with the beacon is an example."

"You are kind," Somnanda said, stepping off the bed as the mess bubbled down into the ground and disappeared. "Your move, Captain."

Chapter 11:___Neutralizations

"**W**e must reunify the ship," Shetland said. "It was my mistake ever to let it get out of hand; now I must redeem my lapse in leadership and bring us all out of whatever heavens or hells the ghost has fashioned for us. As always, I need your advice."

"You are kind," Somnanda repeated. He now held the candle/beacon in his hand, and it glowed without wax. "This is surely a virtue in you. We two represent Captain and beacon; I suspect the minimum would next include the pilot. But—"

"Why the hesitation?" Shetland inquired innocently, though he knew why. That two-dimensional Johns-apparition! "The advice seems good."

"I fear that Pilot Johns would be difficult to reach." Accurate estimate, that! "And at one time you found it necessary to render him unconscious. This time the task might prove hazardous."

Because shallow people were most dangerous when given power, and the ghost represented absolute power of a kind. Yes. "This concurs with my own estimate. The obvious answer is not always the appropriate one."

Shetland glanced about. His giant toadstool had faded away also; they now stood on the large squares of the chessboard. "Let's not repeat our mistake, then," he said. "We'll approach Beeton first."

"Even there—the man is volatile."

Shetland reconsidered. He felt almost certain that this entire predicament was due to Beeton's tacit collaboration. The cartographer could have warned them, but had chosen not to, even though it meant his own demise as well. Why should he help now? "Yes. Bracing him without proper preparation or comprehension could be disastrous. But suppose we recover Alice first, then Beeton?" Too late he saw the conflict there; there was no physical Alice to recover. In fact, Beeton might in some fashion have engineered her original death, perhaps by telling her something that caused her to see the mission in a devastatingly altered perspective. That seemed unlikely— but no more so than her actual manner of death. How would her fiancé react to a physically animated ghost-Alice?

"That was my thought, Captain."

Now Somnanda had agreed. Should he confide the truth of his suspicions? Or play it through, knowing he had to tackle the difficult cases sooner or later? "And an excellent thought it was, Somnanda!" He paused, hoping the man would have some further qualification, but Somnanda merely waited. There was no choice but to proceed. If he failed, he would not be unduly upset; in fact, he was prepared to be quite philosophical.

"Alice!" he called.

There was no response. Was that significant?

"I doubt calling will be effective," Somnanda said. "I barely heard you when you called me, and I am specially tuned for communication. It was easier to answer than to ignore. But the others—"

"Perhaps we can locate them more specifically," Shetland said, glad for the reprieve. "You were on the Rook's square; do you suppose the others have equivalent residences?"

"They do if you say so," Somnanda said with a slow smile.

"Oh? Why?"

"Because you are Captain. Your will dominates. That is why you were able to convert my Castle. You are accustomed to having your way, and the others are accustomed to giving way when any significant issue develops."

Even when their judgment was superior to his, Shetland thought. But he had to agree. "Yes, I am King, rightly or wrongly. My power is far less absolute than you seem to credit, but I may be able to invoke it in this situation."

"Still," Somnanda said, and Shetland recognized the signal of solid advice following the pep-talk, "this is a unique framework, and contact may be more effective if we indulge the natural lines of flow."

"What is natural about being enmeshed in a galactic ghost?"

"The ghost animates our visions, allowing feedback to make them overwhelming—as with me and my slothful nature. If the others—"

"Ah, at last I see! The Seven Deadly Sins—incarnate!"

"That is my fear."

"You are right again, Nanda! We must work out a complete framework—sins, residences, anything—then study how to shape these to our needs. I can, as you say, control things to a certain extent, but I can't change fundamental characteristics of human nature."

"At any rate, it would not seem economical to combat them directly," Somnanda agreed. "Sloth is passive; others may not be."

"I am Envy—and make no mistake, I do envy you your comprehension! I am also, it seems, King. You are Sloth—and Rook. But what are the others, or how may we define them for our convenience and management? Specifically, Alice—assuming she can be recovered."

"Covetousness."

"Your memory is better than mine, Nanda!"

Somnanda seldom laughed, but he indulged himself now. They both knew that no person's memory excelled Shetland's eidetic ability. It was not Somnanda's memory that was superior, but his psionic ability. "A good memory is the lazy way, so that would be in character."

"Covetousness," Shetland said. "As she and I agreed, one envies what another *is* but covets what another *has*. In a chess piece, that should translate to the urge for power, for there are no individual possessions in the game. She should be a Queen—the greatest potential on the board, yet always subservient to the King."

"Her residence would then be a palace," Somnanda said. "Or a boudoir. Sexual power—"

"I wonder whether it is wise to become involved with that, at this stage," Shetland said, once again thinking of the Johns involvement. "We cannot anticipate what might develop."

"She is not unattractive."

"Precisely. She is as fetching a young woman as I can imagine. Should I brace her in the realm of power—sexual power—there could be consequences."

"Space-time code," Somnanda reminded him.

"Not necessarily. We are no longer functioning precisely

as a space crew. We appear to have lost our ship, for one thing. In our present context, young Beeton could feel proprietary rights, and he already represents—"

"Anger. Yes, that could be awkward."

"Because he is our trouble spot. At best, he will be difficult; at worst—"

"Yes. Though there may be some involvement with Sosthenna now. Should Lust go after the Queen before you do—"

Well, he had looked for some alternative! "Yes. Anger would be furious," he finished. "I am forced to concur. I shall summon the Queen."

"It might be better to approach her quietly," Somnanda said. "The less fuss made before—"

"Right again! I shall proceed to Black Queen One."

Once again Somnanda had a reservation. "How can you be certain she is the Black Queen, not the White Queen?"

"Because this is the way the King arranged the chessboard." Shetland began walking, or rather hopping, covering one square at a time. Somnanda, fortunately, stayed behind. Now he could deal with ghost-Alice in privacy.

Each hop was seven leagues. The scenery changed dramatically. He passed Knight's square, where a tournament appeared to be in progress, and the Bishop's square, fortunately unoccupied. He didn't need any complications along the way!

The fourth hop brought him to the Black Queen's square. It was, indeed, a boudoir. There were costly tapestries hanging on the walls, and a tremendous ornate bed in the center. Servants hurried to and from that canopied couch, carrying loaded trays.

Shetland halted outside the tentlike structure. "Ahem!" he said.

"Oh, Captain!" the Queen's voice came. "*Do* come in, why don't you!"

It was not Alice. It was Tibet.

The curtain was flung aside by a stout arm. Tibet lay within, her upper section propped by great fluffy pillows. All about her were platters of food, every type of delicacy. She was stowing food away at an inordinate rate, consuming a roast in great messy bites even as she spoke to him, and it disappeared in cartoon fashion a gulp at a time. In twenty seconds she shoved the exhausted platter aside and reached for another. The hands of a servant snatched the empty dish and bore it off in the direction of the royal kitchen for refueling.

"Gluttony," Shetland said.

"You better believe it!" Tibet said around mouthfuls. This time a tremendous plum pudding was being rammed into her oral orifice, sweet hard-sauce flaking off against her moving lips. "For the first time in my life—mmph, mmph—I'm on the way to getting a bellyful!"

He had looked for covetousness and discovered gluttony. Neither he nor Somnanda completely understood the female psyche! But now that he was here, he ought to get Tibet out of it. Her body was grossly fat already; her two arms were like wrestlers' thighs, her neck had disappeared in the folds marking continuous chins, and her belly was so big it shoved her monstrous meaty breasts up against the creases of her neck. He had never before seen such phenomenal obesity, and the sight revolted him.

That gave him an idea. When she had become nauseous while eating ice cream, she had been turned off the ice cream. If he could make her sick . . .

Tibet was now gobbling down a vegetable dish, cramming radishes, carrots and even whole potatoes into her mouth. She hardly seemed to chew before the mass of nourishment slid down her throat, clearing the pipe for the next rush shipment.

Shetland conjured a servant bearing a gallon pitcher of liquid and a tiny glass. "You must be thirsty," he remarked.

"Thirsty?" Tibet repeated, pausing just a moment to consider the matter. "I'm dehydrated!" She snatched the pitcher, ignoring the glass. "Orance juice! Just what I need!"

"Small doses are best," Shetland cautioned.

But she was already guzzling from the spout of the pitcher. Shetland watched the fluid level drop: three-quarters, half, one-quarter . . . empty! He was appalled.

"Funny taste," she commented. "Not a vintage year. Well, on to the main course." She hauled a tremendous platter onto her ballooning belly: a complete roast pig with garnishes.

"Tibet, you can't go on this way!" Shetland said. "You aren't a literal glutton—"

"Sure I am!" she said. "Always wanted to be, never had the chance before. Captain, I love this! I love being Queen, so I can indulge myself thoroughly. I even have a potty built into the bed, so I don't have to—"

"Please!"

"Captain, don't tell me"—she paused to devour a massive section of the roast—"that you're squeamish about vocabulary! A glutton has to defecate, you know. It's a vital function. In fact it can be a greater pleasure to—"

She paused, the pig three quarters gone. "Oh-oh!"

"I was trying to warn you—" Shetland said.

"What did you put in that orange juice?" she demanded, putting one hand to her tremendous bosom. "Poison?"

"Of course not! I just had to stop you—"

"Then why, all of a sudden, do I feel this way?"

"I didn't think you'd drink the whole thing, Tibet! The small glass was intended for—"

"Forget the glass! What—?"

"Ipecac—half a pound dissolved in the pitcher."

"That's an emetic! Half an ounce is enough to—"

Shetland shrugged. "I tried to caution you."

"You'll be sorry!" she cried. "But not a tenth as sorry as *I*—" She vomited.

It was spectacular. Her stomach did not empty in the inverse order it had filled. The first heave brought out puffy white masses that could be partially masticulated potatoes. The second heave was mainly plum pudding. The third consisted of torn hunks of roast pig. The fourth was yellow liquid: some of the orange juice. The fifth was a bumpy purplish mass that might once have been blueberry pie; it now suggested bleeding hemorrhoids. The sixth was the great red claw of a lobster: evidently she had eaten the crustacean shell and all. The seventh was an ocean of elbow macaroni.

Shetland lost track after that. The bed was covered with vomit, but still it spewed, submerging the uneaten dishes and driving back the horrified servitors. Chocolate pudding—sheep's entrails—corn on the cob (complete with cobs)—fish bones— foaming beer—chunks of buttered rye bread—half a dozen baked apples, one with a baked worm—several rare steaks— pounds of peanuts—brown cola drinks, still fizzling faintly— waffles with thick syrup—pork and beans—gelatin dessert, quivering like jellyfish—several gallons of chocolate ice cream—

Shetland stepped back, startled at the latest revelation, but the heaving stream did not stop. The puke overflowed the bed and dripped lumpily onto the floor. In fact its progress seemed to accelerate as Tibet's stomach muscles found proper purchase. A foul-smelling mass of stuff spread over the tiles, piling high around the bed. The room was being buried in vomit!

Shetland conjured a small barricade and stood behind it as the nauseous semi-liquid accumulated. He could not depart the scene of the crime, because his mission was the recovery of Tibet along with the other members of his crew. If he didn't drown in vomit first!

Next time he took stock, the substance was about thirty inches deep, across the entire boudoir. The bed itself had disappeared under the sickly sea. But the awful sounds of Tibet's retching had stopped.

"There is no pleasure in overindulgence," Shetland called. "Come, be as you were! We have need of you."

"The end justifies the means!" she cried in an accusatory tone. True in this instance, though that was not a precept he normally lived by. He had simply had to use what was available. When Tibet got physically sick of something, she got emotionally sick of it too, as her chocolate ice cream story had shown. This experience might well have cured her of gluttony!

Her ire abated. Her voice became hesitant. "How could you possibly respect me—after this?"

"Respect you? I *envy* you! But we none of us are free!"

"Envy!" she cried, laughing weakly. "From anyone else that would be a cruel joke."

"It *is* a cruel joke!"

The vomitous ocean subsided as if drawn into a huge sewer. The boudoir dissolved into vapor. Tibet stood there, herself again: heavyset but not obese. "Yes, it is, Captain. I'm sorry. Let's go home."

"Now we are three," Somnanda said. There was a faint glow from one breast pocket, where he had tucked the beacon light. "But Alice must still be neutralized."

Shetland sighed internally. He had, in good conscience, practiced to deceive—but here the end no longer justified the means, if that had ever been the case. Somnanda knew about Alice; now he should find a way to convey the truth to Tibet.

"She's covetous, isn't she?" Tibet asked. "Do you think she would be another Queen?" But she answered herself immediately. "Of course she wouldn't! A Queen *has* everything, and hardly needs to covet. It's the peasant girl who truly covets."

"A Pawn!" Shetland exclaimed. "Why didn't I see that before!"

"Because men are basically obtuse about human nature, especially human weakness," Tibet said, smiling. "Bless that obtusity!"

The men exchanged glances. "What approach would you recommend?" Somnanda asked her.

"Oh, I wouldn't presume!" Tibet said quickly. "The sexual gap is as nothing to the generation gap!"

"Generation gap?" Somnanda asked.

"I'm twice her age. Hadn't you noticed?"

"You are younger than I am," Shetland said.

"That's what I like about you, Captain," she said. "But men are ageless. It isn't the same. And between Alice and me—"

Shetland saw his opening and took it without pausing to reconsider. "The gap is no greater than that between any mother and daughter."

Somnanda's head turned to him. One brow lifted.

"Oh, no, I'm unmarried!" Tibet protested.

"Yes. That was why you had to leave her in a strange house—and suffer ever since."

"Oh, God!" she whispered. "Is that what you believe? I

never—my baby was a ghost, Captain! I never—never would have—I thought you understood . . .''

"She remains a ghost," he said.

A light brightened before Somnanda. It was the beacon, now held in his hand.

"I will fetch her now," Shetland said quickly. He could not follow through as he had intended; the beacon would not permit it. "I *do* understand and I'm sorry to have upset you." And he was sorry, and not just because of the beacon. Tibet, for all her failings, was a warm, pleasant, human person, one whose friendship he valued.

He oriented on the Pawn's square, hoping the beacon would subside in his absence—and remembered that there were sixteen Pawns in a game of chess. Which one was Alice? Ghost or not, he had to settle with her now.

Queen's Pawn, he decided. Black. He was the White King in the field of Black, the inversion of his role in life.

One move took him there. Alice was in a field, leaning over a hoe. The harsh sun beat down on her, and predatory flies circled. She was not a ghost; this was a direct, physical Alice, exactly as she had appeared in life. And how could that be?

Then he cursed himself for a fool. If the ghost-substance could form mock people for its other displays, why couldn't it form a mock Alice? Just as it had formed her mock ghost for the ship. He had pondered this matter before, but postponed experimentation; now that experiment was upon them. There was no longer any need to conceal her absence; he could produce Alice herself! And only he—and she—and Somnanda—and perhaps Tibet—would know the truth.

And the ghost galaxy? What would *it* know? What would it tell?

So Alice was indeed the most menial of pieces, a Pawn. No sex queen. But like a Pawn, she had extraordinary potential, if she could only be guided to achieve it.

All the surrounding fields were greener. Shetland couldn't tell the nature of the crop—cotton, corn, cabbages?—he was no agronomist! Tobacco, perhaps. But this peasant certainly had plenty to covet. No doubt she was the daughter of a poverty-stricken serf, or even a slave. Left in a deserted house when eighteen months old? She had nothing of her own, therefore everything to covet.

How to snap her out of it? There was no castle to disintegrate, no banquet to emetize. How could he turn her vision sour—when sourness was its point?

He couldn't. Except by depriving her of the one thing of value she might retain: her self-respect. Yet wasn't it a lack of self-respect that was her problem? Somnanda and Tibet were basically sure of themselves; the shock of failure in a particular endeavor could be accommodated and put into perspective. With difficulty, even discomfort, at times—but it could be done. Alice was a special case; she had no physical foundation. If he impugned her reason for being, she might vanish entirely, becoming nonexistent.

Why had she committed suicide? Why wouldn't she confess her motive? She seemed to have nothing left to lose! Shetland still could not make sense of this, so lacked even that lever upon her.

He would have to try the gentle approach.

He clothed himself in a kindly beard and an archaic suit. "Let me take you away from all this, my dear," he said.

She looked at him dully. "I cannot leave my work. Massa would beat me."

Was *that* the level she wanted to play it? So be it! "Be at ease on that score," Shetland said. "Your master knows I am here. Indeed, I am a prospective purchaser."

This did not seem to reassure her, so he qualified it. "I am looking for a responsible worker to supervise my own plantation. The work will be light."

A flicker of interest showed. The fish was nibbling.

"In fact, it will be a good situation for the right person," Shetland continued, warming to his sales pitch. "Eight-hour days, weekends off, good food . . ."

Now he had her attention. "Lotion to keep the bugs off?" she asked hesitantly.

"Right here." He handed her a pressurized can. The stinging flies, mosquitoes and body lice departed in an irritated swarm as she used it, dabbing it on like precious perfume. "I take good care of my personnel."

For a moment she seemed very little-girlish, eager yet afraid. He smiled benignly at her. "Speak, child," he said in a fatherly tone.

"And a new dress?" she asked with slightly greater confidence.

"Indeed." He conjured a store rack loaded with assorted dresses. He didn't know how to calibrate size, but was sure her imagination would make them fit. She was made of imagination to begin with! "Take your pick."

She gazed on them with wide-eyed wonder. "They're all so beautiful . . ."

"They're all yours, then!" he said generously, feeling even more like an affluent guardian.

"But I have no shoes!"

"Nonsense!" He held out a small trunk of ladies' footwear ranging from riding boots to glass slippers, together with assorted hosiery.

He expected her to be delighted. She was not. Token

gratification of her covetousness only primed her appetite Well, that would do.

"These will be ruined, working in the fields!" she complained.

"My dear, you are not to be a field worker!" he cried with simulated horror. "Your talents are required inside."

"But I'm *not* inside! I'm out here in the hot sun—"

Shetland conjured a small house in front of them. It had a New England peaked roof, pretty shutters and a red brick chimney. Instant creation was fun!

"That's rather small . . ." she said.

He replaced it with a modern one-level house complete with Florida-room and garage. Its neat green lawn was bordered by a small hedge.

"Still . . ." she murmured.

He converted it into an elegant southern mansion girt with columns. She stepped inside and looked about. He noticed that she was now wearing one of the new dresses he had provided, though he had not seen her change; she must simply have rematerialized it on herself. "Not much furniture . . ."

He filled the mansion with furniture, hoping his taste was proper. This really was not his area of expertise.

"Now it's crowded . . ."

He kept the furniture but replaced the mansion with a palace. "But how will I ever keep it clean?" she cried with maidenly distress.

He produced a small army of servants, growing up from the ground as though sprouting from dragons' teeth. "Yours to direct!"

"But none of this is *mine*!" she wailed. "I have to maintain it for some gluttonous Queen—"

The Pawn coveting the status of the Queen! In life that

would be ludicrous, but in chess a Pawn in the right position could actually achieve that desire. Many games were won and lost through just such a conversion—and this one, too, with proper management. "The Queen already abdicated," Shetland explained. "She ate too much and had an attack of indigestion."

"Somebody spiked her orange juice," Alice said, half smiling. Evidently she had been peeking into other squares. In retrospect, it was worth a smile; "indigestion" was a gross understatement, considering that roomful of vomit!

"At any rate, she has sworn off Queenery. You can take her place, if that is not too heavy a burden."

She did not seem to regard it as too heavy a burden. But she had another objection: "I'm not royal born!"

Good point. It was necessary to keep alert when fencing with personal visions; it was hard to outmaneuver a person in his own setting. *Her* own setting. "You can marry the prince," Shetland said, discovering an out. He cocked his ear and the sound of fanfare came, heralding a royal arrival. A storybook prince . . .

Alice looked stricken, and Shetland realized that he had blundered after all. She was engaged to marry Beeton! It did not matter that in her absence, or partial absence, Beeton had shown an increasing inclination toward Sosthenna. That was a temporary liaison, quite in order according to the code of the ship. But the present situation with the ghost, both kinds of ghost, differed from anything anticipated by the manual of space. In any event Alice would hardly be prepared to *marry* another man, even a symbolic prince fashioned from ghost-substance.

Yet perhaps this call of his had been satisfactory, for it set a price on her covetousness that might make it ultimately unappealing. Did she really want worldly possessions, or did she want to marry her fiancé?

In fact, that conflict just might suffice to throw her entirely out of this framework, and she would rejoin the *Meg*'s crew—no longer a ghost, but a temporary person!

Temporary—for once they left the magic ambience of the ghost galaxy, that figure of Alice would fade like the wraith it was. Cruel.

Or would it fade?

"Captain," Somnanda's voice said in his ear.

"Not now! I'm busy," Shetland muttered. The beacon might be fluttering, but this was to be expected. He was handling a difficult case, and didn't want to lose Alice again. One suicide sufficed!

The clatter of horse's hooves sounded in the courtyard, very like—Beeton's simile was apt—castanets. Did horses emulate the hard heels of young women? Which came first: the horseshoe or the high heel?

He had no proof that ghost-substance was unstable when removed from the parent ghost. Their little sample had performed well enough without regard to distance. Why couldn't Alice remain as she was now, a seemingly perfect replica of the mind and body of the original?

Several reasons, perhaps. For one thing, they might not have removed the plasm from the ghost; if they had never actually passed the event horizon, and remained trapped within the ambience of the ghost galaxy, then they had not tested that aspect at all. And if by means of travel in time they escaped the ghost, its bit of captive substance might well fade out as they reached the time prior to its formation, avoiding paradox. Of course they were from another universe, which might not honor a paradox relating to this one, so—

The sound of hooves stopped. Then came the sound of

footsteps of a well-shod young man: quick, solid, with the rustle of princely garb. Alice's eyes watched the doorway, and Shetland watched too. This was the key moment: would she choose to promote the Pawn into a Queen for the sake of gratifying her desire for worldly goods and power—or would she snap out of it and return to her fiancé?

Would either choice make any difference—to the mock creature who might have taken Alice's place? Stable it might be, or perhaps it would have a half-life of thousands of years, gradually decaying into amorphousness. But Alice herself was dead. He could not afford to forget that. Tibet's nightmare had anticipated this too well: how could anyone know the person from the replica?

"Captain," Somnanda repeated urgently.

"For God's sake, Somnanda! This is a crisis point! Wait another minute!"

Somnanda's presence departed. The palace door pushed open and a handsome man marched in.

Alice gave a glad cry. Shetland clapped his hand to his forehead. Why hadn't he anticipated this!

The prince was no stranger. It was Beeton.

Now Alice, real or mock, could have it all: riches, power, royalty *and* Beeton! She would not be jolted out of the system. The ploy had backfired.

Somnanda had tried to warn him.

Shetland reacted immediately, trying to salvage the situation by emergency action. As he concentrated, Beeton's princely robe became a vestment of another nature: the strict dress of religion. The crown was now the divided headdress of a bishop.

Beeton, about to embrace Alice, paused. Gladness was replaced by shock. He was now a clergyman of a religious denomination prohibiting marriage of its clergy.

Shetland, too, paused. He had changed the costume—but would that change the fact? He could put Beeton in robes, but how could that touch the man's mind? Beeton was no malleable ghost! Had he merely compounded his blunder?

Beeton—Bishop Beeton!—pointed a sternly shaking finger at Alice, who was now garbed in an expensive dress showing cleavage. "Woman, what devil's mischief are you about?" he demanded resonantly.

Alice's eyes widened. "Wayne—I don't understand!"

"Do you seek to acquire worldly riches at the peril of your immortal soul?"

Shetland winced. This was no true bishop talking, not even a chess Bishop. This was the crude rote dialogue of one who knew nothing of religion other than what he had picked up in stories and gossip. That explained part of it; Beeton's personality had not been changed to that of a true priest. But why was he constrained to play the part at all? Was his attitude toward Alice now so casual that he could denounce her as readily as he might have kissed her?

Alice, abashed, could not answer. She might be real or ghost, but Shetland found it easier to understand her reactions than Beeton's.

"Do you consort with strange men, profaning your pure body in the damnable sins of—"

"Wayne!" she cried. "This is space!"

That question, again. Was it, indeed, space? Or time? Or merely oblivion in the crushing tide of the ghost?

"God's power extends through all the universe!" Beeton thundered. "All space and time!"

Shetland was not certain what he had wrought. Such small changes of uniform, seemingly, from the secular to the clerical—but such an imponderable alteration of motive! "Beeton, if you would just listen—" he began.

The Bishop whirled on him, the Wrath of God incarnate. "Would you tempt this poor child into damnation? May the righteous fury of the Lord fall upon your abysmal head!"

Suddenly there was an awful invisible weight pressing Shetland down, crushing his internal organs as well as his exterior body: the gravity of the Lord. How could any mere man oppose that?

"Wayne!" Alice repeated.

Bishop Beeton turned on her again, and the load on Shetland lightened. He breathed shudderingly. Where had that eerie power come from? The galactic ghost, of course—but this was more than mere creation of physical artifacts! Fortunately the pressure continued to ease; even God's newly fashioned representative could not concentrate on more than one villain at a time! But the implications—

"Strumpet!" Beeton cried. "Get down on your knees and beg the Lord's forgiveness for your iniquities of the flesh!"

"But all I wanted—" she cried.

"DOWN!"

Then Shetland understood: this was another manifestation of Beeton's rage at his fiancée's liaison with Johns. That outrage must have festered during this entire voyage, and even the man's act of omission that had allowed them all to be trapped within the ghost galaxy could not satisfy it entirely. Alice, herself, directly, had to be punished, to be made to plead for absolution from her sin.

But Alice had more spunk than that. "What about you and Thenna?" she demanded, for the moment casting off her Pawn's role. "Only a hypocrite could blame—"

"Silence, woman!" Beeton roared, stabbing his finger toward her as though it were a weapon.

And a mantle of fire played about her body, consuming her finery.

Alice screamed and tore at her clothing, trying to free herself from the holy flame. But it clung to her like napalm, burning her even as her full, sleek feminine torso was exposed. The Lord had no mercy!

Shetland struggled to abate this disaster, but his mind was too slow. It was hypocrisy, of course; Beeton had blamed her falsely, and silenced the truth with flame. But Beeton now commanded powers of the ghost-energy that Shetland could neither match nor negate. He had only one recourse: to summon help.

Two crewmembers remained unaccounted for; if one of them could distract—

Before he could fully formulate the need, a Black Knight rode into the room, horse and all. His long lance was lowered as he charged at Beeton.

The lance missed, but the horse knocked Beeton down. The fire about Alice winked out at that moment, and she stood there naked.

She sighed with relief. "Oh, thank—"

The Knight paused to raise his visor, and his roving eye fell on her. "Oho!" he cried with delight.

It was Johns, whose salient trait was Lust.

Sir Johns slid off his steed and advanced on Alice. "I'll take care of *you,* lass!" Behind him the horse, forgotten, wavered into fog and dissipated.

Alice had pleaded the code of space to Beeton, and had indulged herself with Johns before. But now she shrank away. She tried to conjure another dress to cover her splendid attributes, but the best she could muster under stress was a translucent negligee. That was worse than nothing, for it offered only the semblance of concealment, making her body more tantalizing than before.

Johns snorted like a caprine buck, eying her. Horns sprouted from his helmet, and his legs beneath the armor were goat-like. In fact he was a satyr in all important respects.

Shetland's brain was pushing through the molasseslike mess of the script he had so blunderingly evolved. Everything he essayed was going wrong!

Alice's negligee puffed into mist as Johns focused on it. Johns' own armor followed suit. He strode forward.

What else was there to do now, except to summon the last of the crew? Things could not get any worse!

"Thenna—Pride!" he whispered.

There was the noise of another galloping approach. This chess framework was determinedly medieval!

The sound halted the satyr Knight for a moment, and Bishop Beeton's Wrath of God gesture hesitated unfulfilled.

Alice used the respite to wrap herself in a voluminous Turkish towel. That was another poor choice, for it compressed the cleavage of her breasts and barely covered her thighs, directing attention to the covered parts.

Another Knight marched in: a shining White Knight.

It was, indeed, Sosthenna. Shetland had hardly expected this garb, but had to admit she was elegant. Every part of the armor was polished to a glassy luster, and the entire uniform fitted tidily. Rays of sunlight reflected from her as she moved, though there was no visible sun inside the palace.

"Whatever is going on here?" Pride demanded.

"Pleasure."

"The Wrath of God."

"Chaos."

Spoken by Johns, Beeton and Shetland respectively, simultaneously.

Then the Black Knight resumed his stalking of the covetous girl, causing her towel to unwind seductively. The Bishop aimed his finger in holy anger, thunder sounding above his head. Shetland ran to break that up, somehow—and saw Sloth's bed in one corner and Gluttony's feast in another. The crew was backsliding!

"Have you no pride?" the White Knight cried. "Look upon me, ye slovenly, and despair!"

Alice screamed as Johns reached her.

Shetland, dismayed at his loss of control and appalled at what harm this scene could lead to, tried desperately to break it up. But it would not break. His will and his vision had been stronger than those of any of the others individually, but he could not prevail against them all at once. Tibet was gobbling steaks; Sosthenna was declaiming conceitedly; Somnanda was asleep, his candle guttering low. Meanwhile Johns had Alice down on the floor while the electric sparks fired from Beeton's finger bathed them both. What could Shetland do?

They all had their characteristic escapes, while he was left with the responsibility for the mission and their lives. He envied them . . .

Envy? That was *his* sin! How could he hope to solve their problems before solving his own? He had not really been motivated for their benefit; he had acted to interfere with their separate contentments! He was a negative influence, and of course that led to destruction, not unity!

Know thyself! he thought. Now he knew where to start.

But first he had to clean up this mess, so that he could start again, properly. He concentrated.

The palace floor became soft, then marshy. Naked Alice screamed again as she sank into the muck, and Johns was thrown off as his hooves lost support. Tibet's servants became mired and unable to feed her, and Somnanda's bed disappeared slowly under the surface. Beeton's Godlike feet were covered with sticky clay. Sosthenna's pride was humbled as she stumbled and got thoroughly soiled.

Then a herd of large animals cruised through, their splayed feet operating in the muck as if it were their natural element. Their elongated snouts quivered to the scent of fresh plushweed, and their tusks rooted busily for the tubers.

Astrapotherium magnum: the creation that unified all the crew, because each person had fashioned his portion.

Someone laughed, shrilly, hysterically.

And all dissolved into proper chaos.

Chapter 12:_____Chaos

Chaos again—the consequence of failure. Not heaven, not hell, not even purgatory. Just a vague swirl, subject to the devastating tide. The almost total entropy resulting from the push-pull of seven different minds. The ghost would form anything anyone could imagine, whether mass, energy or emotion, just as a set of paints would form any scene when appropriately directed. The ghost might even, perhaps, fashion an escape from itself. But there had to be a unified will. There could be no true picture if all colors were dumped together to form an amorphous mass, and no escape if all wills were similarly mixed.

Shetland had tried to restore the old picture by working on one color at a time, and naturally it had fallen apart. Now he realized that all colors should be spread through all parts of the painting, with only their stresses varying. That technique would integrate it into a whole that would hang together regardless of stress. He was not assembling a picture puzzle whose links were two-dimensional; he was working with the multidimensionality of human beings.

They had worked together, creating *Astrapotherium magnum*. The creature had seemed ridiculous in its diverse conception, but when animated in its setting it had become reasonable, even noble. Perhaps it had been doomed to failure. But with more human interaction in the planning stage it should have been viable. Their committee method had been effective, coming so close on the first try. If only they could get together again, to tackle the problem of saving the human group from the ghost!

Astrapotherium—there was the visible linkage. The group had unified on that before—could it do so again? Was that the key he needed?

Suppose Poth, faced with the decline of his specific habitat, had been able to readapt, to adopt another habitat or to regeneralize? Where would he have gone, how would he have evolved?

There was no way to know, now. Shetland could only consider the example of another animal, one who did change and survive. An ape who, losing its forest, sought the water— the rivers and the lakes, perhaps even the shore of the sea. That creature had developed broad, flat feet for treading the bottom muck, but had not specialized so far as to significantly inhibit its ambulation on land. It had also left its heavy fur, and learned to swim, and to feed on fish. The creature had an advantage in hunting, for its body exuded sweat that evaporated and cooled him, so that it could operate more efficiently in the heat of the day. Flat-footed and hairless; an ugly specimen, looking like the rump of a baboon all over. *But it had survived.*

Had *Astrapotherium* left the swamp before becoming fully adapted in such things as the foot structure, he might have been able to return to forest or field successfully. It still would have been a marginal business, for a creature split between environments, imperfectly specialized for either, usually lost out to the more perfect specialists.

Specialization was an asset in a given habitat, but a liability when that framework changed. Most habitats—forest, field, swamp, lake—were constantly changing. The successful species was therefore likely to be an adaptive one, carrying the burden of many false starts and minor liabilities. To be imperfectly suited for any single habitat, but generally suited to survive the changing of habitats. To be able to use the protection of trees adequately, if not as well as the apes, and the cover of the water, if not as well as the marine mammals, and to be able to cover a lot of ground, persistently if not speedily. Second best in all things—and therefore best in long-term raw survival.

A species less like Poth and more like Man.

Know thyself. Fathom the basic nature of man, so that man might be accommodated to the habitat that was the ghost. And thereby, he prayed, survive it.

He concentrated. Chaos remained, but no longer the chaos of nothingness. Things were present now: a skyscraper building, a hairy ape, a seashore, a pile of dung, a tree, a bleeding carcass, a sword, a notebook bearing a picture of a shaggy pony, a book of poetry, the breast of a woman, a flowing sewer outlet.

Shetland surveyed this mélange, certain that it was significant, if only in the way that loose pieces of a puzzle were significant. These must be fragments of the visible product of the confused minds of six or seven human beings, manifested erratically by the substance of the ghost galaxy. Each one might be a single jigsaw piece taken from a complete personal picture, an image from the subconscious.

The subconscious!

The revelation was so fundamental that he had to back off to appraise it, to work it out more properly. The fragment images receded as his backing became more literal: he was zooming seat-first through the swirl at a running pace. No matter.

The ghost could manifest anything imagined by man, consciously or unconsciously. Obviously *Astrapotherium* could not have been animated had his living innards not been designed as well as his exterior, yet those had never been discussed. Creation was a rounded process, encompassing the implied as well as the expressed. The strength of the thought was what counted, and thought was a multileveled function. Surely the strongest needs of the human species were the unexpressed ones.

Animation of suppressed desires . . . physical representations of the secrets of the mind . . . involuntary exposure for all to see . . .

What a psychiatric tool!

He had lost control of his crew because the ghost changed the basic rules for human perception and interaction. The civilized restraints and hypocrisies were gone, and so civilized behavior itself was gone. But the ghost was no monster; it was a mindless entity, responding only to the minds intruding into its sphere. The nature of the seed determined the nature of the grown plant, whether beautiful or ugly, shallow or sophisticated. The fertility of the ghost environment actually offered a far superior comprehension of man by man. If the scattered signs could only be objectively assembled and appraised.

He had to comprehend the real nature of each of his crewmen, and himself. Not purely as individuals, but as aspects of a framework. That was the meaning of the sewer pipe he had seen among the flying fragments; it was from his own mind, a warning from the text on ecology he had read a decade ago.

He smiled. As a symbol of unity, a sewer pipe seemed farfetched. But it was surely so.

He centered on that, calling to mind the text, opening the book, turning the visible pages. He was accustomed to doing this eidetically, but now there was a physical text there, conforming exactly to his mental image. He reread the material, refreshing his thinking memory.

Man on Earth had fouled his environment relentlessly, pouring sewage into rivers and oceans, chemical smoke into the atmosphere and virulent poisons into the ground. The global habitat had been severely damaged before remedial measures had been taken. Why? Because the scientists of Earth had insisted on doing "pure" research: isolating any particular phenomenon in the laboratory, freeing it from contamination by the environment. That very environment many of these researchers were designed to analyze and preserve. Thus they had missed the large picture in favor of the small, the forest for the trees. They had not appreciated, until almost too late, the complexities of the interacting whole.

Shetland had tackled the crewmembers singly, forgetting their necessary interaction as a crew. He had thought he was succeeding—until they came together and exploded. He had blundered by engaging in "pure" research. But now he could profit from that hard lesson. In the manner of his kind.

He could see the pictures drawn from other people's minds. He could deal with their real beliefs and needs, instead of their superficial expressions. He could consider their complete ecologies. If only he had had that ability before Alice died!

Before Alice? Before Maureen!

He had the tool, but there was still a formidable task ahead. He still needed to neutralize the various elements, but not separately. He had to keep them in some unified setting, doing nothing for one that would alienate another.

First he needed a unifying framework: a situation that included all the wild imaginings of every person, from skyscraper to dung. The common denominator.

In mathematics the common denominator was found by multiplying the individual denominators together. $1/3 + 1/4 + 1/5 = 20/60 + 15/60 + 12/60 = 47/60$. Could the same computation be done with seven people?

Why not? But *how*?

Easy, here! "Let it be done!" he intoned, willing it so. The ghost itself would perform the complex multifaceted computation.

The swirling objects slowed and steadied. The skyscraper faded in the distance; the hairy ape drifted up and out of sight. The notebook dissolved into particles that drifted away. Soon there was only a coral landscape: bright-colored rocks, exotic plants and fish.

Fish? Christian symbol, or underwater?

Suddenly Shetland was desperate for air. He launched upward, swimming for the surface. No symbolism, just the ocean!

His head broke water and he saw land not far off. Now he realized that it was after all symbolic: the beach scene had expanded to encompass him in its ambience. And he knew why.

To find a framework that represented the farthest extremes of all the crew, the common denominator, the ghost calculator had had to go back to their common ancestor. To man's beginning, before the species separated into races. To the time when the hairy ape had lost his hair and become a man—by taking a swim at the beach.

Know thyself. For a time ape-man had supplemented his diet by catching clams and fish and crustaceans. Like the ancestors of the whales and dolphins before him he had roved the beaches, wading ever deeper, acclimatizing, until splashing and swimming became second nature. He could escape predators here, too, jumping into the water when big cats came, and out of it when sharks appeared.

Human females nursed their babies in the compromise safety of chest-deep water. Wet body fur only got in the way, so man shed it, developing instead a subcutaneous layer of fat. The well-rounded woman became sexually appealing; she was a better breeding risk. The babies became so well padded they were fat and bald. Grown males, foraging more widely, retained more hair, but carried less fat. The water was the mother; when a man died, his tribe anchored him with stones and dropped him into deep water, thus making an awkward gap in the fossil record. Few bones on land!

But shallow-water existence was too specialized. Shallows could become scarce, like swamps. If man did not want to emulate the fate of *Astrapotherium*, he had either to continue on into deep water, like the whales, or return to land. So he returned, but he retained his aquatic modifications, just in case. For a long time he hesitated to settle far from water. He remained, biologically, at the fringe: the beach. Indeed, the fascination of the seashore never left him; it was part of his species heritage.

Shetland stroked toward that beach. Deep water was no better place for him than for his ancestors! He had found the common denominator; now he needed to simplify the terms, watching for the divergencies that constituted the developing traits of the members of his crew.

He climbed onto land, shaking off droplets. He was hungry. Before him, a little inland, was an orchard, no doubt expanded from the puzzle fragment that showed the tree. A multitude of gnarly trees bearing large fruit.

Shetland smiled: megalocarpous!

Could ghost fruit be eaten? Surely it could, for Tibet had eaten monstrously in the prior sequence. Or had *seemed* to; probably only a fraction of the apparent food had actually gone down her throat. That substance could have been converted directly into her seeming obesity. When she had thrown up, that fat would have remanifested as vomit. An illusion—yet the food itself should have been as real as it seemed. One had to appreciate the limitations of the ghostly propensities, so as to judge where these were being augmented by human sleight-of-hand.

So he would eat, and hope it sustained him even after they left the demesnes of the ghost. For now he was certain they could leave, once he understood his own kind well enough to unify it for the proper effort. If they remained here too long, all of their bodies would become transformed into ghost-material, for a man was what he ate. Eerie thought!

He plucked a full ripe apple from a branch that bore a different fruit on each twig: orange, peach, grape, plum, banana, pomegranate, and on: no regard for type! Man the ape had been a fruit eater, attracted by pretty color and sweet taste, and neither his vision nor his taste had changed. Man's dream of paradise remained essentially primate: to have all his needs grow on trees, that he might simply pluck them down at leisure, never straining. Sloth . . .

He bit into the fruit. Yes, delicious!

But he hungered for more than this. As he cast about, the tree wilted, its fruit shriveling. A sudden intense drought had undone it; the great forest shrank into occasional oases, and now there was not enough fruit to sustain a lone man, let alone a tribe. His hunger intensified. In the distance he saw a hairy ape, better specialized for trees, surviving nicely.

Beyond the declining wood was an open plain, and in that plain were animals: antelope, deer, gemsbok, pronghorn—somesuch on the fleet hoof. Meat, there for the taking—if he could catch it.

He strode out—and the deer spooked and sprang away. Shetland looked down at his stout, slow legs with dismay: impossible to run down a healthy deer! Or anything else beyond the velocity of a turtle. No turtles here!

How did the predators do it? The deer seemed to be faster than anything else!

He watched, and saw a giant cat, a leopard, panther, lion, tiger, clawed and fanged and maybe tusked, like the one who had almost consumed Poth. It lay in wait, so still it seemed dead, and when a small deer wandered near, it sprang. A bleat, a struggle, a victory, a tragedy. The herd took flight again; the cat fed.

Shetland's mouth watered. Hot meat! Man still heated his food to blood temperature, emulating the first kill.

But could he succeed in bringing down a deer the way the cat did? He doubted it; he lacked the patience to lie in wait for many hours unmoving despite the burning sun and biting flies that his naked skin was vulnerable to. If he were able to hold out long enough, his legs would by then be too cramped to enable him to pounce when the time came. Even if he got his hands on a deer, he might lack the strength to bring it down. He had no tusklike teeth, no daggerlike claws; just soft bare unspecialized hands.

He was coming to know himself and his species. It was not a completely satisfying study.

He looked again. Now a pack of canines was after the

deer. Dogs, each a copy of his childhood pet, but not weak or sick. These were wild and free and strong and beautifully vicious: true predators. The dogs did not lurk, hide or spring; they simply ran. The deer bounded away, but the pack followed relentlessly. A cat would have given out in such a chase, unable to maintain the pace, but the canines were distance runners.

A lame deer slowed, losing ground, becoming separated from the herd. The dogs caught up to this one, leaping at its shoulders, slashing its skin open. Now the deer had to stand and fight. It was well equipped to do so. Its feet were like horn-tipped spears, its horns like rapiers. It was an old stag, alert and experienced; dogs had died on those prongs in the past.

But this time it was alone, with one weak leg, and this was a pack of six dogs. If the deer of the herd only acted together for defense, instead of allowing individuals to fight alone, the herd would be impregnable! But this was not the nature of deer. Perhaps it was just as well, for a deer society that preserved its weaker elements would soon degenerate into overall weakness. Its numbers would increase, to overgraze the pastures, and then all would suffer hunger.

Two dogs taunted the buck in front; two more snapped at the hind legs. The last two circled alertly, watching for openings. The deer could not guard against them all. It whipped its deadly horns about, to impale a dog biting at its haunch—and another dog launched at the momentarily exposed neck.

In a moment there was nothing but a snarling, thrashing mound. Then a carcass being torn apart. Hot flesh again!

But Shetland could not do that either. He, too, was alone, though his purpose was to reunify a group. This seemed to vindicate that program: in a pack there was strength.

Meanwhile, he had a problem. He might in the course of several days run down a deer, for men had demonstrated that long-range capacity before. But he was hungry *now*. Also, he was apt to lay himself open as prey for a lurking cat or roving dog pack.

How, then? What asset did he have that could contribute to his survival, making up for his physical inadequacy?

His hands? They were versatile, capable of grasping and manipulating many things. He could fashion and use tools— and weapons. A man with those became the equal of almost any animal on the plain. But that would not enable him to catch a running deer.

His brain? He was smarter than deer, smarter than cats, smarter than any other living creature except another human being. Could that superiority be used to fill his belly?

Shetland smiled. In his hand appeared a shovel. Not a metal one, for this was not the industrial age. A crude hand-crafted wood and bone item, bound with vine. But serviceable. He began to dig near a waterhole, excavating a deep pit with a few magically swift strokes.

A big cat spied him and crouched, ready to spring. Shetland turned, his shovel becoming a flint-tipped spear. He stood his ground, spear pointed toward the cat. The feline yawned and departed, not hungry anyway.

A pack of dogs winded him and charged, baying. Shetland braced against the trunk of a large tree that conveniently appeared, a pile of rocks before him. As the dogs approached he threw a stone, smashing the leader on the snout. The others circled, looking for an opening. There was none behind the broad trunk, and none before it, and the longer they hesitated the more often they got clipped by thrown stones. One yelped as he was blinded by a strike on the eye. They might have had him by charging in a mass, for he could not have killed more than two before the rest got him, but that was not their way. They were not smart enough to revise their strategy to suit the occasion.

Actually, if the pack lost one or two members each time it made a kill, that pack would soon be gone. So it was not stupidity but the strategy of longe-range survival that dictated the dogs' course.

After a time the pack leader decided that this foe was too strong to be taken, and the dogs departed. Shetland finished his pit and covered it over with branches and dirt.

Then he took a walk. At some distance from the trap he yielded to a call of nature, carefully burying it so that there would be no smell to spook the prey. That was another significant change in man: the ape did not bury his dung, for he cared no more than *Astrapotherium* who smelled him. The dog made only token burial, for he did not depend on stealth, normally. The cat buried meticulously. Man tended more and more to conceal his dung, thereby showing the direction of his changing mode of life. It was possible to judge the life-style of an animal by the pile of dung it left behind!

Deer were thirsty. They came to drink, avoiding the man-scent around the concealed pit. Shetland circled to the opposite side of the herd, then charged, screaming. The deer ran—over the pit. One broke through the artful covering and fell in. Shetland ran up with his spear; his meal was at hand.

He did not enjoy the killing, but hunger prompted him. Once it was done and the warm meat separated from the carcass he felt better. He conjured a fire and roasted a portion; the fire also helped keep other predators away.

Fire: there was another thing that fascinated man! The use of fire had had phenomenal survival value for the species, and it left its imprint on man's soul. He could watch it indefinitely, as if soaking up its life.

Shetland ate until his belly was swollen, for he did not know how long it would be before he ate again. As a fruit picker he had never gorged, but as a hunter he had to. Thus he became a glutton in the interest of survival. More so for the female of the species, who generally had to wait at home for the man to return with the kill; she had less control over her feeding, so had to rely to a greater extent on stored fat. Gluttony was no deadly sin, but rather another necessary tool. Up to a point.

More fragments of the puzzle were falling into place: the pile of dung, the tree and the bleeding carcass. All steps in man's ascent to the skyscraper.

A man appeared. His face was not familiar. He could be a camouflaged crewman, or a phantom. He could not be trusted—but also could not be assumed to be an enemy. This called for caution.

"Hello. What can I do for you?" Shetland inquired amicably. He should have realized that the odor of cooking meat would attract human company!

The man did not reply. He stared at Shetland.

The stare: a signal of aggression. Shetland bridled. He had just used his brain to outsmart several animals and get a good meal, and he resented a stranger moving in now to imply that the accomplishment was minor, or to abscond with the winnings. This was his territory!

Territory: many species protected a particular locale from intrusion by others of their kind, reserving a favored hunting area or residential site. Carnivores could not tolerate crowding; the quarry would soon be depleted. Man the primate had been hierarchically organized, ignoring territory; now that he was becoming a hunter he had to modify his responses. In fact he had assumed two sets of responses: he was governed by his most powerful or representative members while reserving private rights to his own domain.

Man was a dual creature, then. Part landbound, part waterbound. Part hierarchical, part territorial. Part forager, part predator. Part flight—and part fight.

This bold stranger threatened both Shetland's territory and his status. Shetland hefted his spear.

The other man sneered. His hand came up with a club. He could smash Shetland before the spear could be brought into play.

So it was like that! Shetland's spear wavered and became a sword. Another puzzle piece fell into place. His heart beat faster and his breath quickened. He had been tired and sated; now he was alert and strong—and angry. No deadly sin there, either: without anger he would have to consider the risks of his position and give way, allowing aggression to prosper. Anger was another and necessary tool for human well-being.

The stranger's club became a bow, one arrow nocked. The muscular arm drew back the string. Before the sword could strike, that arrow would be loosed.

Shetland's mouth went dry. Sweat appeared on his body. He felt the hairs rising on his limbs. His sword became a rifle.

The other's bow wavered into a blaster.

Suddenly Shetland's mouth was brimming with saliva. He felt an almost uncontrollable urge to urinate. His breath caught. He swayed, clinging to consciousness. He was outgunned!

Then he held a laser weapon, capable of holing the blaster together with the man's hand and body, instantly.

The intruder looked. He saw. He cowered. He dropped his weapon and bowed his head. He was beaten. He was making submission. Shetland had outbluffed him and was now the top man of this hierarchy. He had won without fighting: another important ability of the species.

"I was only fooling, Captain . . ." the man said. His voice was familiar: Johns.

A victory, but only superficially. He would let it be, for now. "Carry on, Johns." Before he had been part smart, winning individual battles, losing the campaign. Not this time!

It was the occasion for another burst of thinking. Something about this puzzle was askew. It didn't assemble properly.

This was a framework in which just about anything went. Tools and weapons and animals could be created from the ghost-substance at the behest of a thought. People could mask their features, facial and physical. Yet the overall vision was limited. Why?

Because it had been necessary to retreat to the crew's common denominator, certainly. But now he had interacted directly with Johns—the Johns he knew as the *Meg*'s pilot. Why had Johns joined Shetland's conception, instead of sticking to his own? Why had all the puzzle fragments, the symbols of other visions, emerged into Shetland's own framework? He had been exploring the basic nature of man, so that he could learn how to unify a crew of diverse men and women. But other people should have been doing other things. Something was amiss.

His was not the boldest or most powerful mind available here. But he did have strong motivation, and an excellent visual memory. Were those factors enough to give his own vision dominance? Could he, merely by overriding the scattered views of the others, draw them into his own vision?

Yes, it seemed he could, provided he understood them well enough. All he had to do was continue his interactions, encouraging the others to join him voluntarily rather than involuntarily, as he assembled the vast picture puzzle that was the crew. Now that he had found the key, it was easier than he had feared. So long as he made no serious mistake.

Johns had wandered off. Before Shetland stood a house: a third party's conception. Was someone trying to get his attention?

Shetland sheathed his laser and strode up to the door. It opened at his touch, admitting him to a small, warm vestibule. There was a hat rack, a coat rack and a laser rack, so he placed his accoutrements appropriately. He had not worn formal clothing a moment ago, but this was no doubt an effect of entering someone else's enclave within his framework. He would play the game; he would interact. He had to, in order to accommodate this person into his simplification. He proceeded to the inner door.

The presence within was feminine. She hovered, a swirl of perfumed vapor, awaiting his desire.

Who was she? The ghostly effect implied Alice, but that was uncertain in this compromise framework. Obviously she desired his approach, having made herself available. But Alice had died after contact with him before, and never told him why. Why should she seek him out now?

He concentrated. The mist contracted, becoming firmer as it condensed, like a nebula densifying into a star. Head, neck, shoulders, breasts—there was another fragment, the breast of a woman!—waist, hips, thighs, legs, feet . . . a slowly emerging sculpture. He could not be certain whose influence predominated: his or hers. His desire or her actuality. He merely wanted to strip away the camouflage concealing her identity, so that he could understand.

The forming figure rotated, as on a pedestal. The thrust of bosom and buttock manifested, and the fall of hair. A full figure, slender of neck and waist and ankle, generous of mammary and gluteus maximus. Well proportioned, statuesque. Taller than Alice, more slender than Tibet, darker than Sosthenna. Who? The face remained inchoate.

Now he concentrated on that face. It formed, but not recognizably. He willed it to be what it would be, rather than what he might anticipate, because he wanted to know the truth. A woman was trying to interact with him, but she would not express herself. Veiled by the ghost, she wanted him to guess. Distaff mystique!

He refused to guess at her identity. A mistake would be too costly. Better to have her anonymous than scorned via miscue, considering the phenomenal forces in play. So the face remained nebulous: the features were there, but not the personality. She was Woman, unknowable.

And desirable. Her nudity and her attitude constituted a flattering invitation. There was no doubt in his mind that the present objective was sexual, and he felt himself responding. That was one form of interaction that might betray her identity.

He reached forth and took her by the hand. It was cool and firm. He kissed it, proceeding to her wrist, forearm, upper arm, shoulder, neck and finally her waiting lips. The species of man had developed large lips, their mucous membrane permanently everted, the surface richly nerved. Kissing lips. Couple two pairs of these, and experience the powerful feedback that prepared the two bodies for action.

He put his arms about her, but she turned within that circle and faced away, insisting that he name her. But he could not, yet. He knew without being told verbally that behind this façade was a woman who wanted him, who perhaps loved him, but who would not tell him so unless first assured of his own love.

Alice? He had hardly known her sufficiently, and still had

not fathomed her suicide. Tibet? Pleasant companion, old shoe, but hardly a mistress. Sosthenna? Her, surely—yet she had reserved her private self from him, increasingly.

He stalled. There was a bed beyond her, its sheets turned back for ready occupancy. He placed her on it, face up, arms and legs spread slightly. Whatever clothing he wore dissolved away. He joined her, running his hands over the lush curves of her torso. Sosthenna? This body was most typical of her, and it all felt genuine, but he knew that much of it had to be ghost flesh, transmitting no tactile sensation to the owner. He tried to tell by feel which flesh was human throughout, so as to get a notion of the true shape and identity of the body, but the ghost mask was too good. If it were Sosthenna, so little padding would be needed that it would hardly make a difference. If Alice, *all* of it was ghost, so there would be no demarcation.

Alice—why, *why* had she killed herself? He would gladly have done this with her when she lived, had he known she wanted it. Did it make sense for her to do in death what she had not chosen to do in life?

She stirred, and he realized that his explorations had become somewhat clinical. Hastily he corrected this, and found it no chore. These breasts were marvels of ponderosity, twin hemispheres centered by pigmented aureolas and tumescent nipples. The purist would have it that the breasts of the human woman were exclusively milkers, but Shetland was sure that they, like most of the parts of the body, had dual purpose. They were esthetic beacons for the gaze and touch of the male of the species, erotic billboards. A flat-breasted woman was not attractive, by standard definition, whatever other merits she had. Otherwise the entire development of the mammaries could have been left for the term of pregnancy and lactation, as was the case with other species, reducing feminine vulnerability at other times. No, breasts were sex objects.

In fact, the monkey that had walked away from the jungle, washing its fur coat away in the water, was a highly sexual creature. In proportion to the body, the human penis and breasts outmassed those of any other species. Both were far more prominent than was required for mere reproduction. Sex had become, to a considerable extent, an end in itself. It was the cement that bound together the family.

But there was another organ whose overdevelopment dwarfed that associated with reproduction. This hairless wonder, *Homo sapiens*, possessed a brain that was monstrous, both on the relative and the absolute scales.

No other animal on Earth could match the constancy of man's indefatigable intelligence and sexual drive. Year round, these operated. Truly, he was the superanimal: superbrain and supersex!

She moaned a small moan and writhed a small writhe, reminding him again of the business and pleasure at hand. His massive brain wanted her identity while his massive penis wanted her substance. He pulled her about to face him, close, so that her massive breasts flattened warmly against him. Real or ghost, her physique was certainly—

For a moment he froze. *Could this subject be male?*

What an encounter that would be! A secret homosexual fascination, indulged by the deception of the ghost.

Half numbed by horror, he stalled by running his hands over the body as if in further appreciation, stroking breasts, belly, buttocks and moist crevice. All were completely female. Then he relaxed.

It had to be a woman. The ghost-substance could clothe a woman with richer physical endowments, padding her body and masking her face. Surely it could pad out the avoirdupois about the hips of a man, too, and lengthen the hair of his head. But it could not subtract what was originally present. It might put breasts on a man, or penis and testicles on a woman, but it could neither delete a man's member nor fashion a vaginal canal within his flesh. He had to believe that.

Shetland smiled at himself. He could theorize very frankly on the aspects of human sexuality, but the notion of deviating, even accidentally, from heterosexuality shocked him. Perhaps this was mere cultural bias, but it operated with extreme and fundamental force.

He kissed her again, feeling her body respond, feeling its heat against him, feeling the pulse of it strengthen. His tongue quested between her lips and met her tongue and stroked it. His arms drew her in more tightly, so that the flesh of their chests seemed to merge. He felt her hot breath against his cheek, her arms at his back, adding to the pressure.

Their deep kiss broke at last, and their bodies separated. Both torsos were hot now, gleaming with sweat. Her abdomen was flushed, and as he watched, this color spread to the upper contours of her breasts. Could the ghost emulate that effect?

He put his head against her chest, his ear between the burning breasts, and heard her heartbeat. It was pounding: 120 or 130 beats per minute and accelerating. Th-thud, th-thud, th-thud, th-thud—the rhythmic double beat of the drum, the fundamental pulse of all human music, pounding, pounding, quickening toward climax! Babies responded to that dynamic rhythm—and so did men!

He started to mount her, but she twisted away again. He still had not named her, and she would not allow culmination without that token. A man might indulge with an anonymous woman, but a woman who was not in the business would not indulge with an anonymous man, or with one who found her anonymous. She had to know him, and required that he know her. Yet still he had not fathomed her identity!

Her back was to him now. That did not have to stop him. It was thought by many people that there was only one proper position for the sexual act, but he knew this to be a limited picture, possibly responsible for more human anguish than any other misconception. Effective stimulation of the woman was almost impossible during that conventional connection, whereas with the rear approach it was simple for the man to bring the woman to climax too. Perhaps that was why some religions inveighed so passionately against it: they did not wish sin to be fun.

Yet it would not be fair to claim the back position was nature's dictate. Both front and back had aspects to recommend them, and variety became far more important for year-round activity. Man's copulation, like his habitat, had become dual: he reached for the new without relinquishing the old. Thus he was equipped for any sexual contingency, and the fascination of the act was enhanced.

Still, it was not his way to indulge in anonymous copulation. How could a couple "make love" when there was no love, because they did not know each other? He must name her, and since it was useless to guess, he must name the one he most wanted. The one he could cherish not only in space-time but during all the years of his retirement. The one he could marry.

He named her—and that name as it emerged surprised him. He had not suspected his own subconscious desire, but he knew as he heard it that it was the right one—for him and for her.

She turned to face him, by that action signifying not her preference for position but her acceptance. In a moment they merged. Somewhere deep inside her he exploded: this was nova! A galactic geyser sprouted and clouds of steamy dust billowed outward. It was the ghost again, animating what was in his being, making it splendidly literal.

The little house was gone, blown apart. The steam coalesced into placid white cumulus humilis clouds, cotton puffs floating gently above a soft green meadow. Her vision, and an appropriate one. They lay together in a sweet-smelling garden bower, cooling. The love that had lain dormant for two years, human time, had bloomed at last, and in this power of love was salvation from all ghosts of any nature.

They separated somewhat, physically, and Shetland looked at her face. The mask was gone, though the body was unchanged. The body she had worn twenty years ago—and would wear twenty years hence. She was Tibet.

Know thyself! Shetland reminded himself again. To do that he had explored man paleontologically, learning how he fed and bred. Gluttony, anger and lust—all vital to the species, all present in every man of it. All traits that linked man to the animal world, while tools and language set him apart from it. The puzzle piece with the sword said that only man could preconceive tools for specific purpose, whether for building or killing; the piece with the book of poetry signified his unique ability to utilize a full pattern of symbolic expression. Both were functions of his superior intelligence; without that monstrously extended organ, the brain, neither his facile hands nor his glib tongue would profit him enough for survival.

Yet it was man's brain that caused the trouble. Man still warred with himself, still overgrazed his pastures, still behaved irrationally. Man still believed in ghosts. In fact, his brain was destroying him. It had freed him of natural limitations so that he was consuming himself into oblivion.

Man's intellect had to be disciplined. Shetland had searched for true understanding of his own nature—and found love. And that was the answer.

"Is it too late for us to have a family?" Tibet asked. "I always wanted—"

At that moment another revelation opened to him, a minor piece in a large puzzle that nonetheless made clear what had been baffling and shocking before.

"Alice," he called. "Here to me!"

Alice stood before him, neatly dressed. "Sir?"

Hastily Shetland formed clothing about himself and Tibet, eliciting a tolerant smile from the latter. "I know you," he told Alice. "*We* know you."

Now Tibet turned to him questioningly, while Alice smiled.

"I know why you died," he said. "And why you wouldn't tell me. And how to make it right, now and forever."

"I *couldn't* tell you . . ." Alice murmured, blushing as well as her complexion permitted.

"What is this?" Tibet demanded. "Alice never died—"

"Alice and I had been discussing her adjustment to the code of space—the sexual element," he explained. "She is engaged to marry Beeton, and she—"

"Not any more," Alice said, passing her hand over one shoulder as though feeling a burn. "Wayne needs a more mature woman, and I am but a child. I can appreciate that now." She looked at Shetland, and in that moment there was something so forlornly childish about her that Tibet made a little sound of sympathy. "I was talking with you, and you were so big and masculine and competent, and I was thinking about that code—and suddenly I realized that you were the ideal I had been looking for all my life. And it was hopeless."

"But dear," Tibet said, stretching forth her hand. "During a voyage it is all right: You had only to—"

"No!" Alice cried. "Not as a lover. *As a father!*"

Then Tibet began to understand. "You never had a father—and you couldn't adopt one in space, because—"

"Incest," Alice finished. "The Miseg Act transformed sexual relations, but some aspects it couldn't touch. There was no way out, because of the code of space. Except—"

"So you avoided the fate that was, for you, really worse than death," Shetland said. "By dying. Quickly, before your emotion could pyramid into a threat to the beacon. But your spirit lived on, in the ghost."

"No," Alice said. "Nothing lived—except your memory of me. I am—like your dog, whom you refused to believe was gone."

Shetland felt something that in another circumstance could have been a heart attack. Here it was merely heartbreak. Her death had been unnecessary. Had she understood properly, or been able to explain her feeling to him, he would have welcomed the new status, and certainly not sought any incestuous connection. Sex in space was free, but not required when neither party wanted it.

"You really did die?" Tibet asked, appalled. "Rather than explain?"

"Some things are easier to voice after death," Alice said. "By the time I could have brought myself to explain, the beacon would have . . . and it was so silly . . ."

"But how can anything be made right *now*?" Tibet asked. "Once we leave the ghost, you will fade away!"

"I don't see why our ghost animations have to be temporary," Shetland said. "They should retain their forms as long as we will them to, wherever we take them." But he wasn't sure.

"But I don't *want* to," Alice said. "This is artificial, wrong—"

"No, it is merely temporary," Shetland said. "We shall be mending you at the appropriate time. Tibet and I."

Alice looked at him a long moment, slowly understanding his meaning. "Thank you," she breathed. "You're wonderful!" She faded from view.

"This is all mixed up," Tibet complained. "That poor girl—"

"You do not need to concern yourself," Shetland said, squeezing her hand. "It all started with you."

But her brow remained furrowed. "I am developing less of a taste for the mysterious. It sounds as if you just promised her euthanasia!"

"I promised her *life*," he said. "Now four of us have been recovered—you and I, Johns and Alice. Let's work on the other three. We still have a tremendous job to do."

Johns reappeared. "Captain, you're doing a banner job—but what's the point? Nothing we can do, together or apart, can get us out of a black hole."

So Johns, too, had understood about that. "You're mistaken," Shetland said. "We have all been sadly confused, but now it is coming clear. We are going home—just as soon as we reunify."

Johns shook his head gravely, and even Tibet looked concerned. Both thought Shetland was fooling himself.

"The drive still operates," Shetland said.

"It did last time I checked it," Johns admitted. "But that was before we pitched into this scene. And a black hole—by definition, nothing in the universe can escape it! We can run the drive forever, and never cross the event horizon again. I thought you understood that!"

"I *did*. That was our problem. I could not command the ship and crew when I did not have confidence in our mission. Somnanda!"

Somnanda materialized.

"Does the beacon glow?"

"Always." There was light before him.

"Therefore we maintain contact with Earth."

"But contact is pointless when we can't *go* there!" Johns said.

"If nothing whatsoever can escape from a black hole," Shetland said carefully, "no matter, no energy, no information—how is it that the beacon still operates? *That's* information."

"That's different," Johns said. "It's all in Nanda's mind . . ." Then he twisted his face thoughtfully. "Still—"

"Yes, it's different," Shetland agreed. "Because it is not a signal through space, but a signal through *time*."

"But we, too, are traveling in time—" Tibet said.

"That's right," Shetland said. "That's why I was not at first concerned. But there is a complication: the tide. It is imperative that we act together, because—"

"Because one of us is a ghost?" Alice put in, reappearing.

"Because we *all* are ghosts," he said.

All four stared at him.

"Beeton!" Shetland called, and the young man appeared. "Have you noted the visions?"

"Have I ever! I've gained a whole new perspective on life," Beeton said. "But they're not visions. They're concrete manifestations of human thoughts."

"Concrete," Shetland said. "So that they are in addition to what already exits, not in lieu of it."

"Yes," Beeton agreed. "Except—"

"Except that the *Meg* is gone."

Johns jumped. "By God, he's right! Before we saw Poth from the portholes of the ship. Now we're right *in* the ghost scenes!"

"But the *Meg* can't be gone!" Tibet protested.

"It is and it isn't," Beeton said. "To understand that, you have to appreciate the nature of the black hole. Mass is present—such monstrous mass confined to such a tiny locale that its gravity prevents the escape of anything within its event horizon. That is why we could not even get a reading on mass as we approached, just an indication of a galactic-sized presence."

"We know that!" Johns snapped. "But with time travel—"

"To enter that horizon—the rim of the black hole—is not necessarily to be destroyed instantly. Not when the hole is the size of a galaxy. It could be minutes, hours, or even days before its tidal effects become overwhelming."

"Tidal effects?" Sosthenna inquired, appearing behind him.

Beeton chucked her under the chin—a gesture of possession and pride. Their understanding had evidently reached its culmination in much the way of Shetland's own with Tibet. The code of space had been rendered inoperative; the liaisons were no longer casual. There was no further need to fear the cartographer's passions, as long as Sosthenna was minding him. "Did you think the tide was just something to wash away castles in sand? Tide occurs whenever masses interact, most noticeably when they orbit each other in space. Because—"

"This is going to be technical," Tibet said. "And how does he explain what happened to the *Meg*?"

Beeton smiled. "All right—we'll spare you the fascinating technical detail, except to say that the tide affects all matter, not just liquid, and is inescapable. If you are near a large mass, you are subject to the tide, even if you are traveling in time. And if the main mass is large enough, and you pass within its event horizon, that tidal force will tear you apart. In the case of the black hole that is our ghost—"

"But you said the ghost was massless!" Tibet cried.

"*Seemed* massless. I thought so once. It was conjecture, because of the singularity, the infinite density at a point of no dimension. As it turned out, I was mistaken—and it was too late to avoid it. The *Meg* has been torn apart by the tide, right into its component molecules, which in turn have been fragmented into their atoms, and the atoms themselves have been broken down—"

"But what about *us*?" she cried, horrified. "If that happens to the ship we're in, then it must happen to us too!"

Beeton nodded. "That is why I am pessimistic about our return to Earth, despite our time travel."

Shetland could not restrain a snort of amusement at this colossal understatement. But Tibet was still following the awful trail of reasoning. "You're saying we're nothing! Our atoms are—that we're—"

"Ghosts," Shetland said. "Yes. It happened at the first period of chaos, after *Astrapotherium* became extinct. That was when the ship fragmented, and we developed the power of magical creation and even teleportation. Hardly a talent for solid bodies!"

"But then we're all dead!"

"No," Shetland said. "Only Alice is dead. Our minds live on. Perhaps on Earth such separation of spirit from flesh is only theoretical—but in a black hole physical theory breaks down. It seems that here only our bodies are subject to disintegration; our minds, or if you prefer, our souls, are unable to escape that framework. So they remain, disembodied—but they are able to re-create the bodies from the substance of the ghost. Bodies indistinguishable from the originals—if we so desire them. As we have known them; I don't believe we can generate genuinely foreign forms, such as a female body on a male spirit. But within broad limits, anything goes. Tibet prefers her youth—"

He was speaking to the group now, not just to her. But Tibet remained appalled. "But why doesn't the tide—"

"Tear us apart again? Because we are now *of* it, not *in* it. We are no longer as physical as we seem. And that is why we have to unify our minds and wills and work together. Nothing else remains to us."

Johns shook his head. "I don't see—"

"If we unify our will," Shetland said, "believing in each other, trusting each other, loving each other completely— then our minds are not pulling against each other. We can use the unique qualities of the ghost environment to re-create ourselves and our ship. Literally: mind over matter."

"You're saying we can go home after all," Johns said. "That we can put ourselves together again, just the way we made Poth, and follow the beacon back. Because *it* does still connect to Earth; it's mental, not physical. No one will know the difference."

"No one *must* know," Beeton said. "We have more important things to do than get vivisected in the laboratories of Earth—not that any lab could hold us! We have only to dematerialize and re-form elsewhere. For we shall remain ghosts all the rest of our lives—and I rather suspect we shall find ourselves immortal."

"I hope not!" Tibet said, accepting it at last. "I couldn't stand living forever! One life is dull enough for me!"

"But can we really leave the ghost?" Johns asked. "Here we exist; I accept that. But even if the beacon can lead us home, can we take any matter with us? Any ghost-plasm? Because if we can't, even if we do get there, we'll be no more than real ghosts, with no substance at all."

"That is the question in my mind," Shetland said. "I think that if we shape our mission properly, designing the parameters so that we *can* take it with us, or to find some other way to draw on whatever shadow power our universe has to offer—''

"There is one way to find out," Beeton said. "We can try it. If we find ourselves fading out as we pass the event horizon, we'll have to back off and figure out another approach. If we can't make it, then we're stuck here—in our complete fantasy world. That's really not so bad." He gave Sosthenna another squeeze.

"But there is so much to do!" Sosthenna said, squeezing him back. "Let's assume we do make it. With this power of the ghost we can save mankind from itself. There must be billions of ghosts in space and time—enough to sustain every soul on Earth, living or dead!"

"Provided they can adjust and unify—as we are doing, thanks to Captain Shetland's exploration into human nature," Tibet said. "Without him, we would have merged into that singularity and lost our identities."

"That is called nirvana," Somnanda said. "It is not an inferior condition."

"Nirvana can wait until we have done something useful for our kind," she said. "We must all go back to Earth."

"You're forgetting Alice," Johns said. "Don't get me wrong—you're a fine girl," he added, turning to her. "And I'd sure like to get together with you again, anytime. But you're dead—all-the-way dead. Can you return to Earth?"

"She will live again," Shetland said. "Her substance will return with us in its present form, though she will remain a genuine ghost—that is, an entity to whom the essential propensities of life remain alien. She can only emulate the living state, not participate in it."

"But that's cruel!" Tibet protested. "That's haunting!"

"Only for a while," he told her fondly. "Soon you and I will conceive a child, and that child will host Alice's spirit.

At that point it will cease to be a ghost and will become real—as our daughter.''

"My dream!" Tibet exclaimed. "My lost child—"

"You have found her again," he said. "She was always yours in spirit. And mine. But it took the ghost to make it possible in the way it should have been the first time.''

Somnanda lifted his hands in a benediction, and the light of the beacon shone brightly as a star. "Thus anachronism and paradox become practical," he said. "I suspect we will also discover that the effects of our unity here—once we truly achieve it—become inherent in the larger system. The paleontological texts will claim that there really was an *Astrapotherium magnum* during the Oligocene epoch in Patagonia, and even a *Sebecus* crocodile . . .''

"Naturally," Shetland agreed. "If we succeed. We still have the most difficult task of all, truly unifying, achieving peace among ourselves . . .''

Author's Note

This novel has a considerable history. Those of you who read my collection *Anthonology* will know some of it, but only part. Let's begin, then, at the beginning.

Back in the early 1960's, before I started the full-time devotion to writing that has continued for two decades, I exchanged writing efforts with several other hopeful writers. We would comment on each other's material, seeking to improve our abilities by constructive criticism. Some of these exchanges resulted in collaborations, as was the case with Frances Hall and Robert Margroff and Andrew Offutt, and some in salable manuscripts, and many in continued failures. But I think this program was worth the effort.

I wrote "Ghost" the story, about 10,000 words long, somewhere back around 1961 and showed it to some of the engineers at the electronics company where I worked so they could check my math, but I didn't market it at that time. I dusted it off in 1964 or 1965, when the exchange group was in existence, and sent it around for comment. It was a space-travel adventure, with hellishly complicated calculations for time and distance. Originally the protagonist was Captain Sheet (I mean, when you're writing about a ghost . . .), but I concluded that was too obvious, so I shortened it to Shet—and got an objection to that, perhaps because it sounded too much like an expletive. So I lengthened it to Shetland, where it remained.

I sent it off to *Playboy* in July of 1965, because that magazine was a market for some science fiction and paid about ten times as much as the genre publications did. It can take a long time for material to be considered, which is a frustration to an author, but if the manuscript comes back too quickly there is the suspicion that the editor never bothered to read it. Indeed, I had this one back in just eight days: barely time for the mailings, each way. So I shipped it to *Analog*— and in just three months it came back. Then I tried Damon Knight's *Orbit,* and had it back in all of seven days. Every market was taking either too little or too much time! At last I tried *Galaxy,* where Fred Pohl was on the job, and in three weeks it was accepted for its companion magazine, *If,* for a payment of one cent a word, $100. Writers don't get rich on short stories. It was published in 1966 under the title "The Ghost Galaxies."

In 1972 I reworked the basic story into a 60,000-word novel, adding characters and carrying the narrative on into the ghost galaxy. This was, incidentally, the last novel I typed on the conventional QWERTY keyboard. For twenty years I had typed two-finger on that one, but then I changed to touch-typing on the superior Dvorak keyboard. As I re-typed *Ghost* this time I was struck by the neatness and accuracy of my prior job; the truth is that my touch has never been able to match the accuracy of two-finger. For those who want to learn typing, but don't want to take a class and be forced into touch, I have this advice: go ahead with two-finger. For the average person it is just as good as touch, and relatively painless to learn. For one thing, you can do it your own way, without being constantly chided about where your eyes are. (For the pro, however, touch is better.) Now that I have a computer, my accuracy doesn't matter as much; it's easy to correct. But two-finger would work on the computer, too. However, the charm seems to be on the Dvorak key-board, since everything I've done on that has found a market.

When I wrote the novelette, the theories of the universe in vogue were Steady State vs. Big Bang, and the story version reflects that. By the time I wrote the novel Steady State had been overthrown, to my disappointment, so I had to modify the technical detail. Since the Big Bang theory does not allow for "old" galaxies, I had to shift from space travel to time travel, a devious business. Theories of the universe keep changing and evolving, and no doubt this update will become dated too; that sort of thing can be a problem for a science fiction writer.

At that time I was in contact with another writer, Sterling Lanier, author of *Hiero's Journey*, which novel I recommend to you, who happens to be a distant relative of the poet Sidney Lanier, whose life and work I have reference to in *Macroscope*. He had a little girl about the same age as my little girl (but they don't stay little, alas . . .), and a car of the same make as mine, and a wife the same age as mine (that must have been a vintage year for women!), who had had a disturbingly similar history of miscarriages, and we visited and compared notes on all manner of things. I wrote an article on him for a local newspaper, which was sadly cut for publication, and bought some of his brass figurines, that he crafted and had cast via the lost-wax process. He gave me more than I paid for, in more than one sense, and one of the bonuses was *Astrapotherium magnum.* Yes, that creature did exist, in Patagonia some time ago, and this was my introduction to it. So I put it in the novel. I still have Poth, whom I use for a paperweight to hold down the sheets of projects like this one. It is an honorable profession. It was Sterling Lanier who pointed out the "committee animal" appearance of the creature.

Other aspects of the novel were drawn from my own experience and observation, as is generally the case with my writing. The discerning reader will have perceived themes I have used elsewhere in my science fiction and in my later fantasy, and of course my interest in astronomy and anthropology (Anthony-pology?) shows. The malleable visions are explored more fully in *Tarot,* for example. So *Ghost* reads, unsurprisingly, like a composite of typically Anthony notions, including a certain fascination with death. One item that may seem crazy is not: the progression of taste for flavors of ice cream. It happened to me just that way, and more recently, years after the novel was written, I finally recovered my taste for chocolate ice cream. Of course now I am diabetic and so can't indulge in much of it. The full course of that progression was about thirty-five years.

I had a literary agent then, and he tried the rounds, but no publisher was interested. As I remember, Fred Pohl was then editing at Bantam, and he remarked about having published it in the magazine, but bounced it this time. He later went on to write his own novel, *Starburst,* with a ghost in a spaceship, which was variously reviewed as his best novel and his worst. I hate to seem wishy-washy, but I judge it to be in between: good but not great. No doubt *Ghost* will receive similar reviews.

In 1975 a man named John White was setting up a kind of

co-publishing venture, in which he worked with an established publisher to handle his titles, and shared the proceeds evenly with the authors. I had some dialogue with him, and had my agent send him *Ghost*. (I keep my eye constantly peeled for markets, you see, and I never forget a languishing novel.) He liked it, and talked with Dell about publishing it. Dell liked the novel, but rejected the venture, inviting me to submit the novel independently. Now I did not like cutting out John White, but the publisher was adamant, so we agreed to separate. (I worked up another novel, *Tarot,* specifically for Mr. White, but a series of problems, including loss of the preliminary manuscript, brought that and his company to grief, and again with regret, I had to market it independently— and it had a horrendous continuing history of its own, eventually being published in three volumes by a publisher who had rejected it.)

So we tried *Ghost* on Dell without the third party, and the editor liked it very well. In fact he said he planned to make it a major project. But he wanted some revisions. He sent me a letter detailing them, and I had to agree that it was an excellent commentary. So in February 1976 I completed 17,000 words of additional material for the novel and shipped it off—and it was lost in the mails. So I sent a carbon copy, and my agent sent that in. The editor did not respond. After a time he left Dell, and the novel was returned to us. We had not gotten a contract on it, so the publisher had no obligation and no money invested. The editor went to another publisher, where he gave us to understand he would not be buying new material—then published a note soliciting new material. "What the hell?!" I demanded of my agent. He collared the editor for a lunch—it seems that most business in Parnassus is done over lunches—and asked him point-blank what the story was. It was no sale. Then an assistant editor had a column in a fanzine (amateur magazine), *Thrust,* telling of his experiences, and how there were so few decent or original novels submitted, and how Piers Anthony had tried to foist off an appallingly bad novel on Dell that contained the word "megalocarpous" that he had to look up. (I don't know why; not only was the usage obviously humorous, the term was plainly defined in the novel, exactly as in the present edition.) Thus insult added to injury. It was a hard lesson, but one I learned well. For most of a decade thereafter I flatly refused to do revisions without a contract, and only now, with a couple of projects including this same one, have I made an exception, partly because I wanted to retype the novel into the computer anyway. And of course I have continued to keep my eye open for markets, as I slowly but patiently chip away at my backlog of unsold material.

This, then, is *Ghost,* the twenty-second novel I wrote and the most recent "unsold" one, as revised for an editor who did not buy it. Including this Note, it is now 87,000 words long. I always did believe in it, as I do in all my material. I am a typical writer in that I regard any editor who ever rejected anything of mine as an idiot, by definition. It's amazing how many intelligent people are idiots . . .

SCIENCE FICTION FROM PIERS ANTHONY

☐☐	53114-0	ANTHONOLOGY	$3.50 Canada $3.95
☐☐	53098-5	BUT WHAT OF EARTH?	$4.95 Canada $5.95
☐☐	53125-6	DRAGON'S GOLD *with Robert E. Margroff*	$3.95 Canada $4.95
☐☐	53105-1	THE E.S.P. WORM	$2.95 Canada $3.95
☐☐	53127-2	GHOST	$3.95 Canada $4.95
☐☐	53108-6	PRETENDER *with Frances Hall*	$3.50 Canada $3.95
☐☐	53116-7	PROSTHO PLUS	$2.95 Canada $3.75
☐☐	53101-9	RACE AGAINST TIME	$3.50 Canada $4.50
☐☐	50104-7	THE RING *with Robert E. Margroff*	$3.95 Canada $4.95
☐☐	50257-4	SERPENT'S SILVER *with Robert E. Margroff*	$4.95 Canada $5.95
☐☐	53103-5	SHADE OF THE TREE	$3.95 Canada $4.95

Buy them at your local bookstore or use this handy coupon:
Clip and mail this page with your order.

Publishers Book and Audio Mailing Service
P.O. Box 120159, Staten Island, NY 10312-0004

Please send me the book(s) I have checked above. I am enclosing $ _____
(please add $1.25 for the first book, and $.25 for each additional book to cover postage and handling.
Send check or money order only—no CODs).

Name _____
Address _____
City _____ State/Zip _____
Please allow six weeks for delivery. Prices subject to change without notice.

THE BEST IN
SCIENCE FICTION